WRATH OF THE ANGEL

Archangels' Wrath Series

Book 1

STEALTH BOOKS

TABLE OF CONTENTS

CHAPTER 1

As his mother drove him and his brother to church, Nick Slate shared his thought. "What would you do with infinite power?"

"Smack you until you stop asking stupid questions."

"No, I'm serious."

His younger brother, a new teenager, had surpassed him in size and grew on pace to become a mountain of muscle. Jake's biceps bulged as he lifted his fist. "You're about to feel infinite power rain down on your scrawny ass."

"Don't hit me. You're smarter than that."

The fist opened. "Good point."

"Thanks."

"You want to know what I'd do with infinite power? It doesn't matter because nobody has it. Not even a stud like me."

"In theory, God does"

Jake slid across the '85 Ford Crown Victoria's sprawling back seat, leaned into his firstborn sibling's ear, and whispered. "You don't believe this 'God crap', do you?"

Nick considered his middle brother wise for his age, and he valued his opinion. "Do you?"

"I asked you first."

"If there was someone with infinite power, I'd expect compassion from him. We'd still have a father, and mom wouldn't be an alcoholic. So, I don't see why I have to believe any of it." Nick glanced at the car's driver to verify she kept her eyes forward.

"A lot of people have it worse than us and still believe in God."

"They're making emotional decisions, but I need evidence."

"You talk like you're already a scientist."

"I will be someday. Life only makes sense if you can observe its causes and effects. Otherwise, everything is random chaos."

"What about all the paranormal shit that's always going on around you? You can't measure that stuff's cause and effect."

As a future scientist, Nick always found his psychic powers odd. "But you can talk about it only because you've seen the effects. That means there are causes. They just aren't identified yet."

"Yeah, I can agree to that. But you're not going to prove or disprove the existence of God by cause and effect, are you?"

Nick scoffed. "I guess not. Scholars have had thousands of years to prove it, but nothing yet."

"So we wasted our time being altar boys? We're wasting our time in church every Sunday?"

"We're honoring Dad's wishes, but I'm done with going to church once I'm in college. I need to explore the world."

The lethargic driver turned her head, and Nick smelled vodka as she spoke. "What's a waste of time?"

"Nothing, Mom." Nick knew his mother had sought a higher power when she'd lost the capacity to believe in herself after his father's passing, but it didn't seem to help. He pitied her, but he would avoid making the same mistake.

She stopped the car. "Okay. We're here. Get out, boys."

Nick sprang through the door, stepped onto the pavement, and raced Jake to the rectory entrance. He slapped his palm against the iron handle. "I win!"

"The hell you do."

A vice grip grabbed Nick's elbow, and the tidal force of his brother's back muscles pulled him away. He staggered for balance and watched Jake depress the latch and rotate the heavy portal open on its squeaking hinges.

Scrambling after his brother, Nick smelled the old must of the building's foyer. He joined his brother at a desk, where he faced a middle-aged woman. "We're here for Joe Slate. We're his brothers."

The receptionist adjusted the outdated glasses hanging over her sagging skin. "Oh. Altar boy training ended early today. I called all the parents. Didn't your mother get the message?"

Nick lowered his head, wondering what his mother had digested, if anything, from the voice mail. "I guess not. But Joe's here, isn't he?"

"He's the last boy here. The others were already picked up by their parents. He's with Father Sergius."

"Can we take him home now?"

"Let me check. The father said he was giving him special training while he was waiting." The lady's lethargy highlighted her frumpiness, making Nick question if volunteering behind a church desk accelerated aging.

As she disappeared around a corner, Jake became animated. "Let's go look."

"We can't go back there."

"No, dumbass. I mean let's head outside and see if we can surprise Joe through the windows."

"She'll be back any second."

"Not at the rate she's crawling. Come on."

As his rebellious brother darted out the door, Nick chased him to prevent him from finding creative ways to destroy things.

Around the corner of the building, Jake stopped at the rectory's far corner and faced a low hedge.

Nick caught him and noticed that the basement held the first floor's windows above eye level. "What now?"

"Get on my back."

"I'll get mud on your pants."

"You think Mom gives a shit? It'll wash out. Just get on." Jeans bulged as Jake's thick thighs lowered.

Nick saw that his younger brother's body was surpassing him in its shaping towards manhood. He slid his leg over a waiting hip and then curled himself over broadening shoulders. Weight lifting, football, wrestling, and martial arts were transforming Jake into a machine that lifted Nick like a feather.

"Well?"

Nick peered through a window. "I'm looking."

"I ain't got all day."

"Nothing. Wrong room."

"Damn." The rambunctious steed burst into a gallop and then stopped at the next window.

After gaining his balance, Nick steadied his gaze, and as his mind registered the scene, his heart sank. "Dear God."

"What?"

"Joe's lying on a table."

"That's messed up. Is he alone?"

"No. Father Sergius is hovering around him."

"What do you mean 'hovering'? What the hell's going on?"

"He's walking around him with a weird look on his face, and he's mumbling something."

"Shit. That's enough." Leaving his brother in a freefall, Jake darted away.

The soft earth rose and smacked Nick's feet. As he staggered for balance, he saw Jake racing towards the building's entrance. Wanting to restrain his brother's hormonal rage, he started after him, but a burning in his sprained ankle slowed him.

"Damn it, Jake." Nick stopped and considered distracting the priest, and he sought a rock to throw at the window. Nothing presented itself, and he reconsidered. Then, as if obeying his upset subconscious mind, a dark form streaked overhead and hammered the window.

Nick looked at the grounded raven. Motionless black wings covered a patch of dirt. Feeling a momentary connection with the bird, he knew it had survived the impact, and the eye facing him blinked in confirmation of having served his will.

His first instinct was to thank the stunned animal for distracting the priest, but he needed to tend to his brother.

When he hobbled to the desk, he saw the old lady straining to hasten herself down the hallway from which shot the crack of Jake's foot breaking a distant door. A final snap preceded the clamor of splinters landing against hardwood as Nick envisioned his brother-turned-monster crashing the battered door off its hinges.

Jake's command echoed. "Give me my brother!" A moment

later, the muscular teenager appeared, dragging Joe by his wrist.

The ten-year old boy seemed caught in a trance, and he staggered to keep pace.

Despite Jake's superior physical power, Nick wielded the family's authority. "Stop!"

Jake froze.

"Give him to me." Nick took Joe's wrist from Jake. "Go tell Mom to start the car."

"We need to get him out of here."

"Do it!"

"Just keep him away from that priest." Jake powered through the door.

Nick turned and saw the flustered receptionist lumber forward and balance herself against her desk. "He destroyed the door."

With his father's life insurance and CIA pension, Nick's family had money, and he knew the exact amounts since he managed the finances for his broken mother. "We'll pay for it."

"What gotten into him?"

Though Jake's methods were rough, Nick appreciated his brother's lion-hearted protective instinct and withheld what he knew. "I think Jake's going through a rough puberty."

"Well, you were better behaved at his age."

"I'm sorry for what he did. Please have the door repaired, and I'll bring a check for it next week." Nick escorted his youngest brother into the parking lot.

Joe resisted the pace.

Welcoming the relief in his twisted ankle, Nick slowed to his brother's speed. "What happened?"

Silence.

"Joe?"

The child's voice seemed distant, as if caught in a dream. Or a nightmare. "What?"

"I asked you what happened."

"Nothing."

"Are you sure? What if I told you that I know what happened

because I saw it? Would you feel better about telling me?"

"I don't want to!"

Nick heard the onset of labored breathing that preceded tears. "Okay. You don't have to tell me. Get in the car and put on your seat belt."

The zombie in the driver's seat appeared unaware of her surroundings as her sons took their seats, the youngest beside her trying to suppress tears.

Jake leaned forward and checked their baby brother. "Look. You made him cry."

"No. You did, the way you scared him like that."

"I scared him? I pulled him away from that creep."

"What did you see?"

"That ass had his hands all around him."

"You're kidding."

"Do I look like I'm kidding? Mom, let's go."

The car started moving.

"I hate to think what would've happened if I didn't take care of business."

Nick wasn't ready to jump to conclusions, and he expected to avoid further exchanges with the priest. "Well, don't worry about it. That's the last time Joe will be alone with him. Father Sergius is being promoted to bishop."

"That bastard's being promoted to a bishop?"

"Yeah. But you didn't think he was a bastard until today. You used to like him."

"That was before he tried to touch my baby brother."

"You don't know what was really happening."

"You saw it yourself."

"I'm not sure what I saw."

"Bullshit. I'm going to make you sure." Jake punched his older brother's shoulder, and recoiled for a second strike.

Parrying the next blow, Nick felt a deep bruise forming. "What's this going to prove, other than you're a hormonal disaster?"

"It's going to make you respect my opinion."

Nick tried to remain calm. Experience had taught him that if he yielded, his brother's calmer instincts would overrule his hormones. Sensing his family slipping into an abyss of dysfunction, he tried to restore order and diffuse the attack. "I respect your opinion. You're not respecting mine."

"I don't think you're respecting anyone's opinion—not even your own. You're in denial."

"I'm just trying to be rational, unlike you and your barbarian ways."

Jake slipped a jab through the firstborn brother's defenses. "My barbarian ways just saved Joe from crazy bullshit, and you're trying to pretend nothing happened."

Nick's arm stung. "Nothing did happen, you moron!"

"But it would've happened."

In the front seat, Joe whined. "Stop talking."

Jake scowled. "We're talking about stuff for your own good. Stop being a baby."

"I'm not a baby."

The plea from his half-dead mother issued forth in detached sadness. "Boys, stop."

Jake balled his fist and crashed it down on Nick's arm. "Now you made Mom mad, too."

Nick's humerus throbbed. "You heard Mom. Chill out."

"This is serious and we're not going to forget about it."

"Calm down."

"Don't tell me to calm down, damn it!"

The howl from Joe billowed with impossible power. "Stop!"

The world turned black, and deafness enshrouded Nick. A lance of searing fire shot through him, like the severing of his spinal cord, before numbness engulfed him.

Wanton depression consumed him, and morbid thoughts tormented him. The concept of life disgusted him, and he felt a crushing need to annihilate everything, including himself.

He wanted to rip out his own heart, but paralysis stopped him, and hopelessness told him death would be the beginning of his agony.

Then, the abject misery subsided.

Blurry, his vision returned, and he began to hear muffled sounds. He noticed himself hyperventilating.

Slumped on the floorboard, Jake appeared shocked. "Nick?"

His name sounded foreign as Nick struggled to discern sounds. He glanced at the driver, and his mother remained a zombie immune to Joe's howl. Then he saw his toppled brother's lips move again. "Nick?"

"Yeah?"

Jake crawled to his side. "Did you feel that?"

"Yeah."

"Holy shit. I thought I was going to die."

"It was like I wanted to die, but I couldn't."

In one episode, Joe's paranormal abilities had revealed themselves with a brutality beyond Nick's imagination. Questions flooded him about the abilities he shared with his brothers.

Had he ignored prior signs in Joe? Could he repeat the mental devastation that Joe had just unleashed? If he attained such power, could he achieve the knowledge, wisdom, and restraint to wield it?

Regardless of a god of infinite reach, Nick knew there were powers beyond human reckoning which demanded his exploration. Resolving whether they were good or evil would be part of the ride.

"Jesus, Nick. What the hell just happened?"

"You just said it. Hell happened."

CHAPTER 2

Four years later, Joe Slate stood before the bishop. He felt his confirmation sponsor's hand clasp his shoulder.

Though intended to offer assurance, the supportive gesture combined with his former priest's proximity to spark the repressed trauma of a day long ago forgotten.

Formless and opaque memories flooded his fragile mind with emotions detached from meanings. Darkness and deafness overcame him, and he trembled.

A force beyond his reckoning hijacked his thoughts, and he slipped into an abyss of hideous visions fueled by an unfamiliar depravity. Pornographic violence, torture by blade, mass drowning, burying of the living, and vivisection tormented him as the massive weight of humanity's evil harassed him.

An unnatural scream shattered his skull and endured beyond the capacity of human lungs. When the howl ceased, it evaporated the kaleidoscope of terror, leaving a final perverse image.

Joe saw the bishop burning alive.

Then, worse than seeing, he desired.

He wished to immolate the clergyman who had terrified him years earlier in the rectory's office.

Images of the man combusting into flames filled his mind, and he sensed a sickening hatred. But his hunger for vengeance welcomed his desire to burn the man's flesh.

His vision narrowed and darkened, and a discomforting heat enveloped him. Consciousness abandoned him, and he slipped outside time's limits.

Smelling dirt and must, he awoke on the carpet.

Murmurs and gasps filled the air, and as his vision recovered, his oldest brother knelt before him. "Joe!"

"What happened?"

"You passed out."

An altar server near the fallen bishop cried out. "Call an ambulance! He's not breathing."

Nick examined his baby brother. "Are you alright?"

Blood pulsated around Joe's joints, and his head rang. "I guess. What's going on?"

"The bishop keeled over right after you went into your seizure, or whatever just happened."

"How?"

"I don't know. He just flopped to the ground."

Stress pushed Joe into hyperventilation, and he couldn't talk. His brother helped him to his feet. "Walk with me. Breathe."

Expecting his brother to bring him to the bishop, Joe was relieved when he guided him to the back of the church. As he walked from his agony, his lungs slowed. "Where are we going?"

"Away."

"But I'm not confirmed."

"You won't be. Not today."

*

The next day, Nick awoke with a heightened understanding. His brother's episode at the altar had awakened an awareness of a power that had lain dormant for years.

Sensing a subconscious bond forming with his siblings, he thought of Joe, and a wave of confusion and sadness swelled within him. He then thought of his middle brother, Jake, and confidence and anger ruled. Instead of being one young man, he experienced himself as a triune brotherhood.

While he walked into the bathroom and then enjoyed the distracting heat of hot water against his skin, the emotional, wordless linkage to his brothers dissipated.

After showering and dressing, he ramped up his exploration of the brotherly bond. While driving to his English class at the community college, he thought of a phone call with Jake.

Nothing happened.

He sent out his thoughts to his brother again, but the effort fizzled when he stopped at a light. "I'll try again when I'm not driving."

Once parked at the school, he silenced the engine and stayed seated to envision a call with his brother. "Call me."

Nothing.

Ratcheting up the intensity, he tightened all the muscles of his body and tried to force his brother to telephone him.

Still nothing. "I'm an idiot."

As he gave up and opened the door, his phone rang. Breathless, he whipped the device to his cheek. "Hello?"

Jake was somber. "The bishop died."

"I know. Weren't you listening when Mom told us last night?"

"Yeah, but it just sunk in. You don't think Joe's seizure had something to do with it? It was just a coincidence, right?"

The tone made Nick wonder if his middle brother had also grown aware of the supernatural fraternal linkage. "I have no idea. Your guess is as good as mine. You are just guessing aren't you?"

"Yeah. Why'd you ask such a dumb question?"

"Right. Sorry."

"You apologize too much."

Nick redirected the discussion. "Why'd you call me?"

"To talk about the bishop, fool. What conversation are you having?"

"I mean, why now? Aren't you late for school?"

"I'm a senior at the top of my class."

"So?"

"So, I'm acing Miss Miller's class and she doesn't care if I'm a little late."

"Okay, but what compelled you to call me now? You never call me in the morning."

"Shit, dude. I don't know. Our bishop doesn't die every day. Isn't that enough?"

"Maybe."

"It freaked me out now, and I called you. You're the guy who calms me down when I'm spun up."

"Okay. I get it."

"Look, I don't want to take advantage of Miss Miller's generosity any more than I already have. Got to run."

The line fell silent, and Nick considered the probability that his will had imparted a supernatural request for the call. He accepted that proof would elude him today, but he remained curious. And hopeful. And anxious.

Three hours later, Nick sat in a cafeteria reviewing his class notes, and a compelling desire overcame him to speak to his baby sibling. He grabbed his phone and dialed Joe's number.

No answer.

He tried his other brother.

Jake's voice was strained. "What's going on?"

"I can't get a hold of Joe."

"Me neither."

"Really? When did you call him?"

"About a minute ago."

"Me, too. That's strange."

"I got a bad feeling." Jake's pause suggested he sensed something ominous. "I feel sick."

The phone beeped, and Nick extended it to read it. "It's Joe. I'll call you back." He switched calls and heard crying.

Joe forced his words between sobs. "Mom was in an accident."

"What do you mean?"

"She crashed her car into a pole in the parking lot."

Nick's heart sank. "Picking you up from school?"

"Yes! Come take me to the hospital."

Four hours later, Nick watched his middle brother pace in the waiting area of the emergency room. Then, in a moment of anguish, he felt his mother pass. "You can stop worrying. She's gone."

"Don't say that!" Jake stopped in mid-stride. "Damn you."

"I'm sure of it."

"How could you know?"

"I just know."

"You're an asshole."

"Don't you sense it?"

"The hell I do. Stop being an ass."

Beside him, Joe started crying.

Jake pointed. "Look what you did to him!"

Joining Joe in mourning, Nick felt tears streaming down his cheeks.

Jake glared at his firstborn sibling. "You really are a spooky freak. This is for real, isn't it?"

The surgeon appeared and confirmed Nick's premonition that his mother's alcohol-induced automobile accident had killed her. She was free from her suffering, but shame filled consumed him after he realized his first reaction had been relief.

After two weeks of exhausting his tears, Nick ate dinner with Jake. "I want to take Joe with me to Michigan."

"Uncle Rick and Aunt Jennie said they'd take him."

"They offered out of obligation. They don't want him."

Jake lowered a beer to the table. "Yeah. You're right."

Nick knew better than to rebuke his brother for underage drinking. "That means I need to take him."

"That will make you his legal guardian, right?"

"I guess so."

"This is going to screw him up worse."

"But I have to take him. Even if you could find a way to take care of him while you finish high school, you can't take care of him after that." Nick was proud of his overachieving sibling for earning an appointment to the United States Naval Academy with the intent of becoming a Navy SEAL. But the rigors and constraints of Jake's future precluded him from tending to their brother.

Nick wanted to salvage the remainder of Joe's childhood. Wondering if he could, he chastised himself for having focused on raising Jake at the expense of his youngest brother.

Jake chugged his beer and then lowered his glass. "I don't like it, but I can't think of a better way. Taking him's the best thing you can do."

"Are you going to be okay?"

"Don't worry about me. I'll keep my grades up. I may not stay at the top of the class, but I'll do enough to keep my appointment to the academy. At this point, how bad would I have to screw up for it to matter?"

The rapid and familiar jostling of the household pet barreling through the cat door filled the kitchen. Then came the triumphant hunter's muffled howl.

Looking toward the floor, Nick perceived the proud posture of his old, husky, gray-furred friend.

With canine-like obedience, the feline bee-lined to Nick's feet to present the prize.

Jake leaned sideways and looked under the table. "Way to go, Chester. As usual, he goes straight to his master."

"He knows who treats him right."

"I swear you have some sort of connection with him. It's like he's your dog, and he obeys your thoughts."

"You're exaggerating."

"Not much. Cats have no masters, except that this one has been your puppet forever."

"I happen to like cats, and he responds to it." Nick bent and reached for the captured sparrow. With a combination of a mental command, subtle gesturing, and memorized ritual, the cat's jaws relaxed in perfect synchronization with the cupping of his master's hands around the victim.

Nick sensed the bird's mortal terror as its wings flapped within his hands. Then, while he walked towards the door, the sparrow's terror subsided. As he passed through the doorway, the dryness of the outdoor climate pricked his exposed skin. Releasing the fowl to his fate, he unfolded his fingers.

Wings fluttered and then pumped as the bird ascended to freedom.

Nick returned to the table. "Shouldn't you learn as much as

you can in your last semester in high school to make the first year at the academy easier? I hear the first year's brutal."

"I will. Grant's parents will make sure I study."

Nick was grateful that Jake's friend's family had agreed to house him for the remainder of his senior year. "I suppose they will. They're good parents, but I'm not. I'm not sure how I'll keep Joe in line. He doesn't respond to authority. Or too much of anything, for that matter."

"Sure, he does. He cleans up after himself and does his chores."

"That's only because he's afraid of you clobbering him. I don't have your size or fighting skills or your..."

"Or my what?"

To avoid angering the hair-triggered muscular monster, Nick sought the right word. "Your edge. You always look like you're ready to pummel the next guy who pisses you off."

"That's because I'm always ready to pummel the next guy who pisses me off. It's a useful attitude."

"But it's dangerous with your strength and martial arts skills."

Jake tipped back the beer. "Not anymore, really. The trick was establishing my reputation. I don't have to lift a finger to keep the peace. Dudes back off at the sound of my name."

"That approach is never going to work for me."

"Don't worry. I can't explain it, but somehow I think Joe respects you more than me."

Since childhood, Nick had felt invisible except to his charismatic middle brother. He often wished that Jake had been the eldest, the leader to bear the siblings' burdens. "How can that be?"

"You've got a hidden power, and he knows it. Even I know it, and I'm dense to subtleties."

"You've been saying that for years, but it could all be coincidence."

"Coincidence? Any kid that picked on you in school ended up sick or broken."

"You're exaggerating."

"They called you 'Spookie Slate', and nobody picked on you after your sophomore year."

"They called me 'Spookie' because I was different, and they stopped picking on me when you beat up three guys for giving me a wedgie."

Jake tipped back his glass. "Well what about the kid that beat you up in junior high? His appendix burst the next day. And that football player who beat you up freshman year ended up breaking his leg the next game."

"Maybe I had a guardian angel working overtime."

"More like a revenge angel."

"Whatever."

"And now that Joe killed a priest, I'm not sure it's just you with the spooky power."

"He didn't kill him. At least we can't know for sure."

"Weird shit's been happening recently."

Nick probed his brother's perspective. "What do you mean?"

"When you and I called Joe at the same time. It was right when Mom died, wasn't it? It was like we knew."

"Yeah."

"And when I called you earlier that morning. I didn't admit it, but it felt like you summoned me."

"I did summon you."

"Bullshit."

"It's true."

"If that's true, then you're spookier than I thought."

"But it's not just me. I had nothing to do with you calling Joe the day Mom died."

Jake walked to the refrigerator. He grabbed a beer, twisted off its top, and returned to the table. "Maybe Joe didn't kill the priest. Maybe it was you, and Joe's seizure was collateral damage."

Nick felt his brother's gaze probing him for a confession. "He was a bishop, and I didn't kill him. Nothing's happened to hurt anyone that could be tied to me since the football accident."

"That's because of our reputations. People figured out that

if they mess with you, they'll either get your creepy curse, or they'll get my fist in their face. But it's a new game when you head off to Michigan. Someone's going to piss you off, and you'll see how spooky you really are."

Good grades in high school and a continued performance in community college had earned Nick entry into the University of Michigan, and he looked forward to escaping, even with his baby brother as baggage. "Don't worry about me. I'll be fine."

Jake bit into a pizza slice, chewed, and washed it down his throat with beer. "It's not you I'm worried about. It's whoever's ignorant enough to screw with you that I pity."

CHAPTER 3

Father Lewis Bannen slammed another shot of bourbon.

Remembered demons danced in his hypnotic haze, reenacting their counterattacks to his past expulsions. Dead languages, multi-plexed voices of layered evil, and the bones of possessed victims breaking under the strain of convulsions replayed in his mind.

As the alcohol engulfed him, memories merged with imagined horrors. A fallen angel, its face a leathery mask of wrinkled wretchedness, appeared in a dark corner of the rectory's basement. The stench of sulfur and methane punished the priest's nose, and he hurled his glass at the monster.

The container cracked against the wall, and the apparition vanished.

Lewis lamented his nightmarish lot. "Forgive me, God."

A dull pain reminded him of the explosive device that had broken his back and cost him three lumbar disks. Doctors had fused the vertebrae of then-Corporal Bannen, relieving the intractable sting but leaving him with burning muscles and tensed nerves.

Decades ago, he'd accepted the suffering as his impetus towards a higher power, riding it into the priesthood after his medical discharge from the Army. But the chronic strain on his patience undermined the social aptitude he'd needed to administer the sacraments of Eucharistic Mass, marriage, baptism, anointing of the sick, and confession. He'd considered himself an inferior priest–until a wise pastor had pushed him in a new direction.

The Archdiocese of Detroit had needed an exorcist, and Lewis had wanted a new start. Fifteen years and hundreds of sessions later, he valued his place as God's servant in the spiritual battle-field.

But as his forties yielded to his fifties, his body succumbed to his injury's structural decay while his heart sank under the burden of demonic warfare. Then, three years ago, his downward spiral accelerated when a fifteen-year old girl, pregnant from her father's raping, had committed suicide before he could expel her attacker.

His confidence still compromised, he screamed at the shadows. "Tell me your name!"

"Father Mark Brown."

Lewis faced the imposing figure of his pastor. "Forgive me, Father Mark. I didn't mean to yell."

"You asked for a name. Did you receive an answer from anyone other than me?"

"No. I may have been yelling at myself."

"May I turn on the lights, or do you prefer just the candles?"

Lewis settled his gaze upon the flickering flames, wishing he could live in such simplicity. Oxygen, heat, fuel, fire. No conflict. No free will. No fear of damnation.

"We'll stick with the candles, then." The husky pastor moved with confident compassion towards his ailing comrade. "It's unhealthy to drink alone."

Lewis felt the air shift as his boss sat in the plastic chair beside him. "I'm sorry, Father Mark. I'm in a state of mortal sin."

"Perhaps not. God recognizes your struggle and offers grace as you to work to eliminate this habit."

"I threw my glass at the wall."

"Then you don't mind if I take a swig from the bottle?"

"Be my guest." Lewis slid the fifth gallon of Jack Daniel's Tennessee Whiskey across the table and appreciated his companion sipping to create the illusion of a shared drink.

Lowering the bottle, Brown exhaled. "You're troubled."

"Yes, Father."

"Is it your back pain?"

"That's part of it."

Brown grunted. "You're seeing apparitions, too?"

"Yes, Father."

"Being an exorcist is a burden."

"But I shouldn't be sinning like this. My drunkenness is vile, but I can't stand sobriety and... the pain. What forces are tormenting me, and why is God allowing them?"

"He must be testing you. He must be transforming you into something stronger than you already are."

The words gave comfort that weakened under the whiskey's weight. "You're too kind to me. I deserve Hell."

"We all do, except for saving grace." Brown tipped back another ceremonial sip.

"I need one more gulp."

"Just one more, and then I'll help you to bed."

"If only I could sleep."

Brown examined the bottle. "Is this all you've had tonight?"

"Yes, Father."

"It's a lot, but I think you'll be okay with one more swig, as long as you promise not to drink any more after that."

"I promise, Father."

"Good. You need your rest."

Lewis swallowed a mouthful of bourbon and capped the bottle. Struggling for balance, he drifted into his stocky companion's side and found stability.

The pastor helped him up the stairs and into his bedroom. "I'll be back with a glass of water."

Lewis closed his eyes as Brown departed, and sleep found him immediately.

The next morning, Lewis awoke with a pounding headache and nausea. He forced himself through his toiletry routine and then walked to the kitchen.

Brown greeted him. "How are you?"

"Hung over."

"That's not a surprise. Get some water into you. Some coffee might help, too."

"Thanks." Lewis moved to the sink and prepared his water and coffee.

"I made you an omelet. It's in the refrigerator."

"Thanks again." The exorcist sat and began nursing himself back to health.

"When's your session?"

"One thirty."

"Would you like me to be there?"

"I always appreciate the extra support. We're coming up on sixth months, and I think I can get the demon's name today."

"Are you up for it?"

Lewis swallowed a bite of egg and cheese and washed it down with black coffee. "I'll be fine."

"Okay. I'll take your confession at eleven, then?"

"That's fine, Father Mark. I'll see you then."

His confessed grace restored, Lewis stood with his back to the altar. The high school athlete sat before him, the restraints dangling beside his limbs.

Behind the boy stood his father, an older brother, and two of the boy's Catholic companions–strong football players that Lewis trusted to restrain the possessed energumen.

Beside Lewis, Father Brown held a crucifix. At his other side, a psychologist rubbed his fingers, his eagerness obvious. Aside the anxious shrink, a physician seemed nonchalant, reflecting the possessed demoniac's robust conditioning and minimal risk of succumbing to physical stresses.

However, Lewis knew that sin and depravity had compromised the boy's soul, making him susceptible to the evil entities within him. The physician's presence was a normal precaution Lewis respected in protecting the young demoniac.

After his father had lost his job, the boy had turned to fortune tellers for stock tips. When short-term wins had helped the family, his interest had grown into extensive exploration of the occult. After a Satanic ritual, he'd befriended a female participant and had worked his way into her bedroom. Three months later, he'd convinced her to abort the product of their union.

Then the fortune-telling had faltered, and as his family's finances had failed, the boy had feared for his future. As depression, anxiety, and anger had eaten him, he'd delved deeper into his devilish endeavors, opening the door to the demons.

Lewis began with the instructional phase of the Rite of Exorcism, leading with the Lord's Prayer, the Hail Mary, the Athanasian Creed. He then touched the subject's neck with the hem of his stole while pressing his palm on the boy's head.

He followed with a series of requests to saints for their intercession. Unlike some exorcists who adopted the modern version of the rite, he stuck to the seventeenth century American translation. As a former military man, he adhered to its prescribed path with minimal customization.

While grinding through the routine prayers, he watched the boy close his eyes and reopen them with defiance. Believing he'd invoked the possessing spirit, he reached the second phase and began his first of three series of commands to the demon. "In the name of Jesus Christ, tell me your name."

"Tell me yours, drunkard."

"In the name of Jesus Christ, tell me your number."

"Aren't you dying for a drink?"

"In the name of Jesus Christ, tell me why you entered God's servant."

"We did it because he's strong enough to break your back–again. He'll slam you into a wall, and you won't walk away."

"In the name of Jesus Christ, tell me when you entered God's servant?"

"He's my servant, just as you are, you drunkard."

"In the name of Jesus Christ, tell me how you gained access to God's servant."

"We were in the vaginal fluids of the tramp he fornicated. After he breaks your back, we'll enter you when he comes to know you." The boy curled and writhed in his seat, a sadistic smile plastered on his smug face.

Lewis suspected he'd gained a small victory by coaxing a

truthful answer, and it should've been the fatal chink in the beasts' armor. But the prior night's drinking and fitful sleep made him weak, and he stalled. He welcomed his pastor's intervention.

Brown cleared his throat. "Perhaps a Hail Mary."

Capitalizing on the leeway allowed in the rite, Lewis requested support from the woman all demons hated and feared. When he finished, his mind drifted, and he bought time by leading a short version of a request for support from Michael the archangel. His hangover's lingering toxicity dried his mouth, and he reached for a glass of water.

The demoniac smirked. "What's wrong? Am I tiring the alcoholic?"

Lewis rattled off more commands for the information he wanted, culminating in the rote recital of the rite's order to the demon to depart. But signs of the cross, holy water, and the laying of his hands on the energumen imparted no visible effect.

He began his second of three attempts at commanding the evil entity. "In the name of Jesus Christ, tell me your name."

"Do you remember the night when you kicked a frog, and it died when its lifeless body hit the wall? You realized how evil you are, and you started sobbing. An adult sobbing over a frog!"

The impossibility of the boy's knowledge of the decades-old event compounded Lewis' certainty of the demonic possession. But the memory hurt, and he felt himself losing ground.

"Shall we continue with all your repressed memories? Shall we describe what you did to Jane Smith in the back of your Jeep during your senior year of high school?"

"Silence! You cannot. My sins are confessed, and God has forgiven them. He will not, however, show you mercy." Lewis called a divine timeout by sprinkling holy water on the boy's face.

As unnatural sounds gurgled from his boy's throat, his cheeks extended and narrowed towards a wolfish snout and then returned to normal.

Shocked looks from the assistants confirmed that the restructuring of the bones had happened–whether as an illusion or as a paranormal event.

"We see everything we need to destroy you. You are weak and will succumb. We know you."

"And I will know you. In the name of Jesus Christ, tell me your name."

"Never."

"In the name of Jesus Christ, tell me if you are held in him by necromancy, by evil signs or amulets."

"We're held in him by his need to crush you."

"In the name of Jesus Christ, tell me the sign of your departure, so that I'll know when you have left God's servant."

The boy's eyes rolled back in his head, revealing the full whiteness that separated energumens from those suffering seizures. The veins in his face and neck bulged, and then the eyes rolled forward with dilated pupils glaring at him.

"You'll feel him inside you."

Lewis swallowed. "Silence, in the name of Jesus Christ."

"Would you prefer that we have him spit in your mouth?" The boy launched a wad of spittle that the exorcist dodged, and it landed on the steps to the altar. "Or we could kill him and find our way into you at our leisure. For a priest, you are vulnerable."

Knowing an aborted session invited grave risk, Lewis pressed forward. He labored through the ritual, and the boy slumped into the quick hands of the assistants. Lewis sighed and then inhaled to recite a closing prayer.

The boy interrupted him. "Tell me how a drunk coward thought he could tangle with the likes of us."

"In the name of Jesus Christ, be silent, evil spirit."

The demoniac ignored the name and continued his taunt. "We know how you got here. We saw it."

Lewis wanted to pray to silence the beasts, but the guilt of the invoked memory stymied him.

"That's right. You remember. How could you forget? One of us watched you that day. You were among the first in your squad to see the suicide bomber, yet you did nothing. You froze, like a child."

A wave of shame paralyzed Lewis as the kneeling boy collapsed into a snake-like position with his muscles tightening and straining his joints.

As the solid arms of the young assistants restrained the energumen, the physician stopped them. "No. He can take it. Let Father Lewis battle with them."

The scratchy voice reached a high pitch as the contortions strained the boy's larynx. "This is no battle. This is an annunciation. A failed coward soldier entered the priesthood to hide from his shame, and now he fails to save souls. I expose this sinner, this charlatan!"

Lewis tried to defend himself. "How dare you call this an annunciation! Gabriel the archangel delivered the only annunciation you need to know."

A curled finger unfurled and leveled at Lewis' nose, and black pupils stared at him. "Sergeant Masterson ran out to block the suicide bomber. You let a better man become hamburger. He left a widow and three orphans because he died in your place."

"Silence, in the name of Jesus Christ!"

The holy name instilled stillness for several seconds, but Lewis found himself in a tactical retreat while the energumen pressed the attack. "Sergeant Masterson says he's looking forward to you burning beside him."

"You serve a liar. You are a liar."

The teenager's body went limp. As the assistants helped him sit, Lewis led closing prayers and pondered the accuracy of the demons' final accusation.

Over a quiet dinner, Lewis welcomed the pending end of the day. He ate a steak and recognized the soothing absorption of the toxins in his stomach. He looked forward to evening prayers and a recovering sleep.

As the parish's two other staff priests excused themselves, the husky pastor stood to clear the table and asked Lewis to remain. "Can you stick around a bit?"

"Sure. Do you want some help with that, Father Mark?"

"No, thank you. You've had a rough day already."

"What's on your mind?"

"Your session today. How do you think it went?"

"Poorly, I have to admit. The only bright spot was the demon revealing how he entered the boy."

"That could've been a lie. The enemy's a shrewd liar."

"Sinful sex is a believable entry method, but repeated sessions will verify it."

Father Mark stacked dishes in racks. "How did you feel during the session?"

"I was weak. I was hung over. You know that, Father. There's no need for me to confess it again."

The pastor's tone became ominous. "When the archbishop announced that he wanted a diocese exorcist long ago, I thought of you because you were a warrior. Many people warned me against it. They said you were too troubled. But I saw your fighting spirit, the way you battle through your pain."

"I remember, Father. I see this as my calling, and I'm grateful for your support."

The pastor bowed his head. "God help us both. After today's rite, I'm starting to doubt my decision."

CHAPTER 4

Five years later, Joe Slate stood before the judge, remorseless.

Fate had burdened him since his conception, with his father dying while he'd grown in his mother's womb. Her subsequent depression and drinking while pregnant had established the tone for his existence. He'd decided long ago that whatever he could salvage from his life of despair, he merited.

That included doing what he wanted, when he wanted, to the edge of anarchy.

High school in Ann Arbor, Michigan seemed like punishment far from his childhood home. Having followed his eldest brother to the city, he found his new world a torment.

After countless brawls over trivialities, most of them victories thanks to his tenacity, he'd pushed the laws beyond their limits. His latest fight had placed him in the courtroom.

He stared with disdain at the obese man who appeared to have ridden a silver spoon from childhood to a judge's appointment.

"Joseph Slate, you have pleaded no contest to the charge of simple assault. Given your history of violence, I remand you to the Washtenaw County Youth Center. If you successfully complete the prescribed six-month program, you will be returned to the custody of your guardian, Nicholas Slate."

*

Two weeks later, Nick sat across the table from his uniformed baby brother. "You don't look too bad."

"Prison sucks. But it's not much different than outside. People telling me what to do, people pissing me off, making sure people know I'm the alpha dog."

"You're the alpha dog?"

"I'm in with the alpha gang."

Nick frowned, knowing that Joe had never achieved acceptance with any social group. "You did that in two weeks?"

"I'm not really in the gang, but they've figured out I'm dangerous, and that's good enough."

"How?"

"I stood up to two of them."

"Stood up? I don't see any bruises. Did you beat up two guys?"

"I landed a few punches, but I took a beating. They're smart enough to hit below the neck so that the bruises are hidden. The part where things went my way was when the two guys got the stomach flu the next day. They're convinced I poisoned their food."

"Did you?"

"Maybe."

Nick feared the conversation's direction. "What did you do?"

"I asked Satan to handle it for me."

"Satan?"

"You heard me."

"Specifically for stomach flu?"

"Not exactly. I asked for sickness, but that's close enough, and you can't argue about the speed of service."

"You know that's crazy."

"It worked."

"Come on, Joe. Don't screw around with this. Even if there is a devil and this is somehow working, you'd be flirting with disaster."

"I don't care. It's working for me now."

"It's working, huh? What did you promise in return? As far as I know, if all this is true, you're in debt now."

"I didn't give up anything. You think I held a conversation with the Prince of Darkness? Don't be silly. I just prayed to Satan for what I wanted, and he delivered. I didn't sign a contract for my soul. I just know how to invoke a little help when I need it. Get over it."

Nick shook his head. "I don't like it. But at least you're safe."

"And if I get protection like this, I won't have to fight, and I'll be out in six months."

"But to what end? Or to what beginning? I'm afraid you've gone too far, and you won't have a future. You need to get your life back on track."

Joe leaned back. "You mean like you and Jake?"

"Well, yeah. We're both doing okay."

"And I'm not. That's your point."

Nick felt his brother slipping away. "This detention center helps make my point."

"You're getting good grades in a top university, and Jake's our poster boy at Annapolis. Well, here's my question. Who the hell are you trying to impress? Mom's dead. Dad was never alive as far as I'm concerned. Who gives a shit? Life's about surviving, and I've found a way." Joe's brow cast a sinister shadow over his face

A warning rose in Nick's heart with the realization that his brother hadn't stumbled into Satanic worship overnight. The discussion suggested that his baby sibling had been perfecting rites, rituals, and a relationship with the occult for years–secretly.

Whether the cause or the effect, the occult explained much about Joe–his solitude, his depression, his troubles.

Nick fumbled through small talk until the end of the visiting hour, offered Joe a hasty hug, and marched from the detention center.

As Nick entered his apartment, uneasiness agitated him. An important concept lingered on the edge of his awareness, and he sought its name.

Responsibility.

For the first time in a decade, someone else tended to his siblings, undermining his self-worth. He needed to be needed, but he feared external forces supplanting his parenting role while the military saw to Jake, and now–if he dared entertain it as truth–evil spirits saw to Joe.

The absurdity of the Devil caring for his brother resonated on multiple logic levels. Bizarre events pointing to the preternatural had plastered the periphery of Nick's life, but Joe's reckless leap into Lucifer's lap made him wonder if there were entities exercising their wills beyond mankind's perception.

Nick paced through the living space–a sizeable floor plan for a student, given the generosity of a life insurance policy from each parent. But walking failed to quell his anxiety.

Attempting distraction, he flipped through television channels but remained fitful. As he sought an outlet for his nervousness, the allure of alcohol became gnawing.

School and Joe had curtailed his university social life, and he struggled to develop human bonds beyond his brothers. But as a gifted student with a selfless bent to help others learn, he enjoyed a circle of temporary and convenient companionship with his classmates who studied zoology.

Like himself, those with whom he associated preferred the study of animals to that of humans. He found the certainty of animal behavior preferable to mankind's complexity, and his comrades admitted the same.

He lifted his phone and called a Michigan native, Scott, whom he considered a colleague–for lack of anyone else holding the title.

"Nick! Man, we could use you. We're scratching our heads over this omega wolf thing. I mean, either you're in the pack, or you're not. I don't think the omega really is, because they abuse him so bad. Can you make sense of it?"

"It's complex, but I can explain it. You want to talk about it over some beer?"

"Serious? When did you start drinking?"

"Tonight. Now."

"Uh, sure. I think we need another hour or so of studying. Bill and Rich are here, too. We're in the library."

"Can you make it half an hour?"

"Shit, Nick. What's up?"

Nick sighed. "My little brother's been in juvenile detention for two weeks."

"Sorry to hear that. Hold on." Scott held a rapid background conversation. "Yeah, we'll wrap up here. Let's meet at Nickels Arcade on the State Street side and we'll figure out where to go."

Nick could count on one hand the number of times he'd been drunk. As he lifted his second pint of ale, he expected he'd need his second hand before the end of the evening. But a force stronger than alcohol's euphoria convinced him to slow his pace.

Her name was Deborah.

Tall and elegant, she entered the bar with an endearing confidence. Ordinary beauty eluded her, her cheek bones being less pronounced than commonly desired and her nose reaching a half inch beyond that of cover girls. Young men had to look twice to appreciate her allure, and the minority who did became captivated in absorbing brown eyes, a sultry jaw angling to a narrowed chin, and tempting lips that spread into a captivating smile.

Nick sensed that she knew her destiny, and he hoped to be a part of it.

As a female acquaintance from his advanced biology class led her to the table, Deborah looked to the four men seated at the booth, turned her ankle, and stumbled into Nick's side.

Nick clasped the arm of her jean jacket as she recovered, and then he slid his buttocks into the student beside him to make room.

The acquaintance made the introduction. "That talented example of human dexterity is Deborah."

Nick recognized her. "I've seen you around. Are you okay?"

"I think I sprained my ankle." She crossed her leg over her knee and grabbed her foot.

"How bad?"

"I hate when I do this. It's not fair."

"What's not fair?"

"I'm too tall with small feet."

"You're not too tall. I think you're a perfect height."

From across the table, Scott, his red hair appearing sanguine under neon lighting, shared his insights. "Easy, killer. Flattery won't work. She's got a boyfriend."

"I don't anymore."

The acquaintance flipped her hair and gave a sinister smile. "That's right. We're celebrating her freedom."

"Then we'd better get you drinks, ladies." Scott leaned forward and pulled the group's attention into a discussion about its next episode with alcohol.

A warm cloud rose within Nick. Despite her immediate and uninvited proximity, Deborah seemed to belong next to him.

She lowered her foot and flipped her straightened shoulder-length brown hair over her back. "I didn't get your name."

With her swarthy skin, he pegged her for being of Middle Eastern stock as he extended his arm. "Nick."

She shook his hand. "Deborah. But you already knew that."

"What are you studying?"

"Journalism, but I want to be a lawyer."

"Well, you're in a good school for that."

A peanut bounced off Nick's chest, and he looked across the table.

Scott smiled an impish grin. "This is a good school for everything, you dork. You call that a pickup line?"

Before Nick could retort, the new object of his desires glared at the teaser. "Can we have a conversation without the commentary?"

Scott raised his palms. "Hey, I'm just protecting my buddy from a heartache because you're way out of his league."

"I appreciate the flattery, but we're going to ignore you and hold an adult conversation."

Chides from the other young men ruled in favor of the lady in the battle of wits.

"Where were we?" She smiled. "Oh yeah, what are you studying?"

Nick dared to hope her interest in him would grow. "Zoology, like the rest of these guys."

"Cool. Who doesn't like animals?"

"Exactly."

"You have an accent. Let me guess. You're from New York."

"Not quite. Connecticut."

"Same thing."

Nick found her subtle audacity charming. "How are they the same thing?"

Her blush, smile, and rolling eyes melted him. "Well, I mean, they're close geographically, aren't they?"

"Fair enough. They share a border. Some people commute into the city, but that part of the state's really a Manhattan suburb. I come from the real Connecticut where people work for a living."

"Really? Like what?"

"Well, we lived in a Hartford suburb. There were all sorts of businesses there. Financial services were big, and insurance, too."

"Oh, yeah? How about your family?"

"Not a good story."

"I'm sorry."

He sipped his beer, nursing it to fend off inebriation. He considered Jake and judged him an interesting enough subject to keep the lady's attention. "I have one brother who's at Annapolis and wants to become a Navy SEAL. He's the type of guy who can do it, too. A real stud and a genius."

"That's awesome."

"He's a rare breed. A bit arrogant, but it's hard not to be when you've got the talent he does."

"That's annoying."

"True, but he's got a good heart. He says he's surrounded by so much talent at the academy that it's starting to humble him."

"Do you believe him?"

"I think so. He described the first year like prison with humiliation piled on a serious school load. He had nineteen credit hours on top of an unofficial six hours of military learning."

"That's impossible. That's insane."

"All they do is work, train, and study the first year. He hated it, but he stuck it out because he's not a quitter."

"If you're surviving zoology here, you're no idiot either."

"I imagine not. What about you? Where are you from?"

"Farmington Hills."

Nick gave a blank stare, faltering under the assumption Michiganders suffer about everyone on the planet knowing the location of every town in their state.

Rescuing him, she stiffened her right hand and pointed it toward the ceiling to replicate the map of the state's lower peninsula. Then she slid her left index finger across the meat under her thumb. "Detroit's here. I live here."

"Cool. I see it now."

A waitress brought cocktails and beers, and Nick slid his new ale beside the one he nursed. He intended to ignore the latest drink to retain his focus on the intriguing lady who showed interest in him.

As his conversation with Deborah progressed, will power proved unnecessary to stave off drunkenness. Though he sensed one door closing with his brothers' need for him, he hoped another one was opening to female companionship.

She smiled at him, and the day's anxiety passed.

CHAPTER 5

Nick watched the ladies' shifting curves as they excused themselves.

Scott's commentary brought him back to the table. "I stand corrected. She's hardly taken her eyes off you. You didn't slip her a drug, did you?"

A quiet man, Nick gave a look of stone.

"Okay. I get it. I'll stay out of your business."

"Well, our business is your business now."

"What's that mean?"

"She invited us to a party."

"What sort of party? I thought we were having a party right here."

Nick felt embarrassed and excited about the invitation Deborah had shared before heading to the restroom. "We're going to a session with a Ouija board."

"No kidding? Should I bring milk and cookies?"

Deborah following her, the acquaintance returned. "No, but you may want to lay off the beer. We've decided that you gentleman are worthy of joining us, and you don't want to be drunk for it."

A smile covered Scott's face. "I like the sound of that. Where are we going, for real?"

Nick interpreted the man's lewd look as pathetic, knowing his colleague had been making failed advances at the acquaintance for months.

The acquaintance continued her rejection. "To my dorm room. But don't worry, there'll be plenty of other guys there to keep you away from me. Tonight isn't about your hormones. It's about the dead speaking to the living."

"So, Nick wasn't kidding. You're serious? A Ouija board?"

"That's what we're doing."

"Talking to the dead is impossible."

"If you don't believe me, you're welcome to stay here and drink by yourself."

As the group paid the bill and departed, Scott shrugged his shoulders, muted his doubts, and followed.

The Ann Arbor evening had grown cool, and Nick lingered with Deborah behind the gaggling sidewalk crowd. "Have you seen this type of thing before?"

"Yeah, just once. It was really cool and kind of freaky."

"Isn't this a game by Parker Brothers? I mean, we're just talking party tricks, right?"

"It doesn't matter what you call it. It's something inexplicable, at least if you believe what I saw last time."

"What did you see?"

"I don't really want to explain it."

"I bet you could if you tried."

"I'd rather have you see for yourself."

"At least give me a clue."

She slowed her gait and turned towards him. "It's really better if you see and judge for yourself. But if you just can't wait, I'll tell you what I saw."

"Tell me."

"Two players work the board. They're blindfolded, and nobody reads the letters or words out loud. Someone else writes them down silently. The writer also asks the questions. We flip the board in a random rotation after every latter so that the players can't do anything by memory."

"That's scientific. But what's the outcome?"

"We're pretty sure that we're having conversations with sentient metaphysical beings."

"You can't be serious."

"You asked for it. Now get ready to see it for yourself."

Two dozen people crammed into the small dorm room, and Nick found himself wedged into a corner standing next to Deborah. During a dramatic silence, two blindfolded coeds worked the optics over the board. As the lens landed on each character, another coed scribbled the letters onto a scratchpad.

With their eyes glued to the unfolding scene, two more coeds lifted the board and rotated it randomly before setting it down on the laps of the players. Then the team repeated the process for each ensuing character.

Nick found the scientific rigor admirable. "Have they been this disciplined since the beginning?"

"No, they didn't get hard core about it until they started seeing personalities on the board. Then they had to start ruling out human error and mind games."

"Personalities?"

"Yeah." She raised her voice. "Who's talking on the board now?"

A long-haired engineering student, the apparent leader of the group, kept his eyes on the board. "It's the young boy who says he died during the sixties in a car accident."

"What's he saying?"

"Let him finish. We didn't ask him anything yet other than his name and how he's feeling."

"Well, he's not the one with the crush on me." Deborah shrugged and gave Nick a coy smile. "The one with the crush on me is the teenage boy from the seventies."

In silence, the engineer raised his finger as a final handful of characters came in from the two players. "It looks like you just scared away the young boy. His last words were 'Tom here' and 'bye'. Looks like you're up, Deborah."

"I didn't scare him away. My spiritual admirer overpowered him."

"Either way, it's your turn."

"No way. Tanya doesn't have to use the board when the little boy's telling her he's got a crush on her."

"Okay, then your new guy friend here can play."

Nick felt a shiver, but the curiosity overwhelmed him. He pushed his way through the small crowd and sat in front of the board. After exchanging blindfolds with one of the participants, he sat on the stool and placed his fingertips on the optics.

Trying to debunk the game, he sought tactile clues on the board and the optics, but nothing showed itself. Seeking cracks of light through the handkerchief around his face, he saw nothing but darkness. And having sat at the board before the other new player, he had no idea with whom he was partnering.

He accepted that he had no control over the outcome. The optics started moving, and then they stopped.

The lead engineer called out. "Next letter."

Nick felt him grab the optics as two other people spun the board above his knees. Unsure how the wood landed, he felt a firm hand guide his back to the center of the board.

After several characters, he heard a murmured hush. He sensed that people wanted to announce the discovery but couldn't for fear of undermining the encounter.

After five minutes and dozens of characters, Nick wanted to quit. The presence on the board seemed hostile, and he was relieved when the engineer told him to stand and remove his blindfold.

He was surprised to see Deborah standing by him when he stood. "What's going on?"

"I'm not surprised that two guys are fighting over me, but I'm not used to it when one of them is fifteen years old and dead."

"What did he say?"

"He said to stick to animals and leave the pretty girls to him."

"How did he know I was into zoology? And why the heck are we talking about a dead fifteen-year-old boy like we just had a conversation with him?"

"You want to see the video?"

Half a dozen people raised and wiggled their phones, including the lead engineer. "It's all right, big guy. Welcome to the paranormal."

"Did you get a good video, Deborah?"

"Yeah."

"Let's watch it outside. It's getting stuffy in here."

The cool night air helped Nick regain his senses. "What just happened?"

"Do you want to see the video?"

"I don't need to. An adolescent spirit on a Ouija board just told me to keep playing with animals and to leave you alone."

"Just see it. You'll be impressed."

Nick watched the replay of the session. Nothing struck him as unusual that he didn't already suspect, but the scientific precision of the team surrounding him impressed him. There had been no cheating.

"Don't worry. What's a dead kid going to do? Threaten you on a chalkboard next?"

Nick stopped. "I'm not worried about how a dead boy named... What was his name?"

She appeared surprised but accepting as she broke stride and faced him. "Tommy."

He released her. "I don't care how Tommy communicates with us next. I do care that we believe a dead boy just talked to us."

"Okay, I agree that it's weird, but you have to admit it's adorable."

Intrusions from the preternatural world struck him as fascinating and shocking, but not adorable. What he agreed was charming was Deborah's apparent enthusiasm for anything she encountered. Being alone with her and keeping her attention seemed like an achievement rivaling his best accomplishments.

She walked by his side as giddiness floated him down State Street. Then a warm turd smacked his forehead. "Crap!"

"Hey! Bird poop is good luck in the Chaldean culture."

He ignored her counsel and felt indignant. His quiet rage stirred, and he pictured the offending pigeon plummeting into the pavement. But the touch of her fingers pressing a Kleenex into his skin soothed him.

As he looked up, he saw a curious sight over the quadrangle. The offending fowl appeared to recover from a death dive before tumbling across the grass.

"There. Clean as new." She tossed the tissue into a wastebasket as they walked.

"You're about the most pleasant company I've spent time with since I can remember."

"Oh, shit."

"What's wrong?"

She became a statue on the sidewalk as a dark figure approached under the streetlights. "That's my ex-boyfriend."

A sinking feeling invaded Nick's stomach. "Are you sure?"

"Of course, I'm sure. I'd know that jackass anywhere."

Before Nick could think, the man's quick steps brought him to Deborah. He sounded haughty. "Well, just who I was looking for."

She stabbed her fists into her hips. "You have no business with me."

"You may not be up on current events, but we're engaged."

"Bullshit."

He cracked a sardonic smile. "Your family knows what's best for you. It's taken care of. You're my fiancée now."

"What do you mean I'm your fiancée?"

"I don't know what world you're living in, but traditions matter, and I took care of it. My family and your family agreed."

"You can't do this."

Nick heard her sobbing but kept his silence.

"Don't tell me what I can and can't do. I just did it. If you don't believe me, call your brothers or call your parents. Or call your sister. Or call your aunt. I don't give a shit who you call as long as you realize you're mine."

As tears ran down her face, she looked at Nick. "I'm sorry."

The ex-boyfriend intercepted the apology. "Don't apologize to some guy you just met. You need to start paying attention to your future husband." He grabbed her jacket and yanked too hard for Nick's tastes, but he knew better than to interfere.

As he stood and watched them walk away, he wondered if her civil rights had been violated. But she seemed to accept the rules her culture had dealt her.

In a final act of desperate defiance, he pictured the assailing pigeon diving for the man's back.

For a moment, he saw the world through the eyes of the bird. Trees and buildings moved below him rapidly, and he felt like he controlled the ailerons of a living aircraft.

When he turned to depart, he heard the snap of the bird breaking its neck between the man's shoulder blades. As Deborah's future husband screamed, Nick headed home to make sense of the evening's improbable events.

CHAPTER 6

Nine months later, Deborah's parents wearied Father Lewis.

The mother was incessant. "Are you sure she's not possessed?"

Though it had bishops reporting to the Roman pope, the Iraqi Catholic Church in America lacked exorcists. Suspected cases of possession among its parishioners required intervention from a Western rite diocese, making Lewis their exorcist. He knew the concern when dealing with elderly Iraqi Americans–gossip.

He needed to be truthful and gentle, and he knew he was talking to more than the young lady's parents. Phones would ring, family matriarchs would speak for hours, and a thousand Chaldeans would know his judgment by the weekend. "I can say truthfully that I see no signs of possession in your daughter."

The parents exchanged looks of relief as they uttered words to each other in a foreign language, but the mother expressed doubts. "But you don't seem certain."

"There are some demons, the averti, that can be difficult to diagnose. They remain hidden much longer than the others, but I don't think we're dealing with that. Given that your daughter was able to recite prayers and receive the Eucharist, and given that she's shown no positive signs of possession, I believe she's safe."

"But how can you say she shows no signs of possession when she says she's possessed? What are the signs of a possession?"

Lewis realized the mother was asking the questions because the father faced a language barrier. Though his duties as an exorcist and his support of the Chaldean culture made his Aramaic passable, he withheld that fact. Dealing with the mother sufficed. "Will you translate for your husband? It's important that you both remember."

"Yes. Of course."

"Though each exorcist has leeway in the diagnosis, the Rite of Exorcism identifies three distinct clues that cannot be faked, and they all involve unnatural abilities. The subject must demonstrate impossible knowledge of a foreign language, impossible physical abilities for his or her stature, or unknowable knowledge of events past or future. Deborah shows none of these."

"How can you be sure about her languages? She speaks three at home, and I'm sure she's learned more at the university."

"Demons tend towards older languages, and though I have to discount Aramaic with your daughter, I've heard no Latin, Hebrew, or Greek."

"You mention physical abilities. What about making a bird fly into the back of her fiancé?"

Lewis reclined in his chair and exchanged a knowing look with the psychologist seated by his desk. He and the medical professional had dealt with similar scenarios. "If the action of the bird was caused by a demon, that's an infestation of the demon within the bird. It would not be a possession of your daughter."

"But demons could be attacking my daughter by manipulating the world around her. The bird, her dangerous games with the Ouija board, and God knows what else she's into."

The priest cleared his throat, preparing for the most difficult message. He found it odd that people preferred to learn their loved ones were possessed versus other possibilities. Possession had a cure. The unknown did not.

"What you described is called demonic oppression, which is difficult to diagnose. In fact, it's so hard to diagnose, that there's no practical point to it. I wish I could give you more certainty and comfort. However, a life of virtue and adherence to the sacraments is the best defense against all demonic attacks."

"So there's nothing you can do?"

"If you'll allow me and Doctor Morris some private time with your daughter, we'll do a deeper investigation. I will include, with your daughter's permission, the sacrament of reconciliation. That will be a great help if there is indeed a demonic oppression."

"Of course, Father Lewis. Thank you."

The parents excused themselves and left him with Deborah and the psychologist. Her parents' departure seemed to lift a weight her shoulders.

"Deborah, with your permission, I'd like to make the rest of our discussion a reconciliation. Of course, you understand that I'm bound to hold everything you say as a secret, but so is any bystander to a confession, which binds Doctor Morris. In addition, you have the protection of client confidentiality with Doctor Morris. But if you want to talk to me alone, that's fine."

She shrugged. "He can stay. I haven't confessed in a while, but there's nothing I need to hide."

"May I begin the sacrament then?"

"Well, before you do, are you absolutely sure there's no possession here? I mean, I don't think so, but my parents are driving me nuts."

Lewis leaned forward, smiled, and pointed to the unmarked pitcher of water the group had been sharing. "You've been drinking holy water for the last half hour. If there were a demon within you, he would've complained by now."

She blushed, smiled, and granted permission for the session to begin. Father Lewis uttered the proper lines, allowing her to express her sins for forgiveness. "I hate my fiancée, and there's nothing I can do to stop the wedding."

Lewis knew that the forces driving a traditional Chaldean wedding rivalled those of an earthquake. It was as futile to halt tectonic plates as to derail the girl's fate. He pitied her. "I understand this is difficult. Have you expressed your opinion to your parents?"

"Only once. I don't want to risk the screaming and throwing of objects again."

"I'm sorry you have to go through this. This is a cross to bear. However, the only sin you mentioned thus far is your hatred.

This is one of the most difficult challenges we face. Jesus wants us to show infinite forgiveness and infinite love, even for those in the flock who oppress us."

"I don't even like him. I never wanted to date him. My rights are being violated."

Her pain resonated within Lewis, causing the injury in his low back to ache. He shifted his weight to find comfort. "I will never understand what it feels like, but I've seen this before and can counsel you. I understand if you would prefer counseling from the Chaldean priests. Although I feel capable and would like to help, they may have more appropriate experience."

"Not with exorcisms they don't."

"But you do understand the chance of this leading to an exorcism is extremely remote."

"I know. I have to admit, the possession idea was mine."

"You mean you suggested it to your parents?"

"Yes. And you can see how the slightest fear of it ruining the wedding has turned them into gargoyles."

"Did you suspect it could possibly be true?"

She lowered her gaze. "No. I'm faking it. I'm not sure how to play it out, but I need every option I can to stop this wedding."

"I appreciate your candor. You understand that this is bearing false witness, perhaps not against your neighbor but against yourself?"

"Yes."

"Are you remorseful for this and for hating your fiancée?"

"Yes."

"Is there anything else you need to confess?"

"No. That's all."

"Do you wish to stop committing these sins?"

"Yes. I'm not sure how, though. I don't want to lie anymore, but I don't see an escape."

"It's okay if you don't know how to stop sinning, as long as your intent is true. Can you express remorse for your sins and ask for God's forgiveness?"

"Well, yeah. I don't want to lie. It's wrong."

"Good. You can recite the Act of Contrition if you remember it, or you can express your request for reconciliation in your own words."

She chose her own short prayer.

"Your penance is to read the thirteenth chapter of First Corinthians. Pay attention to Saint Paul's comments about love and how they would apply to people who oppress you, including your fiancé. This is a difficult challenge for anyone, but Saint Paul's words may comfort you."

"I will, Father."

"As for your parents and the possible oppression, you can leave that to me. But I'll need your help."

"What can I do?"

"Will you give me the names of the people that you remember who joined you at the Ouija board?"

"You mean the night of the bird attack? The last night the entities on the board talked?"

"Yes. I mean exactly that, especially the young man you were with prior to the bird's attack."

With the parents back in the room, Lewis explained the plan.

"While I see no sign of demonic possession, I want to see her again in six months. Of course, you can bring her in sooner if she demonstrates dangerous behavior. The family's concern for her well-being has moved me, and I want to be completely sure about this. I'm even going to interview some of the young people who were involved in the strange events."

The mother softened her hard face. "Bless you, Father."

During the family's exit, Deborah mouthed a silent 'thank you'.

The psychologist scowled. "What was that all about? You never get involved in non-possessions like this."

"I'm not sure what happened to me last night, but I may have been blessed with a visitation related to this case."

"We've been friends for years. If you can tell anyone, you can tell me. What happened?"

"It may have been a dream, but it felt real."

"So, who was it?"

"I shouldn't tell you. I feel sworn to secrecy at the moment, if not by direct command, then by a deep humility. I can tell you, however, that it was a creature serving God."

As he paused to assess the psychologist's reaction, Lewis recalled his visitation from Gabriel the archangel.

Knowing Gabriel to be among God's elite, Lewis feared the pride of feeling special after a visit from the one who announces epic matters. The great archangel had appeared in human form, matching the images Lewis would expect from descriptions in Scripture and from antiquity's artwork.

The angel had said little, but through his spiritual sharing of knowledge, he had conveyed much. If it had been a dream, then it was more lucid than any moment in Lewis' life.

But the messenger's source didn't matter.

To Lewis, faith mattered, and his faith told him to trust the messenger.

"Why don't you tell me what he or she said? Then we can assess how you received it."

"That sounds good. The messenger was male, and he said that I needed to exorcise the demon I fear."

"I didn't know you feared any demons."

"There's one that has troubled me. You watched me struggle with him for almost two years with that young high school athlete."

The psychologist nodded, and Lewis appreciated that his professional friend knew better than to utter the monster's name.

"I remember. That's the only time I wasn't sure you were going to succeed."

"I never told you, but that was my second battle with that demon. I faced him once during my early years of exorcist training, before I knew you. I lost the girl to suicide."

"I'm sorry."

"I consider it two defeats. I should've had him and his underling demons out of the high school athlete in half the time.

Speed matters when the demoniac is suffering."

"Why would you fear him? You may consider it two defeats, but the way I see it, you overcame an early loss by becoming a stronger exorcist and winning your second encounter."

Lewis rubbed his eyes. "This demon works against me. Always. He knows he cannot possess me unless I make a grave error, but he knows he can oppress me because I'm weak."

"You mean your drinking?"

"Yes."

"And you're sure that the message of your visitation is particular to this demon and to Deborah's case?"

"Maybe. I felt certain I would get my first clue today."

"Then her presence here was your first clue?"

"I believe so. I believe if I follow the trail of evidence starting with her, I'll find my way to a third encounter with that beast."

"Are you sure you want to chase this demon down? Can't you just wait to see if God puts him in your path again?"

"The fact that I'm hesitant confirms that I am afraid. My fear suggests the truth of the message and the presence of the messenger, as I interpret it. I believe this is a call to action."

The psychologist frowned. "Do you want my opinion?"

"Of course."

"As a psychologist, I conclude it was a dream. Your subconscious mind is posing a challenge to help you stop drinking. In that respect, it's healthy, but only if you can stop. If you'll allow, I've become educated in chemical interventions for alcohol reduction. I have some treatments I can recommend, but you have to be willing to follow them."

"I believe now that I have no choice."

"Okay. I will connect you with a psychiatrist who can prescribe medication. What I have in mind is called The Sinclair Method using the drug naltrexone. It's a harmless, simple, and effective method for tapering off your brain's desire for alcohol."

"I'll give it a try. Nothing else has worked."

"Good. As your friend, I think this is a journey you must

undertake, and I'm here to support you."

"I appreciate it. Thank you."

"And as a practicing Catholic who's seen exorcisms, I know what that demon bastard has done to people. I'll never forget the dislocated jaw of the high school athlete. If that young man had lacked one ounce of strength..."

"Then you understand why I must follow Deborah on the trail to that demon, whether my visitation was a dream, a visitation, or something else."

"You're darn right, I get it. This is a top level demon, and God has chosen you as his champion."

"But what if I find him and fail?"

"You can't. You need kick him back to hell so hard that he stays pinned under the wrath of Jesus until Judgment Day."

CHAPTER 7

Lewis felt misplaced.

He knew how to look like a civilian, but with a dark blue Van Heusen dress shirt and black wool pants, he doubted he fit in. In the academic town of Ann Arbor, he failed to pass as a student, a professor, an administrator, an entrepreneur, or anything else that belonged. The strange glances within the coffeehouse seemed endless.

Worse, Nicholas Slate was late.

As a man of improving patience, he struggled to remain calm while drinking his second cup of bold house blend. He considered calling the young man, but he thought the gesture might appear desperate. Instead, he recited a prayer, and a minute after he finished it, the zoologist student came through the building's front door.

Lewis recognized him from public images on social media, and he made immediate eye contact. The student's eyes sparkled with recognition as he walked towards the priest.

After a quick handshake, he sat across the table from his desired next clue to a demonic possession, possibly the victim himself. "Thank you for seeing me, Nicholas."

"I'm happy to help, Father Lewis. Please, call me 'Nick'."

"Okay, Nick. I appreciate you seeing me. Did Deborah tell you what my interests are?"

"Yeah, she told me pretty much everything."

"Did she explain my specialty in the priesthood?"

The student lowered his voice. "She said you're an exorcist."

"Are you okay with that?"

"Sure. I think it's kind of cool, actually. I'm sure she told you we used a Ouija board and saw things that defy explanation. So you can assume that I'm receptive towards the paranormal."

"Then you don't mind if I ask you several questions along the lines of possible paranormal activities in your personal life?"

"Not at all. I was raised Catholic. So I have a pretty good idea of the ground rules. I figure you're trying to connect the dots between some strange events to biblical teachings, including dealings with angels and demons."

"That's exactly what I'm doing."

"A demon's more or less an angel with a bad attitude, right?"

"Not quite. Every demon is a fallen angel." Lewis reconsidered the teachings. "Well, on second thought, I guess you could say that. For their incredible intellects, angels don't get forgiveness, like humans do. We fall and get back up because we're creatures of habits and slow learners compared to them. But each one of them understood God's plan in a single thought, and then they declared their holy alliance or their hostile rebellion."

"Angels stayed holy, demons fell."

"Yes. And it's a bit of a mystery, given angels' extensive powers, but God took some powers away from demons as they fell."

"Wow."

"My expertise is specifically demons, and they are brutal beyond our reckoning despite any powers lost during their fall, but that's where I'm trying to end up while discussion your interactions with Deborah. You don't need to believe in them to support my questioning, but I wanted to be candid about it."

"That's okay, Father. I'm an open-minded guy. Not to be rude, but that's one reason I left the Catholic Church. I thought it was too closed-minded."

"Well, once you make the leap of faith, you become tied to a truth, and you have to logically rule out possibilities that contradict it. If you run into enough contradictions, you have to take a step back and reassess your truth, but my life as an exorcist has only solidified my belief in the supernatural. Surely you can respect that as a scientist."

"I can. I have my reasons for not buying into your beliefs, but as a scientist, I can't disprove them either. And I find the paranormal fascinating. So, your beliefs are as interesting as anyone's for trying to understand inexplicable things."

Lewis found the young man's perspective relaxing. He'd been concerned that the zoology student would balk at a faith-based worldview. "That's great. Is this booth private enough for you?"

"Sure, Father. Go ahead."

"Let's start with common ground. Can you help me better understand your relationship with Deborah?"

Looking away, the young student seemed heavyhearted. "We definitely had a connection. I'd seen her plenty of times before the night with the Ouija board, and we'd even had a few quick conversations in passing. But something about that night brought us together in a way I thought was meaningful."

"I'm sorry. I can sense your sadness. I understand the history of her engagement. So there's no need to belabor how that came into being. Can you tell me about your relationship with her now?"

"We're friends, but I'm afraid it won't last. I mean, it probably shouldn't last. She's going to be somebody else's husband soon, and my continued presence in her life doesn't make sense."

"This is a difficult matter."

"She's a journalism major, and she found a way to write a series of articles about me and what I'm studying to give us some time together. She's a year behind me, but she'll be married for all of her senior year. So I doubt our cute little way of seeing each other can continue. I'll finish my undergrad degree and graduate in a couple weeks. Then a couple weeks later, she'll be a May bride."

Part of Lewis wanted to find the young lady's parents and speak out against the forced wedding, but Chaldean priests had taught him that any well-intentioned interference into weddings worsened the woman's lot. "So, what's next, if graduation is so soon?"

"I was accepted into a PhD program. So what I've been researching through analysis in my undergraduate degree can now become something I explore in reality."

"Congratulations. That sounds exciting."

"I've been working with electrical engineering students to measure the brain waves of peregrine falcons. My senior thesis was about the possibility of using those brain waves to see if we can digitally map what a falcon can see."

"That's fascinating."

"I couldn't agree with you more. Unfortunately, I've got a couple years of classes to learn more about birds and digital signal processing before I can dive into the fun part."

Having ceased his caffeine intake, Lewis sipped from a glass of ice water. He listened as the student continued.

"As part of my PhD, I'm going to enlist some help from our laboratory animal medicine group, and we're going to actually hardwire electronics inside the skulls of birds."

"Is that possible?"

"It sure is. It's going to take some delicate work and a lot of planning and testing, but the animal medicine group says they can do it. I've already mapped out the interesting areas of a falcon's brain, and they tell me it's easy to implant wires inside a bird's skull."

Lewis thought the student's falcon research corroborated his suspicion of a demon having infested the pigeon that had attacked Deborah's fiancé. When he factored in the strange but revealing comment on the demon-driven Ouija board about Nick playing with animals, he smelled a paranormal trap. "Do you know what you'll do if you can make sense of a falcon's brain waves?"

Nick grinned. "No pun intended, but the sky's the limit. Given the visual acuity of a falcon, the intent is to replicate a high-resolution digital mapping of what the bird sees. That in itself would be an amazing achievement, but I've been warned enough times that it needs a practical application. So, I need to drive it towards that."

"Fascinating. This may be one of the most exciting topics I've ever heard."

As a waitress brought coffee to the student, Nick was blushing and smiling. "I have to admit that's flattering, given that it's coming from someone who fights Satan and his minions for a living."

"I guess neither of us is pursuing a boring career."

"I hope you don't mind if I consider this a two-way interview. I've always had an interest in the paranormal."

Lewis was willing to share insights into his profession to earn the student's trust. "Of course. We can exchange questions, too. Whatever works best."

"Cool."

"I'd like to ask a question about the practicality. I may be ignorant, but it seems to me that military spying with a falcon could be done more easily with a man-made drone."

"Agreed. But it's a matter of stealth. People are smart enough to recognize drones as threats. And, yeah, birds have been used in warfare throughout history, but nobody's used them like this." The student sipped from his coffee, baiting further inquiry.

"Like what, specifically?"

"Spying passively, where the target doesn't know the falcon's an enemy who's watching him."

"I think I see what you mean."

"For example, if a drone or reconnaissance aircraft is high enough, the target doesn't know he's being watched. But falcons can get closer than those systems, and you could use them on protected targets, since anti-air missiles aren't designed for little birds."

Lewis respected Nick's research. "I can only wish you the greatest success."

"That's good to hear. Some people give me grief for trying to turn innocent wildlife into a weapon. I wasn't sure where the Catholic Church stood on this."

"The Catholic Church supports righteous wars. I have to trust that the outcome of your research would be used properly."

"Speaking of wars, isn't that what we're talking about when we look at your work? Wars against evil entities, whether they exist in the flesh or not?"

"Of course, given my perspective, I'm trying to link this all to demonic activity. But it's far too enticing for an exorcist to jump to the conclusion that a demon is involved. That's why we consult psychologists and psychiatrists when someone we're investigating should be getting therapy for mental health."

The student sipped coffee and pondered. "I've never been to a psychologist or psychiatrist."

"I'm not surprised. You seem mentally healthy. How about any periods of blackouts?"

"None."

"Has anyone ever told you about strange behavior that you don't remember?"

"Nope."

"Okay. Good. As you've probably already concluded, you show no signs of being a victim of possession. Oppression possibly, but not possession."

"What's that mean?"

"Oppression means a demon is working against somebody without entering that person's body."

"That still sounds scary."

"It's terrible, and it's difficult to prove. But if someone under attack undergoes a lifestyle change from one of vice to one of virtue, you can retroactively infer that an oppression existed once the oppressive events stop."

"The only occult-like behavior I've willingly even dabbled in was that night over the Ouija board. And as you've probably figured out, I was just following a pretty lady where she wanted to go. I had only a passing interest in it."

Lewis saw an opening. "Based upon what Deborah told me, you must've been impressed with what you saw."

"There's no denying that it defied logical explanation. I just considered it another reason to keep my mind open to realities beyond my five senses."

"Can you describe what you saw?"

"Personalities. I think that best describes it. It seemed like conversations with sentient beings of some sort."

"This is where I have to suggest that they were demons and that any personality the board claimed was an act of fiction scripted by one or more of their kind."

"Did Deborah show you the video?"

"She did."

"Well, you may see that as demons. I don't know enough about demons to say."

"There are few who do. But let's come at this from another angle. How about that attack with the pigeon the night you met Deborah."

Nick shifted in his chair. "She concocted her possession story out of desperation with her marriage. The guy's a jackass, and she can't stand him. But a pigeon committing suicide just to startle a jackass doesn't make any more sense to me than the Ouija board. I'm trying to cooperate, but I'm afraid I'm not helping."

"No, you're helping. Investigations into the paranormal are complex. Did you experience a premonition about the pigeon's behavior, or ever feel as if you were in control of it?"

The comment turned the young man's face to stone.

With decades of counseling behind him, the priest could sense when someone wrestled with sharing the truth.

"No. Nothing like that."

Lewis also had a snout for sniffing lies, and he kept his mouth shut to study the student's discomfort. Sensing he'd delved as deep into the subject as Nick would allow, he let the lie linger unchallenged before changing course. "Perhaps there was something in your childhood that could lend insight? You mentioned you had an open mind towards the paranormal. That can sometimes result from childhood experiences that defy explanation."

The student looked into his drink and then glanced at his phone. "I don't mean to be rude, but we should probably wrap things up. I need to meet with my adviser, and I still have work to do."

"I don't consider it rude at all. I know your education is your highest priority, and it should be. I appreciate your candor and willingness to talk with me."

The student rendered a cordial but quick exit, leaving Lewis with his thoughts.

Stalemate.

The priest believed he'd uncovered the next clue leading to his nemesis demon that the archangel had named, but he sensed an impasse in Nick's instant apathy with respect to the preternatural pigeon and paranormal events from childhood.

If it weren't for the angelic visitation, he would've stopped his investigation. But God's will demanded that he persevere. It would take endurance, persistence, and, as he approached the truth, courage. Unfortunately, the endeavor stirred a compulsion within him.

He needed a drink.

CHAPTER 8

Two years later, Nick carried the bird of prey inside a transparent cuboid into his laboratory. His adrenaline pulsated throughout his bloodstream as he placed his raptor on a table. "Are you here, Andy?"

His lab partner appeared by his side and stared at the feathered focus of their future. "I'm here. Is she ready?"

The bird had become like Nick's pet, and he expected her compliance as he ran his fingertip from her skull to her back, feeling the wires running from her brain to the dime-size transmitter sewn under her skin. "She's ready. Are we?"

"I've got the electronics set up just like every other time. I could do it in my sleep"

"I don't mean to ask dumb questions. I'm just a bit nervous."

"Who wouldn't be?"

"Should we just get started?"

Nick was nervous, too. "Let's get it over with."

"Okay. Help me move the whiteboard."

Nick helped his partner roll the makeshift visual barrier between the bird and his colleague's workstation. Then, as the other PhD student sat, he grabbed a pencil, a notepad, and two customized, oversized cards.

"I'm ready, Nick. Go ahead."

The zoologist flipped a coin. After seeing the results, he wrote on his notepad that his first card would be the red one, which he then lifted to the female falcon's eyes. Knowing the computer needed time to interpret the bird's recorded brainwave signals, he waited for a cue to continue.

Beyond his sight, Andy obliged. "Got it."

Nick lowered the card and flipped the coin again. Getting the opposite result of his first toss, he noted that the second card would be violet. "Next card." He held it in front of the bird and waited.

"Got it."

The duo repeated the process through the tenth iteration.

After the final repetition, Nick's patience proved ephemeral. "Well? How the data?"

"Shit, Nick. I see enough frequency separation to call each one."

Nick's sweaty palms grasped the notepad. "Go ahead."

"Red, violet, violet, red, red, violet, red, red, violet, red."

In a flash, Nick darted around the whiteboard and placed the notepad in Andy's face. Though not a hugger, he accepted his colleague's embrace as they bounced and howled in euphoria.

Ten out of ten were correct.

A month later, Nick watched his partner languish over his thoughts.

A half-empty coffee pot and a toppled two-liter bottle of diet Mountain Dew revealed that enough caffeine pulsated through the man's veins kill a small mammal. Digging his fingers into his disheveled hair while balancing his elbows atop bobbing thighs, the electrical engineer appeared ready to explode. "I know there has to be enough data. I'm just too stupid to extract it."

Nick showed compassion. "You've had enough computer science guys look at it, and you're no slouch in digital signal analysis. At least that's the word on the street."

"What street?"

"You know. Our academic community around here. You don't think I would've partnered with you without doing checking on you first? Everyone knows you're a genius."

"My adviser will disagree when he realizes I can't make heads or tails of this brainwave data."

"We've made heads or tails already. We can duplicate the red versus violet all day. That was breakthrough stuff. We're all but guaranteed to get our degrees now." Nick felt dirty the instant the words left his mouth.

"I hope the shame you feel for saying that is punishment enough. This isn't about our degrees. This is about what we can accomplish. I just don't want to look like an idiot in front of my adviser if we fall short because I can't handle the data."

"His hands aren't clean in this. He's supposed to be helping you, but he can't get our data precise enough to call out discrete colors either." Nick looked to his computer for inspiration. He'd learned to view electromagnetic signals as pulsating waves of information. Before him, the screen showed the frequencies and amplitudes comprising the radiated emissions received from his falcon's brain.

Though they had succeeded in differentiating between the red and violent frequencies which marked opposite ends of the human visual spectrum, they struggled to discern the colors in between. When using seven color cards separated by equal frequency intervals, their data produced useless results. Andy sighed in defeat. "Yeah. Maybe it's too much to try."

Nick believed that if they remained unable to improve the granularity of their results, his research would sputter and die. Consistent with his laboratory partner's defeated posture, he saw nothing usable in the data. "I guess we just keep taking the Edison approach. We consider our work to date proof of what doesn't work, and we keep working towards what will work."

"That only works when you're fumbling through real-world options. We're dealing with the mathematics of digital signals. We only have two ways to fix it. We either get cleaner data, or we find magical algorithms that sort through this shit."

"We're not getting any cleaner data. We've already got three falcons wired up, and we don't have money for more."

The electrical engineer stretched his body from its forward-curled position into a full back arch over his chair. "Maybe it's not our fault. Maybe Peregrine Falcons Three through Five are retarded."

"That's mean. Nobody talks like that."

"Sorry. I'm just pissed off. And I know that the chance of three birds all having the same visual or brain deficiency is zero. I need to solve this with signal analysis."

An idea took shape in Nick's mind that he found both brilliant and absurd. He hesitated to share it. "Huh."

"What are you thinking?"

"Maybe the problem is that even the brain of a bird is too complex to digitize."

"Then we're screwed."

"There's something we could try. Instead of trying to digitize this, let's run this straight from the bird's brain to mine."

Andy rolled forward in his chair. "You don't look like you're joking, but if you're not, you're an idiot."

"I don't mean surgically implanted electrodes. What if you made a helmet that transmitted the raw analog signals to my brain?"

His partner's brow furrowed. "That's actually a pretty good idea. Are you thinking you could see a color in your own mind based upon what the falcon sees?"

"It's got to be possible. Even if it's not perfect, it would be interesting. We could combine the digitization of the data with the human element. We can run the algorithms in parallel to my subjective interpretation, and we can see if I can recognize some patterns."

"I know this is a good idea, but building a helmet like that, even a one-off prototype, is nontrivial. We need to think this through."

"Sure. Of course. We're scientists after all."

"Correction, my friend. You're a scientist. I'm an engineer."

"I was trying to give you a compliment." Nick smirked as he dodged the lobbed whiteboard marker.

"That's what I think of your compliment, asshole."

"Just trying to cheer you up."

"Your idea with this helmet has already helped. Now we just have to come up with some design requirements."

"I guess we start out simple, huh?"

"Yeah. Let's start out with what's already available."

"Makes sense."

"I know they have helmets that read human brain waves in the gaming industry. I could reverse engineer one from a receiver to a transmitter, if you don't mind me microwaving your gray matter while I figure out the power setting."

"Not at all. What've I got to lose? If we can't figure this out, my brain's useless anyway."

"I'll dig up some information on safe radiation doses from our medical gang and start working on the design."

Weeks later, Nick walked on the sidewalk that bounded the university's iconic grassy yard. He headed west on University Avenue towards State Street, where he intended to turn in a random direction in search of a random distraction.

Despite a favorable partnership with Andy, Nick considered himself inept with human relationships.

A drunken dare in high school had relieved him of his virginity, and rare episodes of inebriation at the university had garnered a few other nights of frolic. There had even been an attempt at romance with a nursing student, but a combination of romantic incompetence and social awkwardness had undermined the doomed and short-lived endeavor.

After the spark with Deborah had died, he had kindled nothing.

As for friends, he had none. Andy enjoyed his company but would become a memory after they earned their degrees. Having parented his family, he excelled in survival but sputtered in social skills, and he had failed to reverse the trend despite countless opportunities during his undergraduate years.

He had only his brothers, each a world away.

Joe spent more time in correctional facilities than in freedom, and the Navy had swallowed Jake.

The loneliness saddened Nick, but as he thought of his middle brother, his ringing phone offered temporary relief.

He answered. "Jake? What's going on?"

"I'm on a study break."

"That's three times this week already."

"You're not complaining, are you?"

"No."

"Submarine School is easier than the nuclear power pipeline, and it's the most practical stuff I've studied in a long time."

"You're going to a Trident Missile submarine, right?"

"That's right. The Colorado. It's a good assignment."

"This is the first time I remember hearing you say anything positive about your submarine training."

"For a few months there, I almost wished I'd tried to become a SEAL. I was getting tired of nuclear power training. I mean, a full year of training on the reactor plant before I even see a submarine? It was infinite minutia. It was ludicrous."

Predicting that the conversation would endure, Nick sat on a bench. "But you're still happy you decided to go submarines, right?"

"It would've been interesting to see if I could've been a SEAL, but it's a rough life. You have to love it, and all the field action is for the younger officers. I think it's a job that becomes less fun over time."

"But you think it's different in submarines."

"Of course. It's about evolving into commanding a submarine. That's what it's all about. But enough about me. What are you up to?"

"You remember the red versus violet experiment?"

"I have to admit, that was interesting. Have you made any progress since then?"

Nick could tell the original experiment's success meant nothing to a guy with his ambitions set on commanding a submarine. "Unfortunately, no. We're having trouble with the colors in between. We're kind of stuck."

Jake sounded dismissive and uninterested. "I'm sure you'll figure it out. You're a smart guy."

"I've got an idea or two. I'm sure I'll get through it."

"That doesn't sound very convincing."

"It's hard for me to keep focused when I feel responsible for Joe. I feel like I should be putting less time into my degree and more time into helping him get back on his feet."

Jake grunted. "Any news from our black sheep? Is he in jail?"

"He's on a first name basis with the Washtenaw County Corrections staff."

"That's embarrassing."

"He had a horrible childhood. You know how bad it was for us. Imagine what it was like at his age."

"You make too many excuses for him."

"Maybe."

"Make sure you finish your degree. If you take your foot off the gas, you'll start heading in his direction. I went to a military college so I'd be in a place where laziness and distractions weren't options. Since you don't have that structure, I'm the only guy who can look over your shoulder to keep you focused. I'm looking now."

"I can't just pretend he's not alive. I worry."

"Let him rot in jail."

"He's not rotting. I visited him last week, and he looked fine, at least for him."

"What's that supposed to mean?"

"He looks sad and angry all the time. That's who he is now. Just sadness and anger. He's a monster, and I blame myself for it."

"You can't do that. You have to get that advanced degree. You need to make everything of yourself, if for no other reason than to offset the balance of that little wretch. You can't let him stop you."

"Could you turn your back on him if you were me?" The moment he finished his question, Nick regretted dishing out the ammunition.

Jake became haughty. "Heck, yeah! I worked hard in high school, I worked harder at the academy, and I worked even harder in the nuclear pipeline. Nobody gave me a damned thing. I don't want to hear his sob story. He's just lazy."

"That doesn't mean we have to abandon him."

"Sorry, bro. I already have."

"Can we change the subject?"

"Sure."

In the silence, Nick failed to think of a new topic. "I can't think of anything."

"Girls! The Navy keeps moving me around too much to find a girlfriend. Maybe you're having better luck?"

"I hate to disappoint you, but I've been married to my work for a long time."

"You must see the light at the end of the tunnel. At some point you'll be 'Doctor Slate', and you're going enter the real world. You have to think about your future."

"Nothing interesting ever happens in my social life."

"Well, get yourself a girl. You're in a target-rich environment. You should be beating the ladies back and making them take numbers for dates with you."

"I'll do the best I can."

"Promise?"

"Yeah. Hey, do you mind if I let you go?"

"No problem. See you later." As Nick stood and slid his phone back into his pocket, he regretted his romantic life. Though a scientist, he tried to ignore the evidence of why his sucked.

It had died with the marriage of Deborah.

He allowed himself a rare moment to reflect upon her. He wondered what might have been had she remained free. Did she miss spending time with him? Did she think of him at all?

Half a block later, his phone rang. He didn't recognize the number, but he dared to hope. "This is Nick."

"Hi, Nick. This is Deborah. Do you remember me?"

Wondering if a psychic lure had attracted her call, he choked back emotions and tried to be calm. "Of course. What's it been? Two years?"

"Something like that."

"How are you?"

Her drawn-out sigh framed her answer. "I need someone to talk to."

"And you thought of me?"

"Yeah. Is that okay?"

"It's okay with me, but I'm concerned that we'd be breaking some unwritten rules. You're still married aren't you?"

"I'm still married, but I'm miserable. It's no better than I predicted. It's actually worse. I'm not sure there's any advice you can give me, but I need to talk to somebody."

"I'm flattered you thought of me, but how would we do this without getting in big trouble?"

"Leave that to me."

CHAPTER 9

Nick opened the outer door to the academic building and allowed Deborah to enter the hallway. Instead of greeting him, she turned and gazed through the glass for the spies her paranoid mind feared.

He'd expected joy upon seeing her, but as she faced him, her carriage was forlorn. Concerning him, she'd devolved from an enthusiastic beacon of purpose into a worn beast of burden. Against her curling shoulders, she strained to raise her chin. "Nick!"

"It's great to see you again, Deborah."

"You, too."

He felt awkward hugging her, and she seemed reluctant to accept the embrace. She became lifeless, and he released her. "You seem nervous. Let's get to my lab." He led her up a creaking stairway.

She tripped but caught herself on the handrail.

He reached for her. "Are you okay?"

"I think so. I'm just klutzy."

"Tall girl with small feet."

"Right." He escorted her to the room. Before he could offer to show his work area, she pulled the chair from his desk and sat. "I've only got about twenty minutes. My cousin's applying to the school, and I was able to bring her on campus as her escort. I skipped out while she's in a group presentation, but if I'm not there when she's done, it'll arouse suspicion."

He rolled the chair from Andy's vacant workstation and sat facing her. "They make the women spy on each other."

"Yeah, but that's not my biggest problem. This is my biggest problem." She unfastened her top button and exposed a burn on her collarbone.

"Dear God. Did he do that?"

"He pulled the flat iron out of my hands and pressed the tip into me right through my shirt."

"I'm sorry. This is wrong."

Her eyes welled up. "Thanks. That's all I was really looking for. I showed my mom, and she's in denial. She has no idea how to deal with this."

"This is terrible all around. You're a victim, and you have no concerned witnesses. You have no voice."

"He slapped me a few times in the past, but I had to miss days of work so that nobody would see the marks. So slapping became too risky for him."

"He's an ogre. I'm surprised he just didn't tell you to stop working. That would've been more consistent for him."

She buttoned her blouse and wiped away her tears. "I'm no dummy. I got a job writing for a Chaldean newspaper. It pays peanuts, but it gets me away from him and gives me a public persona."

"I knew you were smart. He can't stop you from working without having to explain it to the readers in your community."

"Bingo. But now he's adjusted his tactics. Assholes always find ways to be assholes."

"I'm not a violent person, but this really angers me. I... care for you."

"I care for you, too." She stood and hugged him.

As she sat back down, her grace and strength under adversity spurred his thoughts towards retaliation. "My brother's a black belt, and he's about two hundred and twenty pounds of solid muscle. I'm sure he'd do whatever you need done to your husband, and he'd make it look random."

"Isn't this your brother who's in the Navy?"

"Yeah."

"That's too much for him to risk."

"But at least you're open the idea?"

"I'm not one of those wives who blames herself for an abusive husband. I know this is wrong, and I'm going to fight back. I have been fighting back."

"How?"

She looked him in the eye. "Can you keep a secret?"

"I think we've sworn an unspoken pact already."

"I'm taking birth control pills without him knowing it. He wants to start a family. I'm doing everything I can to stop it."

"That's got to be hard for a Catholic girl."

"I confess regularly about it, but not to the Chaldean priests."

"They wouldn't breach your confidentiality, would they?"

"I don't think any of the modern priests would, but I've heard rumors in the past, and I'm not taking any chances. In fact, I confess this to only one priest."

Nick probed his memory. "Father Lewis? The exorcist from Our Lady of Sorrows?"

"He advises me to stop and to trust God's will, but I can't. So I've got legit pressure from a priest to stop, and I'm terrified of what would happen if my husband found out, but I have to keep doing it. I don't want babies from this monster."

"This is too much for anyone. Why not just run away?"

"That's an option, but it's last-ditch. I don't want to give up my entire family. I love them all, despite their pressuring me into this stupid marriage. They mean well."

"I'll help you any way I can."

"You already are."

Her response softened his heart in a way he failed to process. To compensate, he switched subjects. "My other brother knows how to fight. He's scrappy about it, but he usually wins, I think. We'd have to wait until he gets out of jail, though."

"It's not that desperate. Many women have been through worse. I need to come up with something better."

"We need to come up with something better. I don't want you to be alone on this."

"I appreciate it. I should get back, though."

"Yeah, let's get you out of here."

"Say goodbye to me here and let me walk out alone. It's safer that way. God knows who he has watching me."

Weeks later, Nick awaited his partner's arrival into their lab.

When Andy came through the door, he carried a box under his arm. "Sorry I'm late. You know how it goes. As soon as you're ready to move the prototype, a wire pops lose."

"That's okay. Let me see it."

They huddled around Andy's workstation, and Nick watched his partner slide the prototype from its box to the desk. The white gaming helmet looked new except for the splicing into its wiring harness. Rubberized plastic, shrunken by a heat gun, protected the wired interface the electrical engineer had created to connect the repurposed toy to his custom control box.

"Looks really nice. You do good work."

"It's a beauty."

"What's inside that?"

"It runs on two small batteries, and I've got a couple boost-buck switching networks to vary the voltage from two to twenty-four volts. It's got a couple low-noise amplifiers that I picked from some radio circuits. I also made a USB interface for the data. Other than that, I've got a bunch of passive elements for filtering and cleaning up signals as needed."

Nick impressed himself as he visualized the basic circuits. "I think I actually understand what you just said."

"You've been studying. They should give you an honorary electrical engineering degree–bachelor level only, of course."

"I don't care about that. I just want this to work."

"Depending how it goes, I may have to make adjustments with the soldering iron. It's pretty much optimized for nothing other than experimenting across the full range of settings."

"You ready to get started?"

"Why not? Who's our bird?"

"Peregrine Falcon Five."

"Why him? We've used him the least."

"I figured he'd be best because he has the strongest signals."

"You're right. Biggest falcon, strongest signals, least amount of noise when amplifying. Maybe someone should get that honorary degree ready for you."

Andy lifted the helmet over Nick's head. "Are you ready?"

"As long as you've got it set on its lowest power level."

"I do. And you'll be sitting beside it the whole time."

Ordered to his size, the helmet was comfortable. Nick sat at his partner's workstation and faced the monitor. "It's a good fit."

"If this works, I'm getting you drunk tonight."

"You know I don't drink."

"But if it works, I'm not taking 'no' for an answer."

"Okay. I won't argue. Go for it."

Andy flipped a switch to energize the battery-driven circuit. He then slid a USB cord into his computer, and a new window appeared on the monitor. "I hope you'll excuse the barbaric programming interface. I didn't bother making it pretty."

"That's fine, as long as you don't turn me into a vegetable."

"There's not enough power to do that. Okay, everything's ready. We're set for gathering data on my workstation, and the data's ready for being fed into the helmet's control system."

"What are you waiting for?"

"Nothing." Andy tapped the keyboard, darted around the whiteboard, and then tinkled an eight-sided die on a table. "First card."

Faster than Nick had dared to hope, billowing plumes of red formed in his vision. He made a note on a scratchpad. "Got it."

Out of Nick's view, the clinking die signaled Andy's next roll. "Rolled an eight. That's no good. Re-rolling."

Again, Nick heard the plastic octahedron dance on the table.

"Next card." With the partners having switched positions, Andy revealed his impatience. "I said 'next card'."

"Hold on. Give me a second." A cloudy color formed in Nick's mind. It shifted, vibrated, and wobbled between yellow and blue, but it settled like a mist of green. Nick stared at the phantom until he convinced himself it represented reality. "Okay. Got it."

They repeated the experiment through all seven cards.

"Read them out, Nick."

"Here goes. Red, green, blue, orange, indigo, violet, yellow."

His partner's footsteps fell like lead. When Nick looked to him as he rounded the corner of the whiteboard, he expected to see signs of defeat. Instead, the engineer beamed. "Show me that."

Nick grabbed and extended the scratchpad.

Andy's eyes devoured the information. "No shit."

"It worked?"

"Yeah. It worked."

"Let's do it again to be sure." After subjecting himself to three more tests–two of them in front of their advisers who hurried to join them upon being summoned, Nick maintained his perfect score. Humoring his partner, he rode the feeling of victory towards his favorite bar.

Six graduate engineering students sat at the table. Andy had gathered them to the celebration, his ease in attracting an impromptu crowd highlighting Nick's inability to call upon anyone.

With two pints inside him, Nick reached for his third. Slipping into the numbing alcoholic abyss, he let his mind float. The initial buzz of the experiment's success waned, and he remained silent as small talk meandered from chair to chair.

A glance across the laminate showed his partner draining his third pint and outpacing him. Andy's eyes drooped as an idiotic smile crept across his face. "If you don't believe me, we'll show you."

The comment that had spurred the engineer's energized retort had eluded Nick's ears, but he sensed an inescapable outcome in the conversation's direction.

A student lowered his beer. "It's not that I don't believe you. I just think it's worth seeing for myself."

The smile fell from Andy. "You mean, like, right now?"

"Sure. Why not?"

After a rapid debate flared and died, Nick accepted the group's decision. For the next hour, his life's work would be a carnival show, and he launched a weak protest. "I've had too much to drink to drive."

Andy shook his head. "That's no problem. We've got a designated driver."

Nick tried to resist. "The falconer's facility is closed now."

"You've got the key though, don't you?"

"Yeah, but I'm not supposed to disturb the birds while they're sleeping."

"Come on, man. After what we did today, our trainer won't mind. You're turning his birds into historical heroes. They're like those space monkeys. What the hell were their names?"

A beer-drinking student answered. "Albert."

"Yeah." Andy pointed at the student's nose. "Like little Alberts, only in raptor form. We've named our falcons by numbers. After what we did today, we should give them proper names."

Nick tried a final dissuasion. "Didn't a bunch of Alberts die?"

"Yeah. But we lost a couple of falcons to surgery, too. That's what happens when you're pioneers."

Nick noticed that people were standing to leave. "Okay. Let's get number five back into our lab. It shouldn't take long to get him back onto the table."

Forty-five minutes later, Nick sank into the chair at Andy's workstation. He heard the crowd breathing beyond his sight, with the falcon, despite their attempt to remain silent.

With the workstation energized, he slid the helmet over his head. Needing liquid courage to muddle through his social awkwardness, he gulped from his fifth beer and then plopped the can onto the table. "I'm ready."

Andy tried to sound sober. "Okay. Here we go. First card."

With his thoughts slowed, Nick expected the experiment to require additional time. But the inverse effect surprised him, and a yellow hue took hold of his mind's eye. "Got it."

Andy rolled, and the die settled. "Next card."

A sea of orange flooded Nick's thoughts. "Got it."

The remaining five cards proved trivial. With the crowd gathered around him, Andy verified the perfection from behind the whiteboard. "Read them off, Nick."

"Yellow, orange, green, red, blue, violet, indigo."

The female student expressed her shock. "Oh my God. That was amazing."

As Nick grasped the helmet to remove it, a vivid image formed and stopped him. He dared to utter what he saw. "He just turned his head towards her, didn't he?"

Andy sounded unbelieving. "He looked at her just when she started talking. Don't tell me you noticed through his eyes?"

Per Nick's memory, this was the first time he'd been the center of attention since being bullied early in high school. With inebriation goading him, he allowed himself the continued theatrical performance. "He's still looking at her, isn't he?"

"You're freaking me out, dude. He's got his eyes glued to her."

"Maybe I'm controlling him."

"You mean you're gawking at a pretty lady using a falcon's enhanced vision? That's a new level of perversion. I commend you, sir."

"I'm no pervert. I didn't notice it earlier, but she's got an engagement ring."

"Now you're doing a parlor trick. But I am impressed the bird's still looking at her. Can you make him look at someone else?"

"I have no idea. But she's waving at him now."

The collective held breaths told Nick he was right. He then heard whispers as his lab partner led an effort to test him further. "Okay, smart ass. How many fingers is she holding up?"

Like a sandstorm of colored dust, and image swirled in Nick's consciousness. For an instant, he saw her three fingers, and then the image faded into opaqueness. "I think I saw three fingers."

"Correct. Now how many?"

"Four."

"Correct. And now how many?"

Nick saw her middle finger. "No need to be rude."

Andy admitted the ruse. "That was me. I made her flip you off. Holy cow, Nick. This is incredible."

Nick heard murmurs and shuffling feet. Expecting the crowd to praise him, he resented the students for walking out the door.

Andy sat next to him. "Okay, they're gone."

"Why'd they leave?"

"You scared the shit out of them, Nick. And I have to admit, I don't know what the hell's going on."

"I don't know, either. I just started seeing stuff I've never seen before. It's like the clarity went up by a factor of ten."

"You think it's because you've been drinking?"

"I hadn't thought of that, probably because I'm too drunk to have thought of it."

"Well, I've had some practice thinking while drinking."

"There might be something to this. Maybe if we can use chemicals to slow my mind, or alter my brain waves, or something along those lines, I can maintain better clarity."

"I'll contact some of my biochemical engineer friends tomorrow and see what they've got for us."

Nick looked to his partner. "This is amazing, you know. This is what we set out to do."

"I know. I'm really looking forward to following up on the chemical part. But I do have a piece of advice."

"What's that?"

"Based upon the reaction of the gang, we've already gone too far to show this to casual observers anymore."

"That was embarrassing at the end."

"Yeah. The next time I talk about bringing random people up here, slap me in the face."

CHAPTER 10

Lewis felt ten feet tall as he loomed over the energumen. Having extracted the demon's name, he anticipated victory. "In the name of Jesus Christ, tell me the sign of your departure, so that I'll know when you have left God's servant."

The possessed responded within an ugly voice. "I've already told you."

"In the name of Jesus Christ, tell me the sign of your departure, so that I'll know when you have left God's servant."

The demoniac, a middle-aged adulteress who had turned to fortune tellers for assistance with her failed gambling efforts, assumed a contrite demeanor. "She will inhale deeply, and then she will sigh."

Using the demon's name, the exorcist ordered the beast from the possessed demoniac.

The lady leaned back in the chair, opened her mouth, and expanded her lungs. When she appeared ready to burst, she curled forward and issued a long-flowing exhale.

After the physician verified the freed woman's health, Lewis led the small team in prayer, completed the rite, and then dismissed them.

Joining Father Mark in the rectory's kitchen, he thought he would help prepare dinner while enjoying his triumph. "These are getting easier since I've cut back on the drinking."

"I thank God the medication has helped you."

"As do I. It's improved my private life, and you just saw how it empowers my work."

"Take care to beware the sin of pride."

"I don't think that's risk for me. Do you remember the powerful demon I struggled with years ago? The one who entered the strong high school athlete?"

"That's one I expect to always remember."

"The demon brought up my injury from the Army."

"If I remember correctly, that's why I didn't ask you about it afterwards. I thought it might be too painful."

"The demon accused me of cowardice."

"Ah, I do recall that now."

"I never told you the details of my injury."

"I'll listen if you'd like."

Lewis hesitated but shared his suffering. The memory played through like a movie. "It was a suicide bomber, a young woman. I don't know how she got so close to our Humvee, but the guy responsible for guarding her sector must've been daydreaming."

"So you weren't even responsible for stopping her?"

"No, but neither was Sergeant Masterson. I saw her coming, and I screaming at the guy who should've been screaming at her. After he did nothing, I shot at her feet, and she kept coming. But Masterson was a third-tour sergeant, and he wasn't afraid to kill. He shot her, and then so did I, but she had a bullet-proof vest and kept coming."

"My God."

The memory hurt as Lewis uttered its description. "Masterson sprinted for her and knocked her over. She knew it was over, and she detonated. Only Masterson and the guy who screwed up died. The sergeant saved a half dozen lives, but the blast threw my back into the Humvee. You know the rest."

"That doesn't sound like your fault."

"But I could've acted along with Masterson."

"Then you'd both be dead, and the world would be short one exorcist."

"I did what my training taught me, but that's just an excuse. Soldiers need to have courage and improvise."

"You have to try not to blame yourself. I know it's not easy."

"It's impossible without God, but with Him, it's possible. I pray about it every day. If nothing else, it assures my humility."

"Well said. It's your cross to bear. Now, how should we prepare these chicken breasts?"

That night, Lewis allowed himself several drinks in the basement. A regimen of naltrexone had curtailed his intake to the minimum to numb his back pain. He also swallowed a prescription neurotransmitter inhibitor, knowing that the naltrexone blocked his opiate receptors and nullified the effect of narcotic painkillers.

The frustration of his war-driven injury and the futile efforts of modern medicine to alleviate his endless suffering angered him. He considered temporary freedom from his pain adequate justification for the dangerous mix of gabapentin and alcohol.

But he recognized the sin in using alcohol to temporarily shrug his cross, and he sought solace and redemption. "God, why do you allow chronic and intractable pain? Your martyrs endured horrible suffering for you, but you strengthened them during their lives. Tt's different for us who endure lifetimes of pain. The pain makes it hard for us to connect with you."

He sipped from a bourbon and Diet Coke. "It's maddening. It drives your people away from you. How can you expect me to love you, when you hold me back with suffering?"

He downed a mouthful. "You've helped me reduce my intake, and I am grateful. You gave me the wisdom to seek prescription medications and to use them to manage my pain. But your servant can endure only so much. Sometimes I need to feel nothing."

He chugged half the glass. "I should feel love for you. I should feel love for all of humanity. This is my calling. Why do you make it so hard?"

Switching gears, he asked someone else to pray for him.

Saint Gemma Galgani had been one of his favorites since seminary. She had endured grotesque back problems without complaint, and she'd even stared down the Devil. "Saint Gemma, please pray for me to the Lord our God. You understand what I'm going through. Somehow, you endured with much more grace and honor than I do. You are an inspiration."

As the medication took effect and the sharp stings softened, he distracted himself with a movie. After thirty minutes of watching, his mind melted away. Walking on the edge of consciousness, he unfocused his eyes from the screen and used his peripheral vision.

An ominous apparition in the corner of the room caught his eye, but when he faced it, it disappeared.

When he felt capable of sleeping, he resisted the urge to pour another drink. He shut down his laptop and went to his room.

A dream of rare lucidity overcame him. Paralyzed, he drifted, unsure if he remained asleep.

The apparition gave no greeting, but Lewis knew it.

Gabriel.

The archangel uttered the name of the demon Lewis feared. The exorcist's voice failed as he attempted to respond, and his visitor departed.

A quantum slice of time lasting a duration beyond Lewis' reckoning passed, and then he awoke. Having discounted the archangel's visit years ago after Nicholas Slate had blocked him, he wondered if the mix of alcohol and prescription medication had fabricated this night's episode.

That weekend, as he rendered the sacrament of reconciliation, he finished his prayer of absolution. Through the privacy screen, he heard an old man struggle to stand and walk out of the small space.

The next believer entered the room and pulled the door closed. He heard the penitent kneel, and then he recognized the forlorn female voice. "Forgive me, Father, for I have sinned. It's been four weeks since my last confession."

He wanted to resist the temptation of predicting the young lady's admissions, but his mind outpaced him and queued her usual penance.

To regain his focus, he recalled the beauty of the sacrament.

No matter the state of his standing with his Lord, he served as a conduit of forgiveness from God. Absolution from an ordained priest assured his penitents a return to a state of grace in exchange for sincere repentance, regardless of his personal weaknesses and failures.

He wished that exorcisms were as straightforward. "Go ahead, my sister. I'm listening."

"I've been using birth control pills and doing so without my husband's knowledge."

Lewis had lost count of how many times he'd heard her confess it. "Is there anything else?"

Her hesitation was a deviation from her memorized script. It startled him, drawing attention to his sore back. He leaned forward in his chair for stability.

"I'm having adulterous thoughts for a friend. I avoided this old friend for years due to my husband's jealousy, but I needed to talk to him, and I did. I think I'm in love."

"I see. Before we discuss this, is there anything else?"

"No, Father. That's it. Before you share your thoughts, can you come out from behind the screen? I mean, you know I am."

"Of course. The privacy screen is just a courtesy. We can do this as you desire." He stood, stooped, and swept his chair into open space. He then sat and faced her. "It's good to see you, Deborah."

"I don't want to get explicit, but you can assume that my marriage is far from the model that Christ defined."

"I remember that you were forced into this. I can't imagine the challenge."

"I won't lie to you, Father. It sucks."

From her body language, he suspected abuse. "You know you can tell me anything, and it has to remain confidential. I can't reveal what you tell me here without your permission under penalty of excommunication."

"It's probably as bad as you imagine. It's your stereotypical one-sided disaster, probably a bit more on the violent side, but let's just let it go at that."

"That's hard for me to let go. But it's your right to tell me to take no further action if that's what you desire."

"I know it's wrong, and I know all the places I can turn, and I know all the support I can get. Just keep it a secret."

He shifted in his chair to relieve his back. "I'll keep it a secret. Let's move on and talk about the confession. Let's set aside the birth control pills for now and talk about your new issue."

"Okay."

"Adulterous thoughts are a form of temptation. It's okay to be tempted. That's not your fault. How you deal with temptation is important."

"I don't want to go into graphic detail. But I'm pretty sure I've gone beyond temptation and am thinking thoughts of my own will that I shouldn't be."

"Okay. That's a good confession on that subject."

"Thank you."

"It's always okay to love someone. But when you say you're in love with your friend, I assume what you really mean is that you're infatuated. There's no sin in having these feelings. Just be aware of them so they don't lead you into sin."

"I understand."

"You don't need me to remind you why taking birth control pills is sinful, do you?"

She shook her head.

"For your penance, I want you to pray five minutes to Jesus for the salvation of your husband's soul. His heart is hardened. Pray for the softening of his heart and his turning towards his Savior."

"I will, Father."

"I will also ask Saint Rita of Cascia, the Patron Saint of Distressed Women, to pray to God on your behalf. For extra credit, you can pray for her intercession as well."

She looked to the ground. "I hate to be a downer, but I've asked her for help a lot."

"I know this is a test of your patience, among other virtues. You'll have to trust that this ties in with God's plan, even if you and I can't see it. The one thing I can promise is that you don't have to go through this alone. I will always be willing to listen."

"Thank you, Father. This is testing my faith, and I'm not sure how much longer I can take it."

In the rectory's lounge, Lewis searched his laptop for archived contacts. After finding the number, he called Nicholas Slate and was surprised when the student answered on the first ring. "This is Nick?

"Good afternoon, Nick. This is Father Lewis Bannen."

"Hello, Father. It's been a while. How are you?"

"I'm well. I hope you don't mind me calling."

"Not at all. In fact, Deborah and I were just talking about you. She says you're the only one she trusts for confessions."

"I'm flattered."

"What's on your mind?"

"I was hoping we could pick up where we left off of a couple years ago about your research."

"I've made a lot of progress. I don't think you'll see much evidence of demons in it, but like I said back then, I'm open-minded and curious. You want to meet at the same coffee shop?"

When Lewis arrived at the coffeehouse, he saw Nick look up from his table and wave. After a warm handshake, the priest sat and ordered a breakfast blend with the blueberry muffin.

"How've you been, Father?"

"If I remember correctly, I think we agreed the last time we met that neither of us does boring work. But thankfully, mine has been pretty routine, which is how I like it. I'm eager to hear how your research is going."

"It's been fantastic. We're right on schedule of where we'd hoped to be. The way we've gotten here is unexpected, though."

"How so?"

"It's been too hard to develop an algorithm to convert a falcon's brainwaves into pixels. However, we realized we can feed those waves into a human being's mind to generate useful data."

A server brought Lewis' snack.

"That's incredible."

"I imagine you're questioning if this is science or paranormal activity."

"I am, indeed. Which do you think it is?"

"I'm pursuing this like a scientist, of course. But if you're willing to come back Thursday, you can see for yourself."

"The school would allow that?"

"You'll have to sign a confidentiality agreement. I suggest you take advantage of it now, before my research gets funding that could close it down to the public."

"I appreciate the offer."

"No problem. Now, what can you tell me about Deborah, without violating anything confidential? I really miss her."

Days later, Lewis entered the academic building and followed Nick to his lab.

For the complexity of the research, Lewis noticed only one piece of interesting equipment. A hospital bed consumed the center of the room, and a suite of stanchion-mounted devices for measuring vital signs rose from the floor.

Other than medical equipment, he found the room simplistic. It looked more like an electronics workshop than a center of science as Nick introduced the two men in the room. "This is Andy. He's my lab partner, and he'll become a doctor of electrical engineering about a year before I earn my PhD."

The young man turned from his workstation and stood. With his sleeves rolled up, he appeared attired for comfort. Lewis shook Andy's hand and introduced himself.

Nick introduced the man in his late forties "And this is Doctor Gerry Ross. He's my adviser."

The priest accepted the doctor's greeting. For an academic man, Ross seemed personable. "It's not every day we get a priest who's interested in our research. I don't remember having a religious professional show interest in my research teams in the twenty years I've been associated with the university."

"I hope I'm not intruding."

86

"There may come a time, hopefully sooner than we all think, where we'll get the funding to commercialize this, and whoever writes the check will probably shut down our work from all spectators. But until then, you're welcome to join us as long as you adhere to the nondisclosure agreement."

"Thank you. May I ask your opinion on how the research is progressing?"

The electrical engineering student looked away. Given Nick's explanation of the roadblocks in digitizing the data, Lewis understood the gesture of defeat.

Ross, however, became animated. "We've had a dozen volunteers who could discern the red card from the violet card, but only a few could discern the more discrete colors. Recognizing patterns is the Holy Grail in this effort, and so far, Nick's the only one who's done it."

"Have you had any insight into why that is?"

"Solving that is almost as exciting as helping push Nick forward into the unknown. If you think of the practical applications, it's useless if Nick's the only guy who can interpret signals from a falcon. So, we need to figure out what makes him succeed and determine if it's something that can be learned, if it's something genetic, or what have you."

"Fascinating."

"We're about to get started. Why don't you pull up a chair? The only rule is absolute silence. So please turn off your cell phone and get comfortable."

Lewis sat and watched the team prepare. With Nick lying on a hospital bed wearing a plastic helmet hooked up to a strange-looking black box, the other two men tended to their workstations.

The adviser announced an update for the priest's benefit. "We're just waiting for the medical response team. They should be here any second."

"What are they for?"

"They'll administer the serum and make sure Nick doesn't die while he's under."

Nick craned his neck to make eye contact. "I'm hardly unconscious during this. It's like I'm in between asleep and awake. There's no danger, and we should go ahead and build a machine to automate the drug delivery so we don't have to wait like this."

Ross killed the dream. "Right as you may be, the university's legal team would never agree to that. As long as you're doing this experiment on the university's dime, you're a medical liability."

A soft knock preceded the door opening, and two women in light blue scrubs walked through. They smiled and wished the priest a good morning as they walked by him, but they had no time for an introduction.

One of them checked the medical monitoring equipment while the other inserted an IV into Nick's arm. A few minutes later, one of them looked to the adviser and nodded.

Ross returned the gesture. "Thank you, ladies. Let's begin."

Andy sounded bored and detached. "I'm turning on the camera."

Lewis looked over his shoulder and noticed an elevated lens positioned to capture the room's activities. As he looked back towards the room, he saw the electrical engineering student walking to a far corner. Focusing his gaze upon the table in front of Andy, the priest noticed the raptor within its clear container.

A computer monitor filled the bird's field of view as it rested on its perch facing forward.

Andy announced his actions. "I'm rolling the twenty-sided die. The die has settled, I have the number, and I am beginning the associated movie clip. I'm beginning the five-minute counter now."

Lewis maintained his silence as he and the others in the room alternated between watching a bird watch movie and watching a doctoral student drift in and out of sleep. The experiment's boredom made five minutes tick away like glacier movement.

Andy sounded the most bored. "The first movie clip is complete."

Ross took charge. "See if he's awake, please."

A nurse shook Nick, and he groaned. She asked him if he was awake enough to continue, or if he wanted more serum. After she lowered her ear to hear him, she nodded at the adviser.

Ross raised his voice. "Keep going. Next movie."

The bird watched a second clip, and then the nurse disturbed her patient again. This time, Nick waved her away. She shook her head and announced that the sedative had worn off and that this trial was over.

Ross walked to the bed and helped the nurses assist Nick in dangling his legs over the side. "How are you feeling?"

"Groggy."

"Are you ready to give your report?"

"The first clip showed Halle Berry with straight white hair and Patrick Stewart in a wheelchair. That's X-Men. The second one had Russel Crowe swinging a sword. I'll go with Gladiator."

The adviser looked to Andy, who announced the results. "That's correct. He got them both right."

Impressed but concerned, Lewis hoped the small team would find a scientific explanation for Nick's success, knowing that failure would open doors to terrifying realms.

CHAPTER 11

Nick finished the most grueling academic test of his life.

Like a sleepwalker, he handed the last packet to the proctor and lumbered towards the door.

In the hallway, he sniffed air that seemed less stifling than the classroom which had caged him for eight hours. Every shred of knowledge he'd crammed into his memory about zoology, biology, and subjects he could never care about, ranging from single-cell organisms to the brain functions of primates, had flowed from his body and through his pencil to stacks of paper.

As he began to feel human, he lifted his cell phone and called his adviser. "Gerry?"

"How'd it go?"

"I think I passed, but it's hard to tell. It's all a blur right now."

"I have confidence in you. I bet you passed."

"I hope so."

Ross tried to lift the student's attitude. "Can you imagine being done with tests for the rest of your life?"

"That doesn't sound bad at all. I'd like to focus on my research and thesis."

"You know it's not just all fun and games though. You still have a huge data analysis effort to figure out what allows some people to see discrete colors while others can't. If you can do that, then you have to figure out what lets you see patterns, and then you have to find someone else who can also see patterns."

Nick found his adviser's instructions daunting. "Do I have to do all that to earn my doctorate?"

"I think you'll be fine if you can propose a credible theory. I need to verify it with some of the other staff, but I think that should be good enough. You'll have to pursue proving your theory, though, to show the proper effort."

"And I have to solve it all if I want to commercialize this and keep my research going."

"That's correct. It's going to take a lot of work, but Andy should be able to help you with the data. I can get you some help, too. I have some undergraduate students who are eager for extra credit."

Three days later, Nick sipped coffee and then placed the cup on his partner's desk. "It's not looking good, is it?"

"It's the same sad story we had with discrete colors. I can't pull anything out of this data. Are you sure we're looking at all the possible biological and genetic factors?"

"We've covered everything you can get from blood samples and DNA. I was afraid of this. You have to figure, though, we're analyzing the human brain. We must be looking in the wrong place."

"Why do I feel like you're about to recommend something impossible?"

"If we're going to do this right, we need to run the experiments while people are undergoing functional MRIs or PET scans."

Andy leaned back in his chair and sighed. "I hate to say it, but this is the beginning of the end for us. You don't need an electrical engineer anymore. You need ten million dollars' worth of medical equipment and a team to run clinical trials."

"I'm afraid I agree."

"It's not all bad. We both did enough to earn our PhD's."

"Yeah. We had a good run, didn't we?"

A week later, Nick entered his lab. It felt empty without Andy's workstation as he pondered options for moving his research forward.

The door opened, lifting him from his thoughts. With his electrical engineering partner gone, he welcomed his adviser's company. "Good morning, Gerry."

"Good morning."

Wasting no time, Ross wheeled a whiteboard in front of him and started writing halfway down the rectangular space. "Here's what you suggested as future possibilities for research."

Nick moved his chair to the board.

Ross doodled a cloud around his scribbled abbreviations for a functional MRI and a PET scan. He then drew an arrow from the billowing shape to a second drawn cloud. Within the second doodling, he drew a large X and several dollar signs. "You'd be facing resistance from your test subjects, you'd need to lease or magically borrow expensive equipment, and you'd need to essentially set up a clinical trial. Very tricky. Very expensive. Well beyond our means."

"I didn't expect it to be easy."

The adviser created a final cloud to the right and then inked a dead end sign. "In fact, it's such a monumental undertaking, you can forget about it as part of finishing your degree. It may be possible for commercialization, but that's a rocky road. It's hard to find investors who are willing to pay for research. Ninety-nine percent of them pay only for proven technologies."

"So what do I do?"

Ross created clouds above the ones with the somber story. Stick figures of people replaced dollar signs, and the abbreviation 'PhD' replaced the dead-end. "You analyze the socio-cultural and environmental factors."

"Are you sure that counts as science?"

"It does for our purposes. I've already cleared the way with some hallway discussions. I've got an idea of how much work you need to do, but once you do it, I'm confident you'll earn your degree."

"I don't mean to complain when you're solving a problem for me, but this is outside my expertise."

"Leave that to me. I'll get you the right experts. All you have to do is understand what they're doing and document it as part of your thesis."

"That sounds easy enough. What factors are we looking for?"

Nick disliked the smirk on the man's face. "I have no idea. It all depends on what comes out of the interview."

"What interview?"

"Your interview. You're the prototype. Whatever factors describe you best are the ones we're looking for."

"I don't want to be dissected."

"You want your PhD, don't you?"

"Of course."

"Then I'll make an appointment for you through my colleague in the sociology department."

A week later, Nick joined his adviser in the lab to review the findings of his interview.

Ross was empathetic. "Wow, Nick. I didn't know that your childhood was so difficult. You've overcome a lot of challenges to come this far."

"There wasn't much I could do except get through it."

"Still, it bears repeating. You've been through a lot. It's impressive that you've turned out as well-adjusted as you have."

"Thanks, Gerry."

"No problem. Okay, let's review the factors. I think they're rather self-explanatory."

The adviser rattled off the outlying conditions that could make Nick different from the average person. "Loss of one or both parents. Abnormal responsibility at an early age. Victim of bullying. Above-average intelligence. Postgraduate-education. Exposed to occult-like practices. No, wait. Seriously?"

"My little brother's into it. For me personally, it's just been one time with the Ouija board, but I got the sense from the questioning that my amount of exposure to such practices was less important than how I perceived what I saw."

"Well, what did you see?"

"Results. Strange events have surrounded my brother for as long as I can remember, and what I saw on a Ouija board defied scientific explanation."

His adviser squirmed and then settled in his chair. "We can review the details later. But I think we're seeing something interesting here. Occult practices may be an indicator of someone's mindset and their willingness to accept the data coming from the bird."

"That makes sense. Do you think everyone has the ability to interpret the data from the bird, but most people are filtering it out?"

"Preconceived limits of what's possible may drive people to subconsciously reject the data."

"I say we run some experiments and find out."

Three months later, Nick reviewed the results with his adviser.

Ross hummed. "Hmm. It's not as good as I had hoped. But there's definitely a trend."

"This is just preliminary work. We had only thirty subjects. A larger sample's needed to find someone who has my level of ability. Weren't you at least impressed that half of them could see the colors and that three of them could recognize patterns?"

"Yes and no. I was impressed overall, but I was disappointed that none of them could approach doing it with the repeatability or certainty that you can."

"We still made a dent in this, didn't we?"

His adviser let down his guard and revealed a smile like Nick had never seen. "I verified that it's good enough for your degree. All you have to do is write it up and defend it."

Relief. "That's great, Gerry. Thank you. I still have a lot of work to do, though."

"I know you can do it. Are you ready for the really good news?"

"You mean it gets better?"

"There's somebody interested in funding your ongoing research. I don't know who it is, but they'll be watching."

"Watching what? Me?"

"I've been told they'll watch some or all of our field tests, either live or recorded versions."

Nick recalled that the scheduled next step was flights on the falcon trainer's land where radio frequency receivers had been set up to relay data from the birds. "We should get started before the existing money runs dry."

Ross gave a knowing smile. "I've already arranged for our first field run for tomorrow at noon."

The next day, Nick reclined into the hospital bed and slipped the helmet over his head. The familiar nurses hovered about him, and as the intravenous serum entered his vein, he slipped into a semi-conscious state.

Ross called out. "Can you hear me, Nick?"

Nick forced a groaning answer. "Yeah."

"Here comes the blindfold. Our new potential investors wanted it. Are you ready?"

"Yeah. Let's do it." Moments later, Nick saw a translucent kaleidoscope of colors that swirled into blurry but recognizable patterns. The transmitted video imagery from the fifth falcon led him on a small journey from the trainer's arm to a perch.

The falcon stopped and rested while facing one of the hundred photographs of celebrities Nick claimed to recognize. A minute later, the bird shot to a new perch where it faced another photograph.

After five stops, Nick was rousted from his semi-slumber.

Ross posed the pertinent question. "Can you identify the five celebrities?"

"Dustin Hoffman. Emily Blunt. Madonna. Al Pacino. Cate Blanchett."

"Are you ready for another run?"

"Yeah. Let's do it." He finished two more runs with the bird. But on the final run, the bird flew to a sixth perch. After waking, Nick identified the celebrities.

"You were fifteen for fifteen. Technically you were sixteen for sixteen, if we count the extra one."

"Excellent."

As the sedation serum wore off, his curiosity grew. "Do you know if our potential investors were watching?"

"I'm not sure if the potential investors had a representative at the falcon trainer's facility, but we have it on video. This was a success, anyway you cut it, and I'm sure they'll be impressed."

His adviser's phone rang, and Nick watched him talk through an animated conversation.

Ross rubbed his forehead. "Oh boy. That was our technical transfer office. I'm not sure how you're going to take this, but you now have investors who want to fund you going forward."

The warmth of hope, excitement, and anxiety filled Nick. "That's awesome, but why shouldn't I be excited?"

"It depends on your opinion of the military. It's the United States Air Force."

"It makes sense and beats letting my research die."

"If you'll allow, I'll help you work out the details. Transition from academic to commercial research can be ugly and disappointing. You need all the advice you get."

"I appreciate your help. If you're interested, why not stick around for some of the ongoing funded work?"

"Thanks for the offer. I'll give it some serious thought."

As Nick slipped from the bed and stood, he realized he was extending his world beyond his comprehension. Working with the military scared him, but he comforted himself with his new secret trump card.

He was certain the falcon's flight to the sixth perch on the third run had been intentional.

He had commanded it.

CHAPTER 12

Joe Slate looked through the glass at his oldest brother. He tried to feel a connection with the only person who gave a damn about him.

Cruel fate had taken his parents, leaving him alone with his brothers. But since their childhood, Jake had regarded him with a fervent disdain that had weakened into apathy, and he accepted that his middle sibling would ignore him forever. Nick, conversely, made the effort to show up, and he wanted to feel grateful.

But he felt nothing.

Emotions were useless for Joe, and he'd abandoned them as life's promises had abandoned him. Efforts to revive feelings within his heart had been fruitless, like trying to activate a muscle through a severed nerve.

He lifted the stale, germ-riddled receiver to his cheek. Joe knew that his brother disliked being in the prison, and his expression of gratitude was sincere. "Thanks for coming."

Nick seemed to force a chipper tone. "No problem. How are you doing?"

"Same as always. My reputation protects me."

"I won't argue if you think worshiping Satan keeps you safe."

Despite his inability to link to his emotions, Joe could feel the weight of a burden, and he sensed his past Satanic worship fueling a lingering anxiety for his brother. If anyone deserved solace, he decided, it was Nick, and he welcomed the chance to alleviate the zoologist's concerns. "It's not Satan worship anymore."

"Really? What is it, then?"

"I've been Wiccan for a while. I just didn't tell you until now."

"Is that at all related to Reiki?"

"I don't know. What's Reiki?"

"It's a healing art. I've had some free time since my comprehensive exams, and I needed a backup plan in case funding runs out on my research. I've been apprenticing with a master."

Joe had expected the conversation to revolve around his Wiccan ways, but he welcomed the Reiki angle. Whatever it was, it would be refreshing compared to the conversations with his incarcerated companions. "What's it all about?"

"Healing energy. It uses the practitioner and his or her hands as tools to manage the patient's energy for optimizing health."

"You're going to have a PhD from U of M, and you're chasing this shit as your backup career plan?"

"I know it's not going to make much money, but I'll find ways to get by if I have to. I'm doing it because it works and I want to help people."

"Fair enough. I mean, it makes sense for you. I guess it sounds cool, but I don't think it's much like Wicca."

"So, what's that about?"

Joe hoped his brother would understand. "It's based on a belief system about the powers that run the world, but that doesn't interest me. I'm in it for casting the spells."

Nick raised his eyebrows. "I assume you've seen evidence of the spells working? You're a smart guy. I can't see you wasting your time on empty promises."

"They work. I've seen enough evidence." The protection spells seemed to work for Joe as curses against those who oppressed him. His victims had suffered stomach aches, injurious accidents, and unsolicited beatings. But he considered the real test to be the spells' effects on his brother.

"Oh, like what?"

"You tell me. I cast a spell on you a few months ago."

"Uh, what sort of spell?"

"A spell for good luck. Have you had any good luck lately?"

"I'm not sure. How would I know?"

"Magick is usually subtle. As long as you think things have

been going well, we'll say it's working."

"I guess it's been fine. I passed my comprehensive tests, and my experiments have been going great. Oh, and I've got commercial funding for my research. So I guess we have a few good data points."

"You never mentioned commercial funding."

"It was a pleasant surprise, and a recent one. I was afraid I was going to run out of money, but then they showed up."

Joe recalled casting a fire-elemental money spell for Nick's funding two weeks earlier. The ritual had been a recitation of the words that expressed his desires followed by a burning of the paper. Quick, elegant, and effective.

He wanted to share the spell's success with his brother, but he questioned if Nick would believe him. Containing his enthusiasm about the money spell's probable success seemed the best option. "I guess my spells are working."

"I guess. How do they work?"

"You can get some effect by just focusing thoughts, words, and energy on something you want to happen. You can make them more powerful if you do certain types of spells on the right phase of the moon and with the right herbs, talismans, and whatnot."

"I do see a few parallels with Reiki. It sounds interesting. I'm going to check it out."

"I'm sure you will. You're a geek."

Nick sounded indignant. "Wait. Is this why you had me bring the jewelry?"

"Nothing gets by my brilliant brother. I need them to cast some money spells for myself."

"Why? Money isn't a problem for you. You've got more than enough to get by from the insurance policies."

The question highlighted the stark difference Joe saw between himself and his altruistic brother. "I'm out in three months. I don't want to just get by. I want some power."

A minute after Nick's departure, Joe accepted the jewelry

from the prison guard and studied the pieces. A simple gold wedding ring accompanied a gold necklace with a small Christian cross. After slipping the ring over his finger and finding it a perfect fit, he judged that Nick had selected the pieces well.

The guard's tone was suspicious. "When did you get married?"

Nick lied. "I guess you could say it was at the same time I accepted Jesus Christ as my Savior."

"That's all the bling inmates are allowed. You're maxed out with the wedding ring and the religious necklace."

"I know. Can I go back to my cell now?"

After bed check, Joe aimed his nose at his cellmate, a young man who had run into trouble during a car theft. "Can you get the candles out?"

"You're not doing that witchcraft shit again, are you, man?"

"I am. Is that a problem?"

"You know that shit's spooky."

"I'll either cast it here with you and maybe throw in a little protection spell for you on the side, or I'll wait until I'm with the other Wiccans in the yard, and you can take your chances on what I do on your behalf."

The prisoner's pause suggested his internal struggle, which ended in Joe's favor. "Okay, man. Look away while I get them."

"That's what I thought." Joe rolled towards the wall and heard his companion rummaging through his hidden stock.

"Okay, man. I got them."

"You got your lighter, too?"

"Yeah. You think I'm stupid?"

"Just wanted to be sure." Rising to his feet, Joe studied the items in his cellmate's hands. Eight empty yogurt containers filled with baby oil and thread served as homemade candles. A small battery with an insulated wire taped to its negative end offered the igniting heat source. "I only need seven."

"You don't mind if I light up one for myself do you? I mean, it's not going to mess with your spells, is it?"

"No. Give me the seven and keep quiet."

"Whatever you want, man. You're too spooky to piss off."

Joe pulled a towel from under his pillow and laid it on the floor with the pentacle he'd inked into it facing upward. After arranging the candles with ninety degrees of separation to represent the four elements, he grabbed the battery from his bunk mate.

Pressing the wire into the positive end to short the leads, Joe moved an exposed section of the wire into a wick. As the metal turned orange, smoke issued from the thread, and then a flame danced atop the yogurt container. After tossing the battery into his cellmate's lap, he used the first candle to light the others.

He formed a triangle with the last three candles, and he placed his gold ring and chain inside it. After lighting the candles, he pulled off his socks and threw them onto his bunk. Barefooted, he stepped into the center of the circle of protection and raised his arms above his head. "I ask that the God and Goddess bless this circle so that I may be free and protected within this space. So mote it be."

As he visualized the center of the triangle filling with prosperity energy and abundance, he realized that his moments during spell casting were his most lucid.

He then pulled the paper with his litany from his pocket, unfolded it, and read it aloud. "Wealth, abundance and prosperity, flow into my life and set me free. It is my will. So mote it be." He stooped and placed the ring on the chain, removing the cross which he tossed to his bunk mate.

"I guess you're done?"

"Yeah. I'm done." Joe blew out the candles and then slipped the gold chain around his neck.

"The guards aren't going to let you wear it like that."

"I'll wear my chain this way whenever I can. That's part of the requirement to maximize the spell."

"You're the one who's going to get in trouble. Not me."

"Don't you think a guard or two respects what I do? Don't you think a couple of them are afraid I might use this power against them?"

"Whatever. Not my problem. What's that 'mote' shit anyway? I've heard you say it before."

"It's ancient English for 'might' or 'may'. I guess the spells just work better that way."

As the cellmate blew out his candle, the soft shadows disappeared. "I saw you ask for money for your brother once. But this is the first time I've seen you ask for money for yourself."

"I'm getting out of here soon. I need to think about my future."

A week later, a man he recognized of respectable rank in a local gang sat across the lunch table, flanked by two lackeys. Wise in prison politics, Joe stopped eating and offered a deferential salutation. "What can I do for you?"

"Listen, Joe. I like the way you carry yourself around here. You've earned my respect."

For his personal safety, Nick shifted into diplomat mode. "I'm honored. Thank you."

"I like your manners, too. You're a smart guy, and I think you're reliable. Are you reliable? Can I trust you, Joe?"

"You know I'm in here for assault. I don't lie, cheat, or steal, and I respect you and your power too much to disappoint you."

As the ranking member broke into a smile, his toadies mimicked him. He wiggled his finger at Joe's nose. "See? I told you he was smart. He knows what to say. I told them you were smart, Joe. I like that you're making me look good."

Although fear for his life compelled his best behavior, Joe was daring to hope for a lucrative offer. "You can count on me."

"Let's talk business. You're getting out, and the guy I had running one of my routes started skimming. I need a replacement, and I been in here too long to trust the young punks out there I ain't met yet. So I want you to be my guy, Joe. This is important shit. You think you can handle it, my man?"

"If you think I can handle it, then I can handle it. I know this is important for you, and I'm honored that you're considering me.

If you let me work for you, I'll impress you."

The leader's smile receded into an inquisitive stare. "Everyone else asks how much it pays. But you didn't."

"Out of respect and good faith. You didn't come here to negotiate. Let me prove myself to you, and I'll trust you to pay me what you say I'm worth."

"Cool. Good answer. But don't you at least want to know how much it pays right now?"

"Sure."

The promised pay doubled his expectations, and it would more than quintuple his historic income.

Two weeks later, Joe spoke to his brother through the glass, but this time, he didn't feel the weakness of dependency. Being welcomed into a gang's service had made a difference. "Hey, bro."

"How are you doing, Joe?"

"Couldn't be better."

"That's the best answer I've ever heard from you."

"I'm getting out soon. Maybe that's got me in a decent mood."

"You know what time yet, so I can pick you up?"

Independence and acceptance into a new family felt good. "Sorry. I've already got a ride." Joe found the pitiful look of surprise on his brother's face priceless.

"What do you mean?"

"I made some friends in here."

"That's good, I guess. What sort of friends?"

"You know. A few doctors, some lawyers, a senator or two."

"Stop messing around."

"Who the hell do you think I met here? You think I'm buddying up with a bunch of school teachers and saints?"

"I'm just concerned, that's all."

"Well, stop being concerned. In case you haven't noticed, I grew up. I'm not your child, and you can stop treating me like one."

Nick looked ready to cry. "You're still my brother. You're still important to me."

"You're still my brother, too, unlike our military poster boy. But you don't have to ride my ass. I can take care of myself."

"Where are you going to live?"

"That stopped being your concern when you kicked me out of your apartment."

"You made me. You know I couldn't tolerate marijuana and the shady characters you brought by. It was too risky for my degree."

"Thank God that's working out. The way you live your life, that piece of paper's going to be your only friend."

Joe noticed a rare emotion in Nick's tone. Anger. "I want to assume you don't mean that."

"It doesn't matter if I meant it. What matters, and what's really sad, is that it's true."

"We're not getting anywhere. Let's try this again next week."

Before Joe could tell his brother not to bother coming back, Nick slammed the phone into the cradle and walked away.

The temporary severance from his brother was cathartic, but Joe promised himself to continue casting spells on Nick's behalf. He acknowledged the debt of his brother's parenting–despite it being a fraction of the care Nick had offered Jake, and he hoped his Wiccan practice could begin repaying it by advancing his sibling's work.

But he admitted a selfish motive. He wanted to profit from his growing spiritual, supernatural powers, and he saw limitless potential in what he could accomplish if his firstborn sibling joined him.

In the future. If and when Nick was ready.

CHAPTER 13

Nick wished for responsive wings, but he went limp and spiraled downward. Stark panic struck as the rocks jutting from the forest grass grew larger, and then his world turned black.

He awoke and noticed his chest heaving, and then he lifted the electro-magnetic interface helmet from his head. Reclined in the darkened room, he felt deathly isolated. He lowered his chin to his chest and gathered his thoughts in preparation to announce them to the microphone that served as his failure's only witness.

The Air Force had bought his new falcons, but he questioned how many he could kill before the funding stopped–especially since he'd started experimenting with them in secret to try to control them. "I sent Peregrine Falcon Eight on a flight path I predetermined. I had total control. I was there. I was driving him. I was flying him."

But he had just flown the animal to its death. "But I'm a shitty falcon. I worked against him. I pushed too hard. There's a natural grace to this I don't get yet. I pushed him into a high-speed diving stoop, and then his entire body went limp. Free fall. No control."

He rolled from his ergonomic recliner and faced the workstation to be sure it recorded his voice into a password-protected, encrypted file. Nobody would hear his notes until he was ready to share. "There's nothing wrong with this setup but me. It's on me now. I have to figure this out."

Unsure if a part of him had died with Peregrine Falcon Eight, he marched out of the control room.

Three days later, Nick watched coeds walking on Main Street

through his second story apartment window. Judging himself too old and socially inept to mix with fellow Wolverines, he lamented his omission from any functional human demographic. There were people who lived normal lives, and then there was him, aloof on the fringe, useless outside a laboratory experiment.

With the football team hosting a conference rival, Ann Arbor was swelling to twice its indigenous population. As the frolicking tailgaters moved toward the Big House, he wondered why he possessed the cursed gift of heightened perception.

His phone chimed on his desk, and he lifted it to hear his adviser. "Hey, Gerry."

"Hey there. I'm afraid I've got bad news. I'm sorry, Nick, but the Air Force is pulling the funding."

"Seriously? Is there any appeal?"

"They gave you a lot of leeway by letting you experiment on your own. They were smart to let you try experiments when you felt like it, to test mood as a factor. But now you've lost your third falcon, and you can't explain why."

Nate thought about revealing his attempts to control the fliers, but he kept it secret. "So my research ends here?"

"Unless you can come up with the cash to train a ninth falcon, cover the equipment, and pay stipends for a support team."

Nick swallowed. "How much? Just for a falcon and the surgery."

"About a hundred grand. But I don't know anyone who'd fund it with the risk of me crashing their investment."

"I can get it."

"What?"

"I need to go." Nick hung up and called his younger brother. "Hey, Jake. I need to talk to you."

His brother spoke with the strength befitting a lion. "Sure. What's going on?"

"It's about my research."

"You're still going to get your PhD, aren't you?"

"Yeah, that's not an issue. My doctoral defense should be

pretty straight forward."

"Then what's wrong?"

"They're about to pull my funding."

"I don't get it. If you're going to get your degree, what's it matter?"

Nick looked out the window as the throngs of football fans grew thicker. He wondered how people could find purpose and joy in sport of such violence. "Meaning."

"Meaning what?"

"No, I mean 'meaning'. Like 'purpose'. I want to continue this work because it feels like something I need to do."

"Okay, I get that. But isn't a lack of funding normal? Don't you always have to apply for grants and stuff?"

"Yeah. But this is a tough proposition. My test subjects have been dying. I've killed three falcons, which ate up three hundred grand of Air Force money."

Jake scoffed. "That's peanuts to the Air Force, bro."

"I know, but it's a lot for my project, and Gerry's told me plenty of times that my work is funded from a finite source."

"That stinks."

Nick persevered. "But I know why. I can fix the problem and keep new falcons from dying. I just can't convince anyone."

"Sorry to hear that, Nick. I know you're working hard. I've learned over the years that all that mumbo jumbo soothsaying and visions you've been sporting isn't all mumbo jumbo. I believe you have some sort of ability. Heck, I remember when you, me, and the asshole could share feelings from across town."

Nick recalled a childhood hinting of psychic power that had faded as his family had entered adulthood. "We probably let them atrophy for lack of use, but we may still have those abilities, and they might be helping me with the falcons."

Jake's silent pause suggested Nick had impressed him. "I've never seen you so driven. I've never seen you so animated."

"When I was flying with the last bird, it felt like I was doing what I was meant to do."

"I've always said I'm here if you need me. How much do you

need?"

Nick cleared his tightening throat. "Thanks for asking. I wasn't sure how to broach the subject. I need a hundred thousand dollars. Maybe a little more."

"I imagine you and I together can get you halfway there. I've been socking away cash with nowhere to spend it. The Navy takes care of all the basics for me."

"Thanks. Do you have an idea how could I get the rest of it?"

"You remember my friend Grant from high school, right?"

"Of course. You lived with him your senior year."

"He's been making big money in the Chicago Board of Trade. I bet he'd be willing to loan us the rest, if not just make it a gift."

Three months later, Nick lay in the lab's recliner and pulled the helmet over his head. His perception bristled as electromagnetic radiation tapped and amplified his brainwaves.

He lifted a jet injector gun, squeezed its trigger, and stifled a grunt as it hissed and pricked his arm. He winced and then relaxed as the serum's warmth billowed. Meditating, he slowed his heartbeat and centered his thoughts on Peregrine Falcon Nine.

Through a virtual private network, a transceiver antenna that graduate student engineers had mounted near the bird's nest, and a wire embedded under Peregrine Falcon Nine's scalp, he connected wirelessly to the bird of prey.

Like dancing on the edge of consciousness, he drifted to pseudo-sleep and awoke miles away. A tree branch materialized before him, and then clouds rolled downward as the expensive raptor took off.

Avian being and man as one. Connected. Heartbeat rising–fast–faster than human. Imperceptible perception becoming real–clear–fierce. Wind over feathers. Wings pumping for altitude and speed. The woodland below coming vibrant in his eyes. Consciousness alive–bird in body–human in awareness–hybrid in instinct.

Nick felt the warmth of rising air caressing the feathers of his belly. He relaxed his wings and soared. Recalling his inherent flying strength, he flapped forward, accelerating to highway speeds.

He flew the bird over a predetermined crossroad which served as his locational reference, and then he moved to his finale.

Noting his hunger, he used it to motivate the bird's action. He glided and angled his vision downward, and a plump quail climbing between the playgrounds of cleared grasslands caught his eye.

Nick thought of feeding, and the falcon dove into its hunting stoop. With his wings and talons compressed against his streamlined body, he drove the world's fastest species through the air. Tripling highway speeds, he was exhilarated.

As he reveled in the freedom, his consciousness slipped, and the falcon wobbled. Nick quelled his joy of flight and refocused on the tactics of the dive. The stoop stabilized, the quail–viewed in amazing clarity–approached.

The moment of truth arrived–pulling out of the stoop. He spoke within his joint falcon-human mind. "Abort the hunt. Quail is good. Better food at home. Abort the stoop."

Nick walked on the razor's edge between dominance and submission within the falcon's spirit. His vision grew hazy and dark as the falcon protested the unnatural bail out. Disallowing another raptor's fatality, he rescinded his pressure. "It's okay–you may have the quail–it's your choice–take the quail or return to the apartment for easier food."

Nick's talon extended, poised to strike the quail. "Wouldn't you prefer easy, better food?"

Nick had staged a feeder for this falcon behind his home, and he wanted him to return to it.

The falcon's hunger tasted pungent, and Nick wondered if his mouth salivated back in his body. "Better food? Easy food? Abort the stoop."

The quail became a target, the falcon's vision in Nick's mind became a camera image from a missile's nosecone. "You can't have both. Quail or easy, better food. More food. Duck and pigeon waiting at home. No more hunger."

To his relief, the falcon angled its body, leveled, and spread its wings. Nick looked over his feathered shoulder and saw the quail flailing through the turbulence of the falcon's wake. Then, with a gentle nudge from his human will, the falcon banked back toward the prepared meal.

Nick awoke and noticed his chest heaving. Excited for having overridden the falcon's instincts, he ripped the helmet from his head and yelled to the empty lab. "I did it!"

Nick sat in his apartment, pondering. The excitement of controlling the falcon in its full range of maneuvers had waned, and loneliness crept into him. A gust of wind chilled him with autumn's coolness, and he stood and closed the window.

To distract himself from ugly thoughts, he turned on his television and learned that two hikers were lost in the Pinckney State Recreation Area. He ignored the reporter's redundant rambling until a park ranger appeared and pleaded for help. The parkland was too vast for existing search teams, and hikers were presumed injured.

Nick checked a map on his phone and recognized that the recreation area was a short distance to the northwest, as the crow flies.

Or as the surgically-enhanced falcon flies.

He looked out the window and saw his raptor on a branch near the empty feeder. Returning to his kitchen, he wrote a note on a pad and rolled it. He then grabbed a spool of string and went into the yard.

The falcon allowed him to approach within arm's reach.

Nick fastened the paper to a leg. "Get ready, you beautiful bird." He headed towards the laboratory.

Peregrine Falcon Nine balked when Nick appeared within its mind and willed it into flight. "I understand no hunger. Fly now, earn easy food."

He questioned if a future promise meant anything to an avian mind, but he repeated the sentiment until the animal moved.

The falcon flapped and climbed into the brisk mid-afternoon sky. Nick placed the sun over his left shoulder, and the falcon covered the distance from the campus to the park with remarkable efficiency.

"Hunt humans."

The falcon rolled into a ballistic free fall.

Nick remembered that his falcons responded to illogical requests by rejecting him through unconsciousness. "I mean seek humans. Help find them. No attack. No hunt. Search."

The falcon recovered and hit a high acceleration turn, followed by an inverse turn with a rapid accent.

Nick sensed the bird trying to buck him. "Fly free." He let the bird glide and relinquish thoughts of human-hunting. "Turn gentle left."

The bird obeyed, and minutes later, the park's southern tree line came into view.

"Turn gentle right. Follow the tree line." Nick took the bird to the northern end of the park and willed it through a zigzag search. Nothing on the planet, he recalled, could search with the speed, agility, or efficiency of a falcon. In flight, he lived.

The falcon cut across miles with graceful ease, scanning the ground under pine coverage.

The falcon saw a squirrel.

"Ignore."

A family of quail.

"Ignore. Reverse course and fly the next leg of your search."

Pigeons.

"Ignore."

Two human figures on foot.

Nick's hope rose and fell as he examined the people. "Uniformed park rangers. Ignore."

Prancing deer.

"Ignore."

A human on a machine.

"All-terrain-vehicle, searching for other humans. Ignore."

A leaf-covered gully approached, yellow and auburn fallen foliage caking the ground.

A broken twig caught Nick's attention. He thought he noticed disturbed leaves leading deeper into the chasm, but the setting sun played tricks on even the falcon's eyes. Then he saw a spec of white. "A child's sneaker. Stoop."

The falcon balked, crumpled into a semi-limp position, and started to fall and roll.

"Damn it. I understand. No prey. No stoop. Descend and see more. Descend at comfortable speed."

The falcon entered a wide circling pattern and lowered upon the white spec while tracing a helix.

"Good."

With amazing clarity, the falcon saw a man lying on the gully below the root of an aged oak tree. Plastic grocery bags acted as tie wraps splinting his walking stick to his jeans. Beside him, a small boy rested his head on his shoulder, halfway between sleep and fear. The shaking of the boy's white sneakers revealed that he shivered in the evening's encroaching cold.

He landed the falcon near the man and walked it toward him. The hiker's eyes widened in disbelief as Nick raised the falcon's talon.

The man reached and tugged the note from the falcon's leg.

Knowing he would make good on the written promise to vector in a rescue party, Nick felt alive when the man smiled and hugged his son.

Then, to guard his work's secrecy, he ordered the falcon home.

Later that night, Nick spoke with his brother. "I know my purpose. I need to use my gift to help people."

"What happened?"

Nick knew he needed to curtail his enthusiasm, or else he'd be cornered into sharing secrets. Nobody needed to know about his ability to control animals. "I had a very positive outcome with the bird you helped me buy. My visions were crystal clear, and he's responding to my training."

"That's great, Nick."

"It's what I've always felt like I needed to do, but I was missing a piece of the puzzle. It's the animals. It's extending my abilities through them."

"Animals? That's rather generic considering you've only worked with falcons."

"Birds have limitless possibility, but I'm thinking about others, too. My mind's racing, and I can't stop thinking of scenarios."

"Sure, Nick. The sky's the limit. Want to call me back after you calm down and have some rational thoughts?"

"Okay. See you."

He lowered the phone, lay back in his chair, and imagined how an animal under his control could do something important for someone, and that it would matter.

For the first time since raising his brothers, he would matter.

CHAPTER 14

Nick finished defending his doctoral thesis.

He closed the door and noticed that the hallway seemed less stifling than the room in which the panel had grilled him.

Though grueling, the thesis defense and years of work behind it were worth the reward. He expected he had passed and would soon be known as 'Doctor Slate'.

His wait until earning his doctorate would be a calm before a storm. Uncertainty dominated his thoughts as he hoped he'd succeeded in defending his thesis, feared that his rescue of the stranded hikers would come back to him, and wondered what life held in store for him with or without money to expand his research.

The familiar coffeehouse offered a quiet sanctuary, but as he enjoyed a Colombian dark roast with a bagel, a stranger walked from the counter to his table. The woman appeared the right age for a young professor, and he found her attractive.

"Hi. You're Nick Slate, aren't you?"

A scan of his memory recalled the two articles written in the years since Deborah's graduation. During his recent need for volunteers, he'd agreed to an interview about his work. He assumed the stranger had read them. "Yes, I'm Nick."

"I've heard about your research, and I have to say I'm impressed." As she placed her latte on his table but remained standing, her mannerisms appeared rehearsed. She wanted something and seemed confident in getting her way. "May I sit?"

"Please."

"I'm Andrea."

He reached across the laminate and shook her hand. "What can I do for you?"

"I'll be blunt. I have a professional interest in your work. I represent a powerful group that wants to fund your research."

Her directness caught him off guard. "I can introduce you to my adviser. He handles the money discussions."

"As you become 'Doctor Slate', you're going to have to make important decisions on your own. The first is who will fund your work. The second is to consider if you've outgrown your need for Doctor Ross."

"How can you know all this?"

She sipped her latte. "Because your achievements fall outside the Air Force's areas of interest."

Hearing a stranger imply knowledge of guarded secrets made Nick's heart race. "How so?"

"They want something you don't care about."

Nick knew enough about psychology to recognize the early phases of recruitment. Ask leading questions. Make him hungry to learn more. Trick him into wanting to champion whatever she was selling. In defense, he turned the conversation back on her. "Instead of games, tell me what you think I want and how you'll help me get it."

Her eyes narrowed. "They're looking for advances in aviation technology. They wanted you to learn about falcons from the inside for their future designs of drones and possibly more."

It was news to Nick, and the attractive stranger was losing credibility. "They never mentioned that." In retrospect, the scientist realized he knew little of the Air Force's motivation.

"Why would they? If they'd sent you in with an agenda to data-mine a bird's brain, you would've overpowered the poor things and turned them into Thanksgiving dinners."

Nick agreed but withheld his concurrence. "Why do you say that? I haven't published anything that would support that."

"Common sense... to those of us who know a few things." She leaned towards him and lowered her voice. "I don't read your reports to learn about your research. I read your reports to learn about you."

Nick's innards quivered. "Are you stalking me?"

She snorted. "Yes, in a way. But that's a good thing, if you'll allow me to explain. The Air Force funded you in hopes of gaining new aviation technology, but that's not what your work is about."

"What's it about, in your opinion?"

Her voice became icy, as if her statement carried more gravitas than he could understand. "You crashed three birds."

The revelation was classified, and he gave her a silent stare.

She leaned back and continued. "You're wondering how I know that, and you're wondering why I care."

Again, Nick remained stone, partly to avoid revealing his agreement and partly to avoid squeaking a pathetic objection from his tightening throat.

She buried her eyes into his, reducing him to her pawn. "You're controlling them."

Subconsciously, he started a slow nod, but when he caught himself doing it, he stopped and sipped his coffee. Dying to affirm her accusation, he tightened his jaw and let the hot liquid silence him as he scowled his lying denial.

"It's about you, Nick. It always has been, but you didn't know it. We've seen this before, and you're not alone. Your talent is rare, but you're not alone."

The pawn squeaked. "What talent? Who are you?"

Andrea pulled a card from her shirt pocket and slid it across the table. "I'm with the CIA. Call me if you want to learn more about who you are." She stood.

Shocked into being, a king rose from the pawn. "Stay!"

His words froze her, and she became the stunned mute.

"I mean, I'd like you to stay. I'm interested. Now. I don't need to wait and pretend that I'm evaluating other options."

She sank back into her seat. "Alright. We need to bring you in for evaluation."

"What sort of evaluation?"

"I can't tell you until we bring in."

"Isn't that circular logic for trying to recruit someone?"

"That's the way we work."

"I don't mean to sound arrogant, but I know my research is special. I'm going to assume that you want me because I'm out-pacing your best efforts."

Her glare was an unreadable mix of sentiments he failed to identify. "This is where you really need us, Nick."

"How so?"

"If you try to sell your services on the open market, you're going to scare people away. In case you haven't noticed, the far-thest that people are willing to go with paranormal services is psychics. You, however, introduce a new element."

"New element? You mean a living creature."

She nodded. "Psychics deal with information. No matter how bizarre or strange their work is, people can always write it off as luck or coincidence or trickery. At the worst, they accept it as a mystery they can live with. But when you deal with a living creature, you've entered a new dimension."

"Is that what your group studies? This new dimension?"

"I hope we can work together and discuss such things. But I can't answer until you become acclimated to who we are and how we work."

"Okay, I get it. Whatever you need done, I'll do."

She paused, a new thought interrupting her speech. "Have you thought about your father? Are you okay with working for the same organization he did?"

The deep question stung. "I hadn't considered it, to be hon-est. I hardly remember him, and I never blamed the CIA for his death."

"That's good. We'll need to fly you to our facilities and do some basic in-processing before the evaluation can proceed."

"Where do we do that?"

"CIA headquarters in Langley, Virginia. Do you need any time to prepare for a trip? We'll need a full week."

"No. I can leave immediately. There's nothing for me here."

The so-called 'basic' in-processing had lasted three days and left Nick feeling like he'd succumbed to a psychological examination replete with endless threats about breaches of confidentiality.

After the final night of questioning and warnings, he retreated to his hotel and enjoyed a steak dinner on his expense account. With his stomach full, he returned to his room and watched a movie.

He thought about calling a brother, but Jake was inside a Trident Missile submarine, and Joe had stopped answering his calls.

Turning off the television, he sensed his thoughts racing towards speculative images of tomorrow's adventure. He stripped to his underwear and slipped between the sheets. As he sank into the mattress, endless conjectures danced in his head and slowed his pursuit of sleep.

After hours of mental wrestling, he succumbed to exhaustion.

The next morning, Nick looked forward to his evaluation.

Inside a basement laboratory room, he stood inside a control room that invoked thoughts of NASA instead of the intelligence community. A Plexiglas shield offered a panorama of the operational floor, and below the clear plastic, three operators sat in front of enough touch screens and keyboards to manage interplanetary travel.

Reunited with his original recruiter, he looked to Andrea to explain the overpowered equipment, but she aimed her arm at the floor.

"I hope you're impressed."

He looked through the Plexiglas and noticed the heightened sophistication that government budgeting had created. Unlike the haphazard evolution under which his university lab room had evolved, the CIA facility appeared designed for comfort, efficiency, and automation.

His eyes started at the far end of the operation floor, where the familiar sight of a falcon in a clear cage was juxtaposed with a large Plexiglas cuboid chamber that surrounded the bird's enclosure and the pedestal upon which it rested. Nick estimated that a horse could fit inside the sparse chamber, but the outline of the door suggested that nothing taller than a human could enter it.

While he pondered the extremes of animal life the CIA had tested, his gaze moved closer in.

In the center of the operational floor, a black leather reclining bed awaited. Monitors for his vital signs and jet injector guns for delivering drugs were molded into the recliner's casing, revealing a completeness of design. A lack of equipment and furniture struck him as odd. "I'm impressed. But why does it look like there's room in there for three chairs?"

"I know a lot, but I don't know everything. And you know I can't share everything I know."

"I understand. I have to be honest, though. I expected more people in here watching me."

"Once you're on the floor, everyone who needs to be watching you will be. Are you ready?"

"I am."

She opened the door and walked him to the recliner. The squishy floor surprised him, and it made him notice the anechoic coating on the walls. He could hear himself breathe.

The leather chair rested low, and he rolled downward into it. Its design helped him relax as she lowered the helmet over his head. "Are you comfortable that low? Or would you like me to raise you up?"

"I'd like it about a foot and a half higher."

"You can do this yourself, but watch me." She pressed a button on a small panel by his forearm that had eluded his detection.

While the bed rose with a hum, he appreciated the quietness of its hidden motor. "What else can I control?"

"Several things. You'll learn more as you go, but you should know now that you can control your injections, both sedation and activation as needed to push yourself deeper into semi-consciousness or to help yourself wake up."

"Nice."

"You can also use voice commands. The chair has microphones and voice recognition software. Of course, I can control this all from the control room, and I'll make sure nothing goes wrong."

"I admit I'm impressed."

The bed became motionless.

"I think you'll remain impressed as you learn what we can do for you." She turned and walked back to the control room.

"Who's going to give me my IV?"

"Nobody. We've progressed beyond that. It's all automatic. We can hit your vein with the injection gun."

"You're kidding."

"I'm not kidding. The gun has an imaging system and can find your vein better than a human. Be still while it injects because it takes up to five seconds. The speed is limited by the needle diameter, which we keep very small to avoid bruising."

"Not that I'm a baby, but if it hurts, it's going to make it tough for me to relax."

"You'll barely feel it."

She left him, and the lights dimmed. Speakers brought her amplified voice into the space. "Can you hear me, Nick?"

"I can hear you."

"I'll guide you through the evaluation. Follow my instructions and answer my questions. Don't try to improvise. Just keep it simple, and you'll do fine. Understand?"

"I understand."

"Are you ready for the sedative?"

"What happens if something goes wrong with that? You said I might have to hold my arm steady for five seconds."

"The gun will retract if you move. So don't move."

Nick became nervous as he tried to envision a technology he didn't trust penetrating his vascular system. "I'll do my best. I'm ready."

"Injection is coming in three, two, one."

Servomotors whirred while moving the silvery gun over his forearm. Tensing with anxiety, he awaited the prick. When it came, it surprised him, and he jerked his forearm. The jet retracted, leaving him with a useless pinhole in his flesh.

"I know it's strange the first time. Are you ready to try it again?"

"Yeah. Sorry. Let's try it again."

The servomotors whirred, the needle penetrated his flesh, and he held firm. Its dose administered, the gun flipped backwards beyond his view, and the warmth filled him.

"How are you feeling?"

"Real good. I don't suppose you'll tell me what drug this is? I like it better than what I was using."

"Not today, but soon, after you're cleared for it."

"What do I do now?"

"You can keep your eyes open or closed. It's up to you. I'm not going to tell you when I start transmitting, but within the next three minutes, I'm going to begin. I want you to remember as best you can when you notice the first transmission from the bird. I'll count off every fifteen seconds."

Nick frowned. "I may not hear you, depending how deep I'm in."

"Your report on the timing isn't crucial. What's crucial is to identify the three movies I'll be playing in front of the bird. Are you ready for the countdown?"

"I'm ready."

"The examination begins now. We are now fifteen seconds into the examination. Thirty seconds."

Nick grew anxious as he saw only the back of his eyelids.

"Forty-five seconds. One minute. One minute, fifteen seconds."

As he feared he was failing, an image formed in his mind. He tried to focus on it, but his nervousness pushed it away.

"One minute, thirty seconds."

Relaxing, he saw the image form again. This time, he avoided the eagerness to take it. Instead, he let it grow.

"One minute, forty-five seconds."

Time ticked away, but the image formed. He had not seen the huge liquid crystal display in the falcon's chamber, but he saw it rendering video now through the raptor's vision.

The Millennium Falcon took laser cannon shots from an empirical cruiser, and he identified the movie as Star Wars. He grasped that the name of the ship being attacked was the CIA's attempt at ironic humor, seeing it through a falcon's eyes.

"Two minutes, fifteen seconds."

Star Wars faded out, and a new movie began. He recognized it as an old film by its black and white coloring. The opening credits played, and the film identified itself as the Maltese Falcon. He appreciated the continued irony.

"Three minutes. That's the end of the count off."

After watching actors with heydays long before his birth, he saw the screen switch again. Instead of a movie, he saw a football stadium. The Denver Broncos and the Atlanta Falcons were squaring off in a game he thought he recognized as a past Super Bowl. After several plays, the image turned black.

"Can you hear me, Nick?"

His voice sounded groggy as it reverberated in his head. "Yeah, I can hear you."

"Can you bring yourself to full consciousness on your own?"

"I'll try."

He had learned that forcing himself to breathe faster helped raise his awareness. Within moments, his shallow breaths helped him open his eyes and see his surroundings.

"I'm going to increase the lighting."

"Go ahead."

The lights seemed harsh as his eyes adjusted.

"Are you ready for me to elevate your head?"

"Yes."

The helmet slid up from him, and then the bed curled his torso.

"It's time to report. Do you remember the approximate time when you saw your first image?"

"It was about one minute, fifteen seconds."

"Can you name the three movies?"

"No, but I can name the two movies and the one sporting event. I like your sense of humor with all the falcons, by the way. Star Wars, Maltese Falcon, and whichever Super Bowl the Atlanta Falcons were in. You'll have to excuse my weakness in football history. I don't remember which Super Bowl it was, but I don't think they won."

"Thank you, Nick. That's all the questions I have. Give me a few minutes, and I'll debrief you."

After minutes progressed like hours of thick suspense, the door clicked open, and Andrea walked in.

"Are you going to tell me how I did?"

"No. You already know how you did. Nobody's surprised, but everybody's impressed."

"I guess that's good. So, what did we just accomplish? I don't mean to be arrogant, but we didn't do anything I hadn't figured out years ago. Did anyone really learn anything?"

"We needed to see it for ourselves. You made it look easy, and that's what we wanted to see. And, yes, somebody did learn something."

"Who learned what?"

She stepped closer so he could see her face. "This evaluation room is a prototype of our field units, and that falcon has more value than just being surgically wired up. He's been trained for the field, too. This may have been an evaluation, but it was also training for the real world with your new partner."

"I don't even work for the CIA yet."

"But if you do, that's the falcon you'd be starting with, and you'd be in a field unit just like this one."

He tested her. "Why can't I control him from here, regardless of where he deploys? Why do I need to be in a field unit?"

"You haven't tested this yet, but we have. There are limits on the range. Electronic signals can travel the world, but the remote control of animals works differently."

"Why is that?"

"I can't tell you."

"You don't know, the CIA doesn't know, or everyone within a stone's throw of us knows except me?"

"I can't tell you until you join us. And as of now, that's within your power. I have your offer."

"After just one evaluation?"

Her smile seemed sincere. "There are escape clauses for us in case you fail to perform, but given your history and what we just saw, I don't think we'll need them. Also, I'm sure you're aware that we're restricted to paying you what's allowed per our pay scales."

"I kind of knew that CIA pay was limited coming into this."

"I hope you're impressed, though, when you look at the packet. You may be young, but you're special. We're bringing you in at a high level to make sure the compensation isn't a distraction."

"Really? I don't know what the levels mean. Can you tell me how high, on a relative scale?"

Her smile became a smirk. "I've been in the agency for twelve years, and if I'm lucky, I'm half way to earning what they just offered you."

CHAPTER 15

Lewis heard the young lady's rote confession. Though a repeat offender, she sounded sorrowful for offending God.

"I've been using birth control pills and doing so without my husband's knowledge."

He rendered his usual support and recommendations, followed by issuing her penance and absolution. As he expected her to leave, she surprised him.

"Are you free for counseling after confessions?"

"We can talk now, unless you need a long conversation."

"I need the time, Father. This issue is complex."

After serving his last penitent, he stepped from the confessional and noticed the other priests had finished their renderings of the sacrament. Parishioners arriving early for the vigil Mass strolled into the building as the recently forgiven exited.

He stepped down the stairs to the church's basement and sat with Deborah at a corner table in the social hall. "What can I do for you, sister?"

"I just filed for divorce."

"This is a significant undertaking. I'll give you any advice or support you need."

"Thank you, Father."

"I normally ask spouses to reconsider and to work prayerfully with the Church to reconcile. But since I know your history, I support your decision without question."

Her eyes filled with moisture. "You're the only one. Everyone else is harassing me. But I've reached my limits. I need to do this."

"I know that you've suffered a history of violence. Do you fear for your safety now?"

"I'm spending each night with a different friend. I'm making myself hard to find."

"I can help place you in a temporary shelter."

"That's okay. I'm going to leave the state soon."

"I think that's a wise move, as long as you have a place to stay where you feel safe."

Tears trickled down her cheek, and she wiped them away. "My friend said that he'll take me in."

"Is this the friend with whom you believe you're in love?"

"Yeah."

"I wasn't aware he'd moved out of state."

"He got a new job."

"I'm glad you have someone to look after you. I do need to caution you, though, that in the eyes of God you're still married until the Church can verify your marriage was invalid. Given that you married against your will, I'm optimistic it will rule in your favor, but you must remain chaste until then."

She shook her head. "Sorry, Father, but that sounds like a load of crap. There's no love. There never was. Why should I be trapped?"

"It's about the sanctity of marriage. Even though it was against your will, you entered into a sacred bond. It's God's will that united you..."

The pain in her eyes said she cared less about God than anyone at that moment.

He changed his approach. "Set aside God's will for a moment. Let's examine your personal healing. You had a definitive event where your marriage started–your wedding, which underneath all the ceremony and oppression was intended to be an eternal bond."

She shrugged.

"To break a bond forged with eternal intent, you're best served by a decree of eternal intent with the power to break that bond–your annulment. To have or even seek sexual relations before then would place you in a confusing in-between state."

"I'm not confused. I was never married in my mind."

Lewis softened his voice. "You were married, you are married, and it matters. I have a back injury with permanent structural damage. I didn't want it any more than you wanted to be married, but we both suffer from our realities and must address them as real."

She seemed unconvinced but willing. "Maybe. I haven't filed for the annulment yet. They take forever."

"They used to, but it's gotten better since Pope Francis reformed it a few years ago. It's still slow, but bureaucracy's not an excuse to avoid it."

Her face became dark. "Isn't it obvious that my marriage is invalid? Do I really need to wait for the Church to catch up?"

"I know this is difficult, but until God speaks through the Church, you're still married to your present husband, even after the court issues you a divorce."

She stiffened her back and crossed her legs. "I don't mean to be rude, Father, but no matter what the Church says, I'm going to figure out if I want to marry Nick before they give me an annulment."

He noticed determination in her eyes. "I think you've already figured it out."

"Yeah, I think I've known for a long time."

"You can date him and get to know him. Just remember that you're still married to someone else while you do." He considered her pending legal challenges. "Have you found an attorney that you trust?"

"I haven't started looking yet. But I don't like my chances."

"Why are you so pessimistic?"

"I'm going to get slaughtered because he's a lawyer, and he's friends with the judges. He's going to make this look like it's all my fault. He'll lie and get people to vouch for him. I'm getting nothing."

"I can refer you to some competent and caring attorneys. I'm sure one of them would represent you, even with the disadvantages you face. They can at least minimize the damage."

She withdrew her phone and asked him for names. He recited the first two he could remember, and she tapped the information into her electronic notes. "What else should I be thinking about?"

"Since you were married in the Chaldean diocese, you'll need to file for annulment at Mother of God Church. I recommend you get that process started before you leave the state."

"Okay."

"I sense your hesitation."

"It's like walking into God's face and telling him his Church screwed up."

"God can handle kicks to the face."

"It's also kicking over a beehive of gossip."

"I see your concern about that. Even though you're leaving the state, it's still a scandal for your family and friends."

"You got it."

"Would you like me to go with you?"

She looked at the ceiling as she considered the offer. "Can I get back to you on that? I'd like to try it on my own."

"Of course you can, but whatever your decision is, I urge you to start the process before you leave. It will be a burden off your back, probably bigger than filing for divorce in court."

"Do you mind if I call them now to set up an appointment?"

"That's a good idea. You might have to go upstairs to get reception. I'll wait here."

Alone, Lewis wondered if her movement towards Nick Slate could shed light on the location of the demon of his dreams and nightmares. His vacillating judgment on the veracity of the archangel's visitations challenged his sanity, and he hungered for clues.

He invoked his spiritual strength. "Gabriel, I sense that you've been guiding me in my service to God. Please share your further insights with me to help me carry out the Lord's will. Amen."

After his prayer drifted into the universe, despair overcame him. He slumped forward in his chair, digging his elbows into his thighs and resting his chin on his palms. The stretch in his lower back alleviated the nagging tightness.

Each time he'd concluded that Gabriel's interventions were delusions of his subconscious mind, an event had interrupted him to contradict his negativity. But years of slow progress tested his patience, and he wanted Deborah's divorce and flight to Nick Slate to constitute a positive sign.

He felt foolish hope when she descended the stairs, closed the door, and returned to her seat. "They said to come by early on Monday."

"I know this won't be easy, but you can do it."

"I'm going to show up when they open just to get it over with. Then I'm going to leave the state."

"Are you driving? I don't mean to pry, but if you haven't had a chance to share your plans with anyone, I'll be your sounding board."

"It's pretty simple. I've taken out a few thousand dollars of cash. I beat my husband to the punch before he could freeze everything. Of course, the cars are in his name, and if I took one, he'd report it stolen. But I'm going to rent one, stuff my things into it, and drive to Nick's apartment."

"You've done an admirable job so far."

"I'm also going to find a job waiting tables near a police station or some other place I can run to for protection if I have to."

Lewis thought about asking her if she would seek work writing for a newspaper, but then he realized the absurdity. A lady in hiding wouldn't publish, at least not under her established brand name. "It sounds like you've thought this through."

"It's enough for me to get away and get stable. I also think Nick won't mind the company. I think he's lonely."

"I hope you don't mind me asking how he's doing?"

"He misses his brothers. One of them is on some submarine somewhere, and the other has gotten into Wicca or witchcraft or some crazy occult practices."

The news hit Lewis in the face, and he chastised himself for failing to investigate if Nick could be a stepping stone to a possessed family member. "I wasn't aware he had brothers."

"He's worried about his youngest brother for the witchcraft. Plus, he thinks he's in a street gang and selling drugs. He got out of jail about six months ago."

"I understand how that could create stress in Nick's life."

"I think he'll be okay while his brother figures out his life. From what he's told me, he thinks it's just a phase." She looked away and apparent deep thought.

"You're processing something."

"You don't still think there's a chance that Nick's possessed by a demon, do you?"

"I never really did. He doesn't show any signs."

"He told me this in confidence, but I'll tell you anyway. He admitted to being scared by his own research. He's not sure if he's deluding himself, but he thinks the birds sometime obeys his commands."

Her revelation wielded an initial shock, but the exorcist processed it against his huge inventory of paranormal observations. "I keep track of articles about him. There haven't been many, and none of them mentioned that."

"I'm the only person he's told."

"What sort of commands?"

"He said whatever control he might have is minimal, like making the bird turn right or left."

"Even as minimal as that, this is becoming difficult to understand as having a scientific basis."

"He said he wasn't sure about that, and that's why he was scared. I don't understand the technical details, but he said it's possible that the energy of his thoughts was being accidentally transmitted over the wires in the wrong direction to the birds."

Lewis remembered basic radio training from his military past. "I'm no expert, but that sounds highly speculative. Did you say he's shared this with nobody but you? Not even his adviser?"

She shook her head.

"That's how I know he was really scared. He said his lab partner may have suspected, but they parted ways before it could become a topic of conversation."

"You say he was scared. Does that mean that he's fine with the concept now?"

"This is where it gets really weird, Father. He was scared at first, but after his brother helped him buy his own bird, something changed. I wouldn't say he became arrogant, but he certainly became a lot less humble."

Alarms whined in Lewis' mind. "That's a potentially dangerous combination. If confidence becomes arrogance, it can mask and exacerbate a lingering fear. I know you're heading out of state for your own needs, but this may also be a chance for you to help look out for his mental health."

Her look was quizzical. "Not really."

"Why not?"

"I'm pretty sure his new employer's handling that. I'm not sure if I should be telling you this either, but he didn't say to keep it a secret. He's gone to work for the CIA."

The exorcist's mind raced to connect the few data points he understood. A steady history of paranormal occurrences, secretive abilities, and inclusion into a clandestine organization left him confused about the powers that drove Nick Slate.

Considering himself helpless to pursue him under the dark umbrella of the powerful American intelligence entity, he conceded that any demon haunting Nick would elude him. But he allowed himself to believe that his destiny remained within reach. Somehow.

Then, it clicked.

Nick had a younger brother who practiced witchcraft and lived a high-risk lifestyle for demonic possession, and Lewis believed that someday, God would give him a reason to find him.

CHAPTER 16

Curiosity had hastened Nick's acceptance of his new employer. He wanted to know what they knew, and he needed to see how he compared against them. He'd taken the job, even though he didn't know his boss' name until Andrea walked him across the carpet towards the man's office.

Wearing a fitted suit that conformed to her curves, she provoked Nick's lust as she outpaced him.

At first, he'd found her mysterious as she'd recruited him. But during the evaluation sessions, she had shown him compassion, validating her humanity. She'd even seemed vulnerable, as he'd grasped that her success relied upon his. Their growing, multifaceted connection was undeniable.

The suit, however, along with her braided hair and precise makeup application, highlighted their differences. It brought out her credibility, and it accentuated her authoritative allure.

As she stopped at the door and faced him, he found her desirable. He wanted her, and for the first time, he wondered if his control of birds could extend to imparting his will on higher forms of life to get something he wanted.

He wanted to control her.

"I probably should've told you about your real boss already."

"Okay. What should I know?"

"He's not all bad. Don't talk much, and don't ask him questions. Just act like everything's going okay."

"Everything is going okay. I'm just getting started."

"I mean, be confident."

Nick surprised himself with his growing self-assurance. "I am confident."

His abilities in the lab had impressed her, but now her gaze signaled that she began to appreciate his character. "I see that you are. You'll do fine. Let's go."

After thirty minutes of formalities and a memorized recitation welcoming him to the CIA, Nick found his new boss disinterested in his work. The budget for his special project with his falcon came from a secretive account, leaving his supervisor uncaring about the outcome.

As Nick left the office and Andrea closed the door behind him, she confirmed his intuition. "I know that probably seemed odd how little he cared. But that's really a good thing. The only reason you want people caring is if you need money, but we've got enough to last us a long time."

"I know what it's like to worry about the money. I was running out when you found me."

She blushed. "Lucky I found you."

He awoke the next day, and his first thoughts gravitated towards firearms.

Andrea had left him with a weapons expert the prior day, and his head spun trying to memorize the names and images of the small arms he'd see in the field. As his mind sought a familiar thought, it focused on her.

He decided to push through the barriers she had erected, real or imaginary, to get to know her.

After his morning of memorizing military uniforms and ranks, she entered the conference room to check on his progress. Having reverted to her business casual attire, she seemed approachable. "This must be a lot to digest so quickly."

"I haven't digested data at this rate since my comprehensive exams. But I'll get through it."

"I'm sure you will."

"Are you hungry? I could use a lunch break if you could."

She leaned towards him and lowered her voice. "I can't make it for lunch today, but how about dinner? I know a great Italian place, if you're up for it."

"I'm up for it."

"How about you follow me there after your training session this afternoon? You're done at six, right?"

"That's right."

The seduction over dinner had happened easily as she had reciprocated his every flirtation. As he'd ridden back to his apartment with her in a cab, the wine in his bloodstream made him feel invulnerable, and in his bed, she had complied with his every wish.

When he awoke the next day, he remembered her leaving late the prior evening when he was done with her.

He felt like a king. He felt like a god.

At work, Nick finished a training session about the capabilities of CIA satellites.

She met him in the conference room as his lesson ended. "I don't suppose you're free again tonight?"

He found her demeanor unchanged, and he respected how she compartmentalized her emotions. "I need to handle something at my apartment after work, but I can head out later."

"What at your apartment could possibly be more interesting than me?"

"I have a friend who's going to stay with me for a while. She's going through a rough divorce, and she needed to get out of state and stay someplace safe."

A cloud fell over Andrea's face. "I'm not getting in the way of something, am I?"

"No. She's just a friend."

"Good. I'll let you have your way with me at my place, then."

Nick returned to his apartment that evening to find Deborah sitting in a rented car. He walked from his vehicle to hers and knocked on the window. She smiled, opened the door, and jumped into his arms.

He hugged her and then released her. "How was your trip?"

"Long."

"Why didn't you call me?"

"I didn't want to bother you at work."

"How long were you waiting for me?"

"Not even an hour."

"Come on. Let's get your things into my apartment."

Twenty minutes later, he finished helping her empty the vehicle's contents into his guest bedroom. "When do you need to return the car?"

"Not until tomorrow. I didn't know how soon I'd get here, and I didn't want to rush things."

"Okay. Good thinking. You probably need to rest tonight."

"Actually, I could go for some food. What are you in the mood for?"

Nick felt uneasy rejecting her. "I'm sorry, but I've got plans already."

Deborah's face darkened. "You knew I was coming."

"I know. Things have been happening so fast with, uh, my new... I sort of have a girlfriend."

"Oh."

"This doesn't change anything for us. I already told her about you, and you can stay here as long as you'd like."

"No, I get it. You have your life. Just let me get a job, and I'll look for my own apartment."

"What are you talking about? I'm still your friend, and I'm here for you. You don't have to go anywhere."

She stiffened her back, and her face became plasticized, reminding him of a lady accustomed to enduring disappointments. "I appreciate that, but I can't be your charity case. I've never lived on my own, and it's time I figure out how."

Nick and Andrea ate Chinese food and then repeated the prior night's episode of casual sex. Then the next evening brought Indian food followed by another recreational session at her home.

At the end of his Friday morning's training, his CIA quasi-girlfriend escorted him to a private conference room. "I've got some good news."

"I'm all ears."

"I can tell you where we're headed for our first mission."

"We? You're coming with me?"

"I thought you'd assumed that."

"I've made a lot of assumptions, but nobody can confirm nor deny them."

"You're getting the hang of it."

Nick smirked. "What about our new habit?"

"You mean the sex?"

"Yeah, the sex."

"It happens."

"In the field?"

Andrea crossed her arms. "We're staffed by young people. Sex happens. Just follow my lead on what's acceptable or not. I'll keep us from getting in trouble."

"No problem."

"You can separate work from your personal life, can't you?"

"Of course."

"Then we're going to have some fun during our down time."

"Where are we going?"

"Iraq. It was either that or Afghanistan, and from what I understand, we got the better end of the deal."

Two weeks later, Nick watched the ending credits of a second movie through a falcon's eyes. During daily sessions, he had improved his endurance in the recliner, and his falcon had accepted the conditioning.

As he reached full consciousness, Andrea stepped onto the operation room floor. "Four hours was the goal. You made it. You and your bird are ready."

"When do we leave?"

"Tomorrow."

"You're kidding?"

"Have you ever heard me joke?"

"This is definitely a job for a bachelor."

She leaned into him and whispered. "You want to spend your last night in civilization doing something special?"

"Look, Andrea. I figured since we're going to be together in the field, and since I'm leaving Deborah all alone, I should keep her company tonight."

"So, her name is Deborah, and you're going to keep her company on our last night?"

"I told you she's just a friend, and I have an obligation to her."

She scowled. "You didn't even know this was your last night until I just told you."

"I promised her I would take her to dinner and say goodbye on my last night. She's really lonely."

"You're breaking my heart."

"I'm just going to take her to dinner and head to bed early."

"And if she's with you in bed, that's fine by me."

"She's Catholic and married. So you have nothing to worry about."

"Why would I be worried? I can always find another dick if I get bored with yours." She stormed away.

For dinner, Nick shared a small Mediterranean platter with Deborah. He chased a piece of shredded beef with a bite of hummus-dipped pita bread. "I took Arabic food for granted when I lived in Michigan. I'll never make that mistake again."

"I thought you might like it for your last meal."

"Great call. It's delicious."

"Your girlfriend or whatever she is didn't get jealous, did she?"

"I don't think she's going to be my girlfriend or whatever for much longer. I have no idea where it's going, and I'm not sure I care. My first lesson in dating her is that she's an empty shell outside her career."

"I'm sorry."

"Don't be."

"If you're looking for a silver lining, it's better that you find out now than later."

"Yeah, that's true. I'd say she's the opposite of you." As he realized he'd verbalized a private thought, he met Deborah's gaze.

Her eyes told him everything, and his heart agreed that she was the right person. But his mind said it was the wrong place and time.

After returning to his apartment, Nick sought solitude with a walk throughout his apartment complex. Five minutes of strolling brought him near the clubhouse, and he was achieving his goal of being alone with his thoughts.

Then, in the moonlight, a small creature scooting about the bushes caught his attention. The animal's dark fur made it appear like a void, but he ascertained its identity as a cat.

Liking felines, he watched it prance, dart, and dig its way across the edge of the hedge. "Hey you! You chasing something?"

Per its instincts, the animal ignored him.

But as Nick began to walk away, a smaller form moved at the far end of the landscaped shrubs. He recognized the elusive mouse as the cat's prey.

The rodent then became an instinctive statue.

Nick decided to do the feline a favor.

Staring at the cat, he concentrated upon its playful need to hunt and kill. Nothing happened, and he intensified his focus.

A rush of simple excitement rose within him as he sensed a connection with the furry hunter. Ceasing its dashing, the cat rested on its belly, and Nick interpreted its posturing as submission to his will.

He then looked to the motionless mouse and spurred the feline forward. Though the foliage obscured the hunter's view of its target, it moved from its belly and began its skulking assault.

Guided by Nick's perspective, the cat employed stealth to close the distance. When it turned the corner and saw the mouse, it accelerated and pounced.

With a muffled howl of victory, the cat turned and trotted towards Nick. It dropped the motionless rodent at his feet and awaited its congratulatory petting.

Nick crouched and ran his fingers over the soft black fur, and the hunter arched its back in appreciation.

He questioned if the animal had offered its quarry as a gesture of deference or gratitude, and the animal's strange behavior left him uncertain. But he knew one thing with clarity.

He had connected with an animal more complex than a bird, and he sensed his power growing.

CHAPTER 17

Wearing combat fatigue pants and a drab olive T-shirt, Nick trotted to catch up with Andrea. "Why are you walking so fast? The rest of the team's still behind us."

She maintained her stride. "Do you think the marines around are staring at my armpit stains or my tits?"

Nick could only speculate about her being a quasi-military professional and a woman on a military base. "I guess they don't see many women in the camp."

"There's a few, but I stand out, especially since they can tell I'm CIA."

"It's that obvious?"

"Yeah, it's obvious for all of us. They put up with us because we find the bad guys for them, but if they knew what our small team here was really doing, they'd box us up and send us home."

"Some marines must know what we're up to."

Andrea reached the chain-link fence and reached through a hole in the camouflaged tarp to work a combination lock. As she jiggled it open and ushered Nick into the tight perimeter, the climate-controlled field operations structure came into view. "Only our liaison."

Nick took three steps in the desert dirt and reached the building. He waited for the other three members of his team to pass through the fence and for Andrea to lock the gate behind them before tapping a code into a cipher lock and dragging open the structure's heavy door.

He walked in and gulped hot, stifling air. Having grown familiar with the control room's buttons during his training, he located and flipped the switch to the external generator. Sound-isolating walls shielded him from the engine's vibrations, but the illumination of lights confirmed the building's energy source.

As the first person to enter, he carried out his next obligation of turning on the air conditioning. Fans spun to life pushing coolness into the space while his colleagues moved to their seats.

One of the men on the technical support team received an update and shared it with the group. "They're still half an hour out. Let's get a poker game going."

Thirty minutes later, Nick folded his weak hand, and then the loudspeaker brought an update from the falconer's observer. "We're ready with the bird."

Andrea raised her voice. "Let him know we're ready, too."

Nick stepped onto the operational floor and energized his vital sign monitors and jet injector guns before reclining into the black leather bed. He could hear himself breathe as he pressed a button on the panel by his forearm. While the bed rose with a hum, he ordered the helmet lowered over his head.

The lights dimmed, and speakers brought Andrea's voice into the space. "Can you hear me, Nick?"

"I can hear you."

"We're ready if you are."

"I'm ready."

"On your command."

"Inject sedative." The servomotors obeyed his voice, the needle penetrated his flesh, and then the gun flipped backwards beyond his view. Surging warmth filled him.

"How are you feeling?"

"Fine."

"We're fifteen seconds into the operation. Thirty seconds."

Knowing the connection took time, Nick remained calm as he saw the back of his eyelids.

"Forty-five seconds."

An image formed in his mind.

"One minute."

Dangling a stuffed quail, a small drone came into view.

Nick recognized the drone and its bait as the falcon's lure. As the raptor's peripheral vision tracked the desert below, the bird followed its symbolic meal. Nick watched the drone climb while deploying the thin line that held the fake quail at a steady altitude.

With minutes remaining until the falcon overflew the city, Nick reached a semi-conscious state back in the field lab. "I'm here."

From the speakers overhead, Andrea's voice filled the room. "Was your connection good?"

"Yes."

"What did you see?"

"The bird's following the quail. The drone went high while I was watching."

"That aligns with the trainer's report. He says the drone is climbing above two thousand feet and holding the quail at one hundred feet."

Nick recalled the unmanned aircraft's tiny dimensions and hoped it would fly unnoticed at its operating altitude.

"You've got five minutes before the bird's in the city. How do you want to wait?"

"I'll just chill with the bird." He relaxed, drifted in and out of consciousness, and settled with the raptor's view. Specks dotted his window on the world, but his flying host blinked its nictitating membranes to clear the dust and moisten its eyes.

With the destination to the northwest, flat plains passed under the bird's belly. Mountains spanned the horizons to the north and east, and a green line defined the city's irrigated land.

As a secret test, Nick willed the falcon to look to its left and then to its right. It obeyed. Satisfied by the bird's shift in focus, he released it to its own volition, and it followed its lure.

The raptor passed the city's southeast boundary and continued two kilometers to the border the marines would cross. The influx of visual data to the falcon's cortex showed shallow angles—the sides of buildings and patches of their interiors through the windows–beyond the reach of higher-altitude man-made spy craft.

A gentle turn brought the bird back the other way, displaced one block to the west, and then the falcon continued its westerly sweep until reaching the town's far edge. The fake quail reversed course and enticed the raptor to patrol the city back towards the east. Nick compared the real-time view against his memory of the latest satellite photographs, but nothing stood out as representing an improvised explosive device or other danger.

After four repetitions back and forth across the section, the falcon began flapping its way home towards its trainer. Nick disengaged. "I'm here."

Andrea's amplified voice was welcomed familiarity. "How was your connection?"

"Strong. I had great visual the whole time, but I didn't see anything worth reporting."

"Nothing?"

"Too much, really. I lost count of the parked cars."

"Any dead animal carcasses? Boxes? Containers? Mounds of dirt? Broken concrete or rubble on the roadside? Anything where a bomb could be planted."

"No. I know what to look for. Sorry, but there's nothing."

"It's still early, if the insurgents even know we're coming. Keep looking on your future flights."

"I will. Is that it for the day?"

"No. You've got two more flights. You need to be ready again in half an hour. But we're on a break now."

The lights became bright as Nick freed himself from the recliner.

Andrea opened the door and pulled up a chair in front of him. "We've got some private time."

"Okay. Can I ask you something?"

"Of course."

"Aren't you concerned that the insurgents will see the drone? Even at high altitudes, it's visible."

"They aren't looking. And even if they are, we're still a week ahead of the attack. They'd chalk it up as general surveillance."

"I hear what you're saying, but it's an unnecessary risk."

"The drone looks like just another drone. The real risk is if someone sees it and connects it to the bird, but that would require someone looking in two different places at the same time from far away. It would be nearly impossible to make that connection from inside the city."

"I guess you're right, but I don't like it." He needed to confess a burning secret. "What if I told you I can control the bird?"

She narrowed her eyes. "I know."

"Seriously? You knew?"

"I suspected."

In retrospect, he assumed he'd been intimate with a professional spy. "How? You didn't grill me about it when you had me at a disadvantage in the bedroom?"

She snorted. "You have great abilities. It was only a matter of time until you tested them. Then it was only a matter of time until you had to tell someone."

"Wouldn't this be easier if you let me control the bird and leave the drone behind?"

She frowned. "We'll be done with the drone by tonight. Your bird will be conditioned to the flight path."

"I know, but that's still an unnecessary risk."

"You're not to impart any control over the bird."

"But what about in an emergency?"

"What possible emergency? If the falcon dies, we'll have a new one overnighted here."

"I don't know why you're so uptight about me making this easier on us and giving us flexibility."

Her tone harshened. "Do you want to show off a remote-control falcon to the insurgents? They'd start killing off every bird they saw, and we'd lose the entire surveillance advantage you've dedicated your life to."

He raised his voice. "That's a bullshit excuse."

"Nick!"

He brought down the volume. "This species isn't even indigenous to this area. It exists to the north, but if you're afraid of a hypothetical genius birdwatcher, you're already on shaky ground."

"That's an apples to oranges comparison. Someone can find a bird's behavior suspicious whether he knows the species or not, and especially if the species stands out as foreign."

"My point is, I can do this. And the way you have your arguments against it so well thought out tells me you've thought of it already. You have other people who've achieved control before, don't you?"

She looked away in thought and then faced him. "You're not ready for control."

The veiled admission made him feel less special but also less a freak. "I've already controlled falcons with enough restraint that nobody could tell. I'm impressed that you even suspected."

"Control is a different department with a higher classification. After you prove yourself, you may be invited to join."

"Prove myself? If I didn't invent control, I'm sure as hell one of the first. You're holding me back."

"It's out of my control. I'm sorry."

"Do you expect me to believe that?"

"Yes. It's true. And you have no choice."

"Fine. I'll believe you, even if it's not entirely true. I guess that secrets and half-lies are the way things go down around here."

"Well, duh." Her smile diffused his anger, but he began to harbor resentment for his new employer.

"I got it. Right. I'm in the CIA now. I'll chill."

"Are you chilled yet?"

"Enough. Why?"

"I needed to tell you that I didn't mean to be such a bitch last week."

"You mean before we left the States? I hardly noticed. No need to apologize."

"You're too sweet, but if you didn't notice that as bitch behavior, you were sleepwalking."

"Sure, I noticed. I mean it's okay."

She smiled. "Good. I was hoping we'd be on civil terms."

"We are, as far as I'm concerned. Maybe better than civil."

"In that case, haven't you been wondering where I sleep?"

He liked her directness. "I assumed they put you up with some female marines, but I'm curious now that you brought it up."

"You and the guys sleep in your own tent because there's a formal division between us and the marines. It's the same for me."

As he realized he was regaining his sex partner, his ego grew. "I didn't know that, but I like where you're going with this."

"It's small, but I get a private tent."

"Because you're a lady or because you're our team leader?"

"A little of both, but mainly because I'm a lady. But since I am the team leader, and since we're in the field, I can order you around."

"Really? I don't see it that way. I'm the star. I'm sure that counts for more than the team leader."

"That would be a shame, because I was just going to order you to my private tent tonight."

"I can reconsider my position."

"I thought you might. See you tonight."

Nick stretched his legs in the afternoon sun, keeping distant from the marines and trying to talk with his CIA technical team. Knowledge of electronics carried him through a few minutes of conversation, but as the heat took its toll, the men sat in the shade outside their compound and sought simpler topics. As his companions talked about sports and electronic gaming, he realized he shared few interests with them.

On the next run over the city, he saw nothing unusual but confirmed the bird's proper path. The last run then took place without the lure, proving the falcon's ability to handle its memorized trek in return for its meal after the day's final flight.

During the week leading up to the attack, Nick joined the

falcon in several confirmation runs, including three trials in the dark. The raptor's vision remained viable in the moonlight.

He spent his time away from the bird studying satellite photographs of the city, and he judged himself ready when the marine liaison summoned him and his team.

On the day of the mission, he joined the marine officer and his CIA colleagues in the back of the operation center, behind the far Plexiglas where the group could watch an overhead view of the city on the liquid crystal display.

The colonel reminded Nick of himself. He was the lithe academic type who probably had a PhD, and he appeared too young for his rank.

Andrea made the introductions. "Gentlemen, this is Lieutenant Colonel Robinson. He's our liaison to the strike team. He knows what he needs to about us, and he's going to share what he can about the upcoming operation. The operations team just finished its brief."

The officer's voice seemed too absorbed in thought to have issued from a marine as he tapped a handheld pointer against the screen. "As you can see, the lead convoy will be in sight of the city in three hours. They'll be taking the main road from the southeast, and improvised explosive devices, or IEDs, will be a major concern until they reach this point here."

Andrea interrupted. "May I ask the question?"

"Yes, ma'am."

"We can watch the road on the flight in, but we'll only get one pass. Will you have drone coverage for the convoy at that point?"

"Yes, ma'am. But when the convoy reaches this point, it'll be within range of rocket-propelled grenades, or RPGs. Those can be launched from positions at ground level or within buildings that are in the drone's blind spots. I've identified the blind spots on the map. Next slide, please."

Andrea tapped her phone, invoking the next image, and then amorphous blotches of blackness dotted the city. Nick recognized them all as being within view of the falcon's future flight.

Robinson looked at Nick. "I trust you find these areas familiar."

"I do. I know what to look for."

The officer turned to Andrea. "You understand that your communications must be directly with me, do you not?"

"Affirmative, colonel."

"You'll speak as if you're using a secret drone technology. If you make a mistake and mention anything about a bird, continue talking normally as if it were slang for a drone. Nobody suspects what's really going on, and it will remain that way."

"Understood, colonel."

"Is the bird ready, ma'am?"

"I just got a report from the trainer. It's still sleeping, which is normal. He'll wake it an hour before the convoy's in sight of the city. The bird will overtake the convoy right here." She aimed her finger at the display.

"That's acceptable, ma'am. I'll conduct a comms check with you in two hours. Good luck."

Three hours later, Nick watched the convoy slide below his view. Nothing on the road appeared dangerous, and he stayed with the bird during its first pass over the city. His adrenaline subsided as the second pass revealed normalcy.

But the third pass spiked his heart rate and catapulted him to a semi-aware state. "I'm here."

Andrea's voice was tenser than the rehearsal and reconnaissance runs. "How's your connection?"

"It was great until I saw an RPG."

She barged through the door, marched to the side. And opened a photograph above his face. "Where? Point."

As the falcon's information merged with Nick's memory of the map, he discerned the building and its location. He jabbed his finger into it. "Right here. It's inside the top story window facing the street. I saw only one insurgent, but I didn't have a good angle to look deep into the room."

"Are you absolutely sure?"

"Yes."

"If you're wrong, you're going to stop the entire convoy for at least half an hour. This is dangerous shit that'll leave the marines in a bad position. Are you sure enough to bet their lives and your career on it?"

"Yes, damn it. I'm sure."

While she walked away, he wondered when swearing had become habitual.

Her voice came over the loudspeaker. "You may as well calm yourself and go back in. You won't do anybody any good in here worrying."

"Who said I was worrying?"

"I'm worrying enough for both of us. Just get back in there and see if you can find something else."

After returning to his altered reality, Nick's visual perception drifted with the falcon over the city, finding nothing unusual. As the bird prepared for its second sweep to the west, he awoke to being shaken.

Andrea glared at him with fiery eyes. "They sent a sniper team into a nearby building to get a visual on your RPG."

Her unreadable glare made Nick question his original assessment. "Well?"

Her smile burst forth. "Confirmed. Confirmed and neutralized. You did it, Nick. You kept marines from dying."

CHAPTER 18

The successful mission earned Nick a private celebration with Andrea, and it also brought new looks from the marines. Though they remained standoffish, he met their inquisitive stares with a confidence that broadcast his newfound value to them.

Though the truth remained beyond their grasp, he made sure his body language conveyed his importance in himself and his small team that had saved their lives. Those who compared his face and swagger to those of the other CIA personnel in the camp knew Nick was the star player.

He figured they took him for a gifted drone operator, and that suited him. In his pensive moments, he found that version of his heroism accurate. When he interfaced with the falcon, he turned it into a piece of reconnaissance technology.

Two weeks of mundane security flights over the city helped prove its dearth of insurgents. Once it was declared safe, Nick's team was set free. Lacking an immediate assignment, he and his CIA colleagues were heading home for two weeks of training and time off.

The day before his departure, a muscular officer with full-bird colonel emblems on his starched collar stepped into his path. The man's broad shoulders filled his uniform, and he created a vacuum of scurrying marines in his vicinity.

The colonel presented what Nick construed as an attempt to smile, but his mouth's tightness combined with his hard eyes to convey the marine's disdain for pleasantries. His tone signaled the foregone conclusion that any question it might carry was a de facto command. "Young man, may I have a word with you in private?"

"Sure, colonel." Nick stopped and waited for the word that never came.

Instead of speaking, the officer reached into his pocket and handed him a satellite phone.

Nick raised the phone to his ear. "Hello?"

His CIA boss in Virginia identified himself and told him the colonel knew about his recent mission and his abilities. He also made it clear to keep his upcoming talk with the marine private.

Nick returned the phone. "Should we go somewhere?"

"No. I'll be quick. I wanted to introduce myself and make you an offer. I'm Colonel Meyer, Force Reconnaissance. I know who you are, what you do, and what you're capable of. When you get frustrated with what you're doing, call me. I can get you what you want."

Nick expected to feel more surprised, but since meeting Andrea, unexpected disruptions had become normal. "Thanks, colonel, but I'm quite happy with my present job."

"I know. That's why I approached you now. Think about my offer while you're happy so that you don't sign up in the future out of desperation. You can answer me when you're ready."

"You said you could get me what I want. What does that mean, specifically?"

The marine placed a hand on Nick's shoulder, paralyzing him with its authoritative weight. He leaned forward and whispered. "Control–of any animal you want." He straightened his back, stuck a business card into Nick's hand, and marched away.

When he landed in Virginia, Nick parted with his team and called Deborah from his car.

Her voice soothed him. "Welcome back to civilization."

"Thanks. Where are you?"

"Working."

"That's great. You got a job. Where at?"

"I'm working as a waitress, just like I said I would."

"Yeah, but where?"

Her hesitancy concerned him. "Far away."

"I don't understand."

"I moved out while you were gone. I have my own place."

"I said you could stay as long as he needed."

"I know. But I don't need to stay with you anymore."

"Where are you staying now?"

"Somewhere far away. I'm on my own in a different state, and that's where I need to be."

As she claimed her independence, abandonment weighed on him. "You're not even going to tell me where you are?"

"Not now. The less you know, the better. My soon-to-be ex-husband probably wouldn't come after you even if he knew you helped me, but I wouldn't put it past him."

He blurted out a comment that weighed upon him like an unexploded bomb after speaking it. "You're the best friend I have."

Silence. Discomfort.

He qualified his statement. "I mean, look at my life. What do I have? My brothers are distant now. I was a lone wolf during my undergraduate days and postgraduate research, since Andy was more a partner than a friend. Now I'm a lone wolf in my job. The only consistent person in my life I give a damn about is you."

"I don't know what to say. Now's not the time, Nick. I've got four tables to deal with right now. We'll talk about this later. I've got to run. Bye."

Loneliness overcame him as the line went dead. To compensate, he sought the ego boost and thrill of sexual release.

He called Andrea.

Her tone was teasing. "Miss me already?"

"You're not surprised, are you? You can't blame a guy for wanting to be with someone as hot as you."

"Flattery works sometimes, but not now. We agreed to take time apart."

"It was more like you were the boss telling me we'd spend time apart."

"I can be a bit bossy, can't I?"

"I kind of like that about you. I think it's sexy."

She chuckled. "Flattery and sweet talk. Nice try. Even if you were good at it, it still wouldn't work."

"I'll be direct, then. You want to hang out tonight?"

"What's wrong? Did your woman in waiting leave you?"

The words stung, and he knew he'd never receive any compassion from her outside of her professional responsibility. "She was never my woman in waiting. I told you she was just a friend."

"Then shouldn't you be spending time with your friend, after three weeks in the sand with me?"

He salvaged what dignity he could by pretending Diane hadn't just pushed him away. "You have a point. I was being selfish and looking for a good time, but you're right that I should pay attention to her. She's probably lonely."

"We had enough good times in the desert to last us for a while. Wait a few days before you call me again."

As an exercise in restraint, Nick minimized his interactions with Andrea during the week at the office and ignored her outside of work. To address his loneliness in his free time, he sought a new project.

He called the medical team at the University of Michigan and inquired about applying the falcons' electronic implantation procedure to a domestic cat. His surgical contact agreed it was possible, but Nick would have to map the feline's brain and pay one hundred thousand dollars for the experimental effort.

Seeking money, he called his brother, Jake.

"How are you doing, Nick?"

"Good. How about you?"

"It's a tough life, but at least I get to give my submarine to the other crew when I come back from deployment. I can't imagine what it's like keeping this pace on a submarine with only one crew."

"Is that how other submarines do it?"

"Yeah, at least in America. It's insane, but that's how our attack submarines are staffed. You really have to love this type of work to do it for a career."

"Are you looking to make it a career?"

"I am. I'm so glad I picked submarines instead of trying to be a SEAL. Now that's a hard life. Compared to that, I can handle anything a submarine can dish out. How's your new job?"

With his brother sounding happy, Nick made his request. "It's pretty good, but it's limiting. I want to do some research on the side to make up for it. I could use a little financial help, if you have the money or can get it from Grant."

"How much?"

"One hundred thousand dollars again. I'm looking to take the next step to the more complex brain of a cat."

"Shit, Nick, that sounds cool, but that's a lot of money. I think we've exhausted Grant's goodwill."

"I understand. I know I'm asking for a lot. Would it be okay if I came down there to visit you for a few days?"

He hadn't seen his brother in years, and he expected the hesitation. "I'm sure we can work something out. It's been too long. What did you have in mind?"

Nick had nothing in mind other than painful scarcity. He needed money, and he needed human interaction, and since he had to deploy back to Iraq in a week, and he had to move fast. "Just a couple days with you. I don't care what we do."

Two days later, his brother met him at Jacksonville International Airport, Northern Florida's gateway to Southeast Georgia, and crushed him with a hug.

Nick reckoned that weight training had expanded his brother's body mass to twice that of himself.

The ride to Georgia in Jake's Jeep Grand Cherokee was quiet. Each sibling's work in secretive jobs limited their topics of conversation. Nick enjoyed the warmth and the tropical foliage that lined the highway.

As his brother angled the vehicle into the city of St. Marys, he broke a long silence. "You don't mind if you meet one of my buddies, do you?"

"You mean to have him hang out with us?"

"I figured Riley could hang out while we chill at a bar."

"You mean to spend all our time drinking?"

"Well, we are sailors, after all. He's the only guy whose wife lets him hang out with me, and that's most easily achieved on special occasions, such as your arrival. It stinks being the only bachelor in the wardroom."

Nick wondered what other activities they could do in the area, but he realized he had no aptitude for golfing or fishing. He was boring, and he accepted it. "Drinking is all we have, huh?"

"Unless you want to go dirt biking. I would never put you on my bike because you'd kill yourself in five minutes, but Riley's bike might be okay for you."

"Why not just put an apple on my head and shoot arrows at me? That would be a little safer. You know I'm not athletic enough to handle a golf club, much less a dirt bike."

"I was just thinking out loud."

"Well, no thanks on the dirt biking. Chilling at a bar sounds just fine."

From an upstairs patio of Trolleys Food and Spirits, a favorite watering hole in St. Marys, Nick watched the sun touch the horizon over a southern Georgian tributary of the St. Marys River. Around him, a mix of young locals, imported retirees, and sailors ate bar food and drank beer.

Across the table, Jake's shipmate, Riley, gulped from a glass and then plopped it down next to a plate of cheese sticks. "You must have one of the few jobs that's more secretive than ours."

Jake intercepted the question. "That's right. He can talk even less about his job than we can. But his research is public and is really interesting. Go ahead and tell him about it, Nick."

While he watched his brother inhale hot wings, Nick was content to pick at the finger food and leave room in his stomach for beer. Between swigs, he explained the published portions of his experiments.

Riley interrupted Nick's opening. "Whatever job you have, I

want it. It must be so much cooler than what we're doing. I either babysit a reactor or drive the submarine in circles."

Jake smacked his shipmate's shoulder. "It's not that bad. We also train to fight. Where else are you going to learn submarine combat tactics?"

"I agree that part's cool, but I could do without the routine that fills up two thirds of our day–and I mean sixteen to twenty of our twenty-four. It's like the military has no concept of sleep."

Scowling, Jake nodded at his shipmate's beer. "Quit whining and keep drinking."

A party of sailors with their wives climbed to the patio and paraded by Jake and Riley, offering handshakes and fist bumps on their way to a large table. One new arrival caught Nick's attention. "Who's she?"

Jake's face lit up. "Funny you should ask. That's the sister of one of the guys. She's studying biology at the University of Florida."

Nick remembered a shy version of himself, but that had been the pathetic creature who had yet to taste success. He welcomed the attention of the attractive coed. "What did you tell her?"

"Just about your research, that you were a PhD, and that you were working for the CIA. I threw in a flattering picture as well."

"You think I need that much help finding women?"

"I have no idea, but in this town with the short notice you gave me, I'm doing you a favor."

"I'll take the favor and thank my monster of a so-called little brother." Nick raised his beer, and the threesome tapped their drinking glasses.

Jake waved his shipmate to the table with his sister, beginning an evening of conquest.

His brother served as an admirable wing man, easing the evening's conversation and getting Nick to a hotel room with the object of his desire. He left him his car and gave him his freedom for the night, and the young coed gave him freedom with her body.

When the visit ended, Nick found himself in another bear-like embrace with his brother's hydraulic vice-grip arms. While he walked to the terminal, the sadness of isolation arose within him, and he distracted himself with his recent memory of dominance over an object of his lust.

But deep thoughts consumed him during the flight to Virginia, and when the plane landed, he concluded that loneliness was an inescapable and universal fact.

He realized Andrea was nothing more than a fellow player in a game. When her next move aligned with his, they would enjoy mutual satisfaction. When their moves diverged, emptiness.

Seeking a connection, he pushed Andrea from his mind and thought of Deborah.

She sought him when she needed him, but it wasn't him that she needed. It was anyone who would be a crutch. She was just another player in an ugly game.

Life was about using people to satiate desires, and nothing else, he decided. His brother had helped him scratch an itch, and it felt good.

But he wondered how long the distracting relief would last before his isolation destroyed him.

CHAPTER 19

Nick and his team returned to the Marine Corps camp in Iraq. Success on the prior mission had been exciting, but now he wondered how repeat performances would tax his endurance.

He watched the desert pass underneath the falcon while it followed the fake quail towards a new city. The bird flew over a smaller section of urban area than that of the prior mission. The pending strike would be surgical, taking out a few insurgents in their apartments.

The days of training leading up to the mission had been uneventful, and Nick had considered Lieutenant Colonel Robinson's briefing a dull, shrunken repetition of its prior iteration. As he reclined into the bed on the operations floor, only the hope of discovering another unseen danger offered him interest in his job.

Again, he watched the desert pass underneath the falcon. As he overflew the lone assault vehicle, the dirt road leading to the city tested his patience with its normalcy. No hidden trenches, no unexpected berms, no disturbed piles of dirt.

The bird then crossed the border into the urban setting and began its patrol pattern. Moonlight illuminated the quiet town, and Nick recognized the challenge of sustained field operations–minutes of exhilaration separated by days of training and hours of boring flying.

He welcomed the distraction when he awoke to being shaken.

Andrea glared at him with fiery eyes, but unlike their triumphant mission, her mouth curved downwards. "They were ambushed. It's over. It's a disaster."

"What? How? I know I didn't miss anything along the road."

"It's not your fault. From what it sounds like, there was a

small cave and tunnel network beside the road. There was nothing out of the ordinary for you to see."

Nick got angry. "Maybe not my fault, but I could've prevented this if you'd let me control the damned thing and keep it a hundred yards ahead of our guys."

"I doubt you could've prevented this."

"I sure as hell could've given them more warning than whatever they had."

"Stop trying to be a hero. It's time for us to be quiet and help the colonel protect our interests."

Nick got angrier. "What do you mean 'protect our interests'?"

"There's a protocol for problematic missions. We need to be quick and definitive in presenting the evidence that this isn't a CIA failure."

"This is our responsibility. I could've prevented this."

"I understand your perspective. It's a fair one. Why don't you take a bathroom break and we'll talk about it after you settle down?"

Nick accepted the opportunity to calm himself and walked towards the tight facilities tucked behind the rear section's Plexiglas. After relieving himself, he returned to the operations room and found himself alone. He raised his voice. "What gives? You locked me in here?"

She answered over the loudspeaker. "Your perspective may be fair, but it's dangerous for the next couple hours. You're on lockdown. I suggest you stream a movie and start watching."

"So that's it? You'd have me watch the Maltese Falcon while you and the other supposed adults play politics to cover your asses?"

"The entire team's on lockdown, Nick. You're just the only one who isn't in a state of mind to obey the order. Believe me that it's for your own good. If I let you out of this box in your present mood, you'd find a way to eliminate all our jobs."

The next day, Nick hid inside the tent with his male CIA colleagues. Wisdom dictated that his team avoid a camp of bitter marines while their desire for vengeance could spark upon accidental victims. He powered through magazine articles to distract himself from the boredom and to break up into small chunks his analysis of an important decision.

Before he fell asleep, he had decided.

He would seek employment with the mysterious special forces marine colonel.

When he finished his morning toiletries the next day, he risked a trip to the communications center. But a sign posted on the door proclaimed that personal communications were shut down while the camp recovered from its loss.

Nick returned to the safe secrecy of his CIA tent to commit himself to a day of reading. But when he returned from a quick and quiet lunch, he found an envelope with his name tacked to the door.

He pulled it off, opened it, and read it. The note was permission from the camp's communications officer to use a satellite phone in the center. Curious about his newfound special privilege, he marched towards the equipment.

With restrictions on individual usage, the communications center was quiet. When he stepped into the depths of the tent, an officer hailed him to a desk. Nick presented the paper and in return received a code to use a satellite phone to call one outgoing number. The officer handed him a sticky pad with the digits, and Nick recognized them as belonging to the Force Reconnaissance colonel.

He sat and dialed, and on the third ring, Colonel Meyer answered. "I thought you might be running into trouble trying to find a phone."

"That's true, colonel, but how'd you know I'd want to contact you now?"

"I didn't know, but if I were a gambling man I would've made a large wager."

"You don't strike me as a gambling man."

"Let me rephrase. I didn't know that you wanted to call me,

but I would've been surprised if you didn't. So I made it possible by getting the camp's commanding officer to give you permission."

As he began to understand the colonel, he began to like him. "It seems you know me quite well."

"I know what happened out there, and I know you were capable of preventing it."

Hope rose within Nick as someone understood him. "You're right. So what's next to take you up on your offer?"

"You'll go to work for a military contractor for a twenty percent raise, and then you'll work for me. You can sign the paperwork during your travels."

"Can you get me out of the CIA?"

"I have relationships well above your boss' level. I'll take care of the CIA and the details like your apartment and state residency issues."

Nick wanted to challenge those promises, but the marine seemed above reproach. The colonel offered him more than the CIA and his university could accomplish if combined. The invitation felt right, but it was happening fast. "How soon do you need an answer?"

"I believe I have one. But if you need time, take a few days."

"A few days in this misery? I'm useless here. My entire team is useless. We're eye sores and reminders of an intelligence community failure. I don't want to be here another minute."

"That's why I approached you when you were fresh from a victory. Did working for me sound like a good idea then?"

"Yes, colonel. It did. How much detail can we discuss on this line? I want to go over my particular interests and see if they match what you're doing."

"This conversation's not the place, but I do need to inform you of a few possible detriments. You won't be working in an air-conditioned building. You'll be working with the Marine Corps, and that could mean outdoors in the middle of nowhere, possibly behind enemy lines."

Nick hadn't considered the danger of hostile territory. "I

wasn't aware of that, but it makes sense. I can't consider that a deal breaker since it's obvious in retrospect."

"Good. If you give me your word that you'll join me, I'll have you flown on military transport, and I'll set you up with a secure phone for us to talk during your travels. If you don't like what I have to tell you, I'll fly you home, and you'll never hear from me again."

Nick sighed and cleared his mind. "Count me in, colonel. You have my word."

"I know this is a lot to digest quickly, but you'll be happy with your choice."

"I think so, too. By the way, where am I going?"

"Camp Pendleton, California. You're training with special operations commandos."

Though a contracting firm wrote his paychecks, Nick knew he worked for Colonel Meyer as he followed him through Camp Pendleton's security checkpoints. Wearing a working uniform, the colonel appeared both immaculate and ready to get dirty with anyone foolish enough to slow him.

The marine officer brought Nick into a private room deep inside a windowless building where he introduced him to his new colleague. Given the leeway extended to special forces in grooming standards, his coworker's shoulder-length raven hair left Nick wondering about his military status.

But the man's sultry voice confirmed his status as a civilian, and Nick thought he may be an actor. If not, then his new colleague fancied himself a vampire. "Welcome to the real game."

Nick awaited the handshake that never happened. "Thank you. I'm happy to be here."

"You're happy now, but you won't be once you've had a full taste." The would-be vampire examined his fingernails.

Meyer frowned. "That's enough, Damien."

"'Damien?'"

"He changed his name when he realized he had the connection. His parents named him 'Oliver'."

With a slow theatric flair, Damien rolled his eyes. "Why do you have to always tell that story?"

"Because you always try to scare away the newbies. Get on with the program."

"Right. The program. You're a zoologist. So you already know the advantages of each species."

Nick's curiosity spiked. "Wait. You're talking about controlling animals like it's a foregone conclusion. As far as I've seen, I'm the only guy who's ever done it."

"Can I tell him?"

The marine nodded. "Go ahead."

"We've had four people who could do it."

Not alone–one of four, and maybe more at the CIA–and no longer a unique freak, Nick needed to know about the others. "You're talking in the past tense. Where are they?"

"They all quit, except for me."

"Why? Where'd they go?"

"I have no idea where they are now. But they quit because they couldn't take it. They're no longer in the game. They're just normal people now."

"What's so hard that they couldn't take it?"

Meyer answered. "It's a hard job at times. They just weren't disciplined enough, but you've got the dedication to make it. Your PhD and CIA training prove that."

"Dedication, sure. That's why I'm here. This is what my life's work's about. But you still haven't told me how other people have been able to control animals."

Damien droned dramatically. "The science is simple. You use micro-antennas on the animals' brains to capture their thoughts and send them to you. Then, for the few of us who are truly gifted, we harness our thoughts into commands that are transmitted back to the animals. The elegance is in the performance. It is a dance."

Nick had expected the explanation, but it took him into areas beyond his understanding. "I get it. That's what the colonel called 'the connection'."

The wanna-be undead raised his chin and looked down upon Nick. "Yes. You've been dealing with an inferior arrangement where the information flow was just one-way. In our sophisticated two-way arrangement, you have to turn your mind into a supercomputer. The information flow is staggering. That's why so few of us can make, much less sustain, the connection."

Meyer waved his hand. "Enough with the sermon."

"Right. Our three primary species are eagles, wolves, and leopards. You'll need to become proficient in controlling all three."

"That's amazing!"

Allowing the display of emotion, Meyer sounded proud of his program. "The Navy provides veterinarians who tend to the animals and perform the implantation surgeries, and we get our trainers through civilian contractors, the same way we get your services."

The vampire took over the bragging. "Eagles are our spies. But in the spirit of the Corps, every marine's a rifleman, and every one of our animals is capable of combat. Your falcons would make ideal spies if they could fight humans, but they are rather smallish."

Nick ran through his mental checklist comparing the qualities of the two raptors. "I agree. Peregrine Falcons are a bit too small."

Damien seemed to warm up to his new colleague. "You're getting it. The species of eagle you'll control in the field depends on the geography of the mission, but once you've trained on one eagle, it's easy to handle another."

"Yeah, it was the same with falcons."

"Bird brains, after all. Once you've been inside one, you've been inside them all. Of course, you give up speed for size when you shift from a falcon to an eagle. I think you'll also find that eagle vision is about half as good as falcon vision, but I'm speculating, since I've never tinkered with falcons."

Nick caught the condescending tone with regard to the vampire's opinion of the smaller bird. "I think that's fine. It's a compromise. But what about the other species? We're dealing with larger and more complex brains."

"After you handle an eagle or two, you'll move on to wolves, just like I did. They're hierarchical, and that means you'll meet initial resistance. But over time, you'll prove that you're the alpha, and you'll be in control."

Meyer qualified the claim. "It's harder than he makes it sound. We capture only the alphas so that when you deploy with them, you get the power of the pack behind you."

When Nick's new undead colleague spoke of the action, enthusiasm lit up his speech. "I've done wolves in the field three times, and a handful of the pack followed me instinctively each time. Unfortunately, I had to win back the pack once since another wolf declared himself the alpha while I was training the real alpha."

Nick liked it better than the nonchalant fake vampire attitude. "Did you have to do any other fighting, like against humans?"

Raven hair caressed the vampire's shoulders as he shook his head. "No. Wolves are great for spying from a couple hundred meters away, but if you get closer, an enemy might see them since you're usually coming with an entire pack."

Again, the marine qualified the statement. "Don't get him wrong, Nick. There's plenty of tactical value in wolves. They can spy, they can distract, and they can attack when needed. We just haven't needed it yet. This is a relatively new program."

"How new?"

"Three years. The breakthrough was in the microelectronics and surgical techniques that allows the telemetry connection."

"This picture's becoming clear. What about the leopard, though? Is that your stealthy ground-based spy?"

"More or less. But I like to think of them as my assassins. Wolves hunt in packs, leopards hunt alone."

Despite the undead man's odd mannerisms, Nick liked him. "Sounds cool."

"It is, in theory, but I've argued the risk versus reward with the colonel, and he keeps telling me that I've lost the argument. But I don't think we should use cats."

"Why? Because they don't acknowledge masters?"

"Right. They aren't bound by any set of social rules, and each one thinks it's a god. I did one field operation with a leopard, and it was exhausting. I have no patience for them."

Nick shrugged. "I'm sure it's demanding. But I like cats."

The vampire glared at him. "If you survive a field operation with one, you'll come back and tell me how much you hate them."

CHAPTER 20

A month later, Nick reclined in a Humvee's cloth-lined bed. Though Spartan compared to his CIA-era equipment, the vehicle made for better surroundings than the open air. A portable generator hummed on the ground beside the wheels, and a small air conditioning unit blew heat out a customized hole in the rear doors.

Lacking an automated injection system, Nick welcomed the Navy corpsman, and he didn't mind having a battlefield trauma expert by his side. The young man leaned over him, blocking the cabin's dim overhead light. "Are you ready for the sedative, Doctor Slate?"

During his training, Nick had found the Marine Corps' version of the drug comparable to that of the CIA, and he concluded the organizations shared the serum. "You can call me 'Nick'."

"Sorry, I'm used to working with marines."

His vampire-like coach sat beside him for his first mission. "I've asked him many times to call me 'Damien', but he keeps calling me 'Mister Crowley'."

After months training with him, Nick still found his colleague's name absurd. "Then we should get a new corpsman."

"Are you aware of the security procedures to get one cleared to work with us? I'm afraid we're stuck with Petty Officer McKeever."

The corpsman shared a smirk with Nick.

The vampire coach continued. "Remember. You're looking for IEDs, RPGs, and snipers. You know what to do."

"Got it. I'm ready. Inject me."

The corpsman shot the hissing gun into Nick's arm, and he drifted into the eagle's perspective.

His gentle commands convinced the bird to carve slow zig-zags across the road in front of the convoy, watching for the type of sophisticated ambush that had doomed his last mission.

Betsy, the six-pound female golden eagle that Colonel Meyer had forced Nick to name, obeyed his commands. The freedom to impart his will on a raptor thrilled him, and he drifted from his body and flew with her.

When he surmised that the distance between the city and the lead vehicle approached RPG range, he released the bird to fly ahead. There was no pre-planned flight pattern–only Nick's experience and control.

He used the same U-shaped patterns he'd employed with the CIA, and on his third leg, he saw an unusual reflection in an open window. He lowered Betsy and made her flap her wings to get a closer look.

A sniper rifle.

Nick thought about becoming semi-aware to inform his team, but there was no time. He expected approaching marines to be within the weapon's range any second. Colonel Meyer had instructed him to use his judgment, and Damien had confirmed the independent action approach as best.

He thought of the rifleman as a threat to Betsy's nest, and she pumped her wings with vigor. He considered the risk of hot metal to her talons but ruled it out for the silence of the weapon's barrel.

The window would present a tight fit for her six-foot wing-span, but he decided that her flapping feathers would hold her altitude with half-strokes and that her resilient bones would handle the beating against the sandstone wall.

He spread her wings to glide, and he extended her legs towards the elongated metal. As her talons grabbed the rifle, the surprised sniper tightened his grip on the stock.

She flapped back and pulled upwards, yanking while torqueing the weapon from the enemy's grasp. In the heightened awareness of the struggle, Nick felt tactile feedback and realized the eagle's outer talon had lost its grip.

But the other talon held, and the bird's surprise and thrust rotated the barrel over the window. To avoid dropping the rifle back into the room, Nick ordered her to dive and use her weight to drive the stock upward over the fulcrum of the sill.

The weapon approached vertical as it tumbled and fell. During a moment of vainglory, Nick wanted to recover the firearm from the street, but common sense took over, and he made the raptor flee. The weapon would mark the location of the sniper, and he knew a trophy was unnecessary to prove the victory.

He was controlling animals and protecting marines.

Three months later, Nick's phone rang, and his adrenaline raced when he saw the name and answered. "Deborah!"

"Happy New Year!"

"I'd almost forgotten." He'd enjoyed a few dates, but his isolation on the year's final day highlighted his chronic loneliness.

"Yeah, I know. I'm not going to complain about last year. I found my independence, and my divorce was finalized. I'm hoping this year is even better."

"Me, too. Congratulations on your divorce. I don't think you told me."

"I didn't. I needed time alone."

"I've been giving you your space. My new job has been keeping me busy, anyway."

"What new job? No more CIA?"

"I'm working for the Marine Corps through a military contractor, doing more or less the same thing, only much cooler."

"That's awesome. Can you tell me about it?"

Her voice made Nick desire her. "They make me run twelve miles a week and hike twenty. Who knew exercise was so meditating? I'm getting in great shape. I can see the outlines of my leg muscles."

"Awesome. What are you doing for them?"

"I can only tell you in person."

"That may be possible. Where are you?"

Hope rose within him. "California, at Camp Pendleton. I live in Oceanside. It's nice, probably better than wherever you are."

"Sounds great. Can I come out and visit you?"

"Of course. Not now, though. I need to head out for a few weeks. But you can come in about a month."

"Um, that sounds good but–"

"Don't worry about the cost. I'm buying the ticket for you as soon as we're done talking–sooner, if you'll let me grab my laptop."

Six days later, Nick woke in the middle of the night. A terrible pain pierced him, and his hands shook. "What the hell?"

As he began to question if he suffered a heart attack, his phone rang. The caller identification pushed him closer to the edge of his body's stress threshold.

He forced himself to answer. "Hi, Joe."

"Did you feel it?"

"If you mean waking up like I'm having a stroke, yes."

"Of course, that's what I meant. Something bad just happened to Jake."

"You're sure?"

"Am I ever wrong?"

"Not about premonitions."

"You know some serious shit's going on. He's in danger."

"What can we do about it?"

"Nothing, but I didn't know who else to call."

Nick hadn't heard from his brother in years and wanted to remind Joe to call him, or at least accept calls, outside of a sibling crisis. But he knew the talk's focus was Jake's safety. "I'm listed as his emergency contact with the Navy. They'd contact me if something was wrong."

"They will."

Nick distracted himself from worry with what little small talk Joe would allow. As expected, his baby brother was silent about his life other than his prideful progress in Wiccan practices. Probes about his other ambitions went nowhere.

He let Joe go and then tried to sleep. Stirring in bed an hour later, he felt a sense of relief, but also of sickness. Unsure what it meant, he heard his younger brother calling him back and lifted the phone. "Yeah, Joe?"

"He's out of immediate danger."

"It's amazing how you know this so clearly. I just get blunt feelings."

"There's still a horrible future danger, though I don't know what it is."

"How should we react to that?"

"He's fine for now. We can rest. But don't be surprised if something horrible happens to him in the next year."

Two days later, Jake called Nick to tell him how close he'd come to bleeding to death after a hydraulic plant on his submarine ruptured near him. But a skilled corpsman had saved him, and he was expected to make a full recovery.

A week later, Nick's thighs burned as he finished his climb to the top of a steep hill in Afghanistan. The four marines patrolling ahead of him declared the area safe and told him to get ready. With the corpsman beside him, he found a flat patch of dirt and lay down.

The hard earth complicated his relaxation, but the serum was powerful, and his training had prepared him. Within minutes, he saw the world through Kevin, the alpha male of an Indian wolf pack that had been returned to the edge of his territory an hour earlier.

The sensations he felt through the wolf were extreme, like extensions of his flesh. As he questioned if the thrill of real danger accounted for the accentuated sensitivity, his wolf approached the den—and met resistance.

A younger wolf had assumed leadership.

The rival approached Kevin's snout. Nick felt his host's back stiffen, and he saw the competitor leap.

His host animal impressed him with his speed, rising to his hind legs to meet the challenge. Letting nature take its course,

Nick observed Kevin roll on top of the usurper, and then as the youngster backed off, he heard the victory howl.

It was the first time he recalled auditory feedback from an animal he controlled, and he credited his extreme emotions during the challenge for opening his mind to the sounds.

As the heat of the rapid battle for alpha status subsided, Nick thought he felt the dirt under the wolf's paws. But the sensation disappeared as he led the hunter on his spying mission.

Having reclaimed dominance over his pack, Kevin trotted in the direction Nick chose. He ordered the wolf to roust his pack's followers towards a local village to look for a ranking member of Al-Qaeda.

After three hours of patient observation, Nick saw his target emerge from a house, and he returned to his body to confirm the data.

Another successful mission.

Days later, he joined Colonel Meyer and Damien for a debrief in their program's private discussion room. They reviewed the details of the wolf operation, and Nick added that he'd experienced both the eagle's and the wolf's senses beyond visual.

"That's happened to me, too. It can happen when an animal gets excited."

"I see that now."

"Well, you're two for two. One success with an eagle, and one with a wolf. Now for the hard part."

"I know. Cats. You've been warning me for months."

Meyer nodded. "Despite Damien's theatrics, he's right. Cats are tough. You'll have time to work with a leopard when you get back. You'll want to be fresh. Take some liberty and come back Monday."

Nick met Deborah in the airport terminal. She ran to him, hugged him, and then locked eyes with him.

Before he could speak, she kissed him, and time stopped as he tasted her warm mouth. He pulled back for air. "Where did that come from?"

"Don't ask me. You started it."

"No, I didn't. Well, maybe. Why are we arguing about it?"

"We're not arguing."

"Does this change anything about us?"

"Not if you've been paying attention since we met."

The weekend passed as a whirlwind of trips to the zoo, Sea-World, and the USS Midway Museum. The thought of bedding her seemed vulgar, and he slept on the couch each night.

When he dropped her off at the airport, he realized he'd found someone he belonged with. He hugged her on the curb. "We never did get around to a serious conversation about our relationship."

"It's okay to enjoy just each other's company."

"We're going to have to get around to it."

"I know, but there's no big hurry. My annulment is just reaching the first interview phase."

"God damned religion."

She pushed back. "That attitude's going to be a problem."

"I'm sorry. It's not my belief, but I respect your position."

"Not based upon that comment. If there's going to be anything between us, we have work to do."

Monday morning was chilly, and Nick saw his breath as he watched a gorgeous black leopard pace behind iron bars. She wore an oversized collar that prevented her from scratching the surgical tape encircling her head.

Two animal trainers stood outside her cage, observing her.

"That's my panther?"

Meyer smirked. "Not until you name her. Those are my rules."

Damien agreed. "You always have to name your animal."

"She beautiful. I think she looks like a 'Terry'."

The vampire spread his arms and looked into the gray sky. "So let it be known to the entire universe that Nick now takes ownership of the Mighty Terry."

"I've got a long way to go before ownership."

"I'm declaring it for you."

"Sure. Thanks. Where'd she come from?"

Meyer answered. "She was procured last week in Myanmar. Her surgery was done immediately when we got her here.

"Wild."

"Enough chit chat, men. Let's get started. Grab your equipment, and I'll get McKeever out here." Meyer marched away.

Ten minutes later, Nick slipped his soft electronics helmet over his hair, rolled onto his back, and let the dirt absorb his weight. The corpsman knelt by one side with his serum, the vampire by the other with the communications pack.

Though outwardly aloof, Damien proved attentive to details as he checked the equipment. "The transceiver is locked onto hers. Whenever you're ready, Nick."

"I'm ready. Go ahead with the serum."

Nick drifted into the connected trance, saw a blurry view from inside of the leopard's cage, and then returned to himself to see the sky above him. "I saw a little, but you're right. She's tough. She didn't tolerate me in her head for long."

"Do you want another hit? You'll be groggy through lunch, but speaking from experience, it might help."

"Let's do it."

"Loading the injector." The corpsman lifted the serum as he prepared it. "Okay. Ready."

"Go ahead with the serum." After a prick, Nick drifted into Terry and saw a foggy view of himself lying outside the cage. The people around him were translucent blobs.

Then the world became the ground upon which she paced as she walked to the far end of the cage. While his hopes rose that he'd make feline control look easy, she turned, sprinted towards his human body, and rattled the bars with her claw.

He awoke to find his arm across his chest with outstretched fingers aimed at the wide-eyed vampire.

"You just swiped at me."

"Sorry. Wow. That was strange."

"Yeah. It was." Meyer crouched in Nick's view.

"If I didn't know any better, I'd say that she just controlled you for a second."

Nick couldn't deny it. "Maybe. My swipe could've been a random reaction to her throwing me out of her head."

Damien chuckled. "She did toss him out with authority. She is a lively one, this Terry."

"Regardless, he'll learn to control her. I have faith." Meyer stood. "That's enough for today."

Two weeks later, Nick finished a five-minute ride in the leopard's head, and as he awoke, he suspected she'd give more intense feedback than any other animal he'd managed.

Damien was encouraging. "Five minutes. That was good. We'll try seven minutes tomorrow."

"That's fine. There's one thing I need to tell her trainers. If I felt it correctly, she'd really like to scratch her incision. Do you think they can handle it for her?"

"She gets her collar off in a couple days, but I'll ask if they're willing to risk it."

Two weeks later, Nick approached his thirtieth minute inside the cat's head, and he attempted his first command.

He ordered her to lift her paw.

Nothing happened.

He remembered that cats acknowledged no masters, and he turned it into a request.

Nothing.

Then he tried to think like a cat. He imagined dirt on the back of the right forepaw that needed removing.

Nothing.

He imagined again, and he kept imagining.

As she raised it and licked it, the exuberance sent him back to his body. "Did you see that?"

"Indeed I did. I'm not sure that counts. The mission was to raise the paw, not raise and lick."

"That was me, though."

"If you say so, but that's still blunt. You're going to need more precise control before you take her into the field."

"You know how to ruin a guy's happiness."

"I didn't mean to. You did good. Cats are hard. You just have more work to do. But once you break through and can really connect, you'll feel more alive in her than in any other creature."

Two months later, the colonel asked Nick to join him in the private briefing room. Damien was in Iraq on an eagle-based mission, and Nick thought little of the one-on-one until he heard the update.

"I just found out terrible news. Our program's in trouble. We need a victory, or we're going to lose our funding."

The words were a punch in the stomach. "What can we do?"

"Take the assignment that just got dropped on me. Apparently, our benefactors understand the concept of a squeeze play. In one breath, they threaten the program. In the next breath, the give me an emergency mission as our only chance so save ourselves. Bureaucratic bastards."

"What's the mission?"

"You and Terry. ASAP. This one's a ticking bomb, and we need to move fast."

Nick panicked. "I'm not ready. I just got her to follow my walking and running directions."

"Those are the most important commands."

"I know, but it's too early."

"To make matters more challenging, she'll have to deploy with you. Due to anti-air defenses, we can't airdrop her in any deeper than you're going."

Nick's fear compounded upon itself. In addition to working with an untrained animal, he'd be beside her side, within range of her angry swipes. "Her trainers taught me the basics of handling her, but this is dangerous on many levels."

"I hate it, too. But it's now or never. For all of us."

CHAPTER 21

A V-22 Osprey aircraft carried Nick toward a war zone. Tapping his fingers against sheet metal, he pondered the stakes. Success in rescuing two American prisoners of war would salvage the animal control program. The thought of failure twisted his guts.

A young Marine Corps officer nudged him. "You going to throw up, Doc?"

"I'm fine, lieutenant"

Lieutenant Dillon was lean muscle with a thin face of stone. "You're not ready for this. Colonel Meyer's a great man, but he's an optimist about this shit."

Nick glanced at the aircraft's occupants. Including Dillon, six seated marines rocked with the aircraft as rainfall echoed throughout the cabin. His gaze dropping downward, he saw the Osprey's final occupant, his one hundred-pound female leopard pacing in her small cage. He tightened his grip on the pole holding her collar. "You think the Marine Corps wasted its money on us. But you can't find our downed pilots without us."

He felt his stomach in his throat as the Osprey's wingtip rotors tilted and lowered the craft into a clearing. A door rolled open and became a ramp, inviting marines to race by him into the darkness.

Nick jogged down the ramp with Terry at his flank, and damp grass squished under his combat boots. Joining a circle of warriors behind a rocky mound, he knelt with Terry held to the distance of her collar's polearm.

Two marines held Tasers as insurance against the leopard's temperament.

Behind him, the silhouette of the Osprey rose and departed,

and Nick felt exposed.

Over the drizzling rain, Dillon's voice cracked through his earpiece. "Listen everyone, satellites lost track of four hostile soldiers escorting our captured pilots to Omega interrogation camp. We don't know exactly where Omega is. We only know it exists from the horror stories of local friendlies. We don't have much time." Dillon turned to Nick. "You ready, Doc?"

"Yeah."

Dillon grabbed the cat's pole and handed it to another marine. He then jammed an antenna into the earth atop the mound. "Lay down and plug in."

Feeling dampness through his camouflage fatigues, Nick lay in the grass. He pulled from a satchel a soft helmet that was wired to a signal relay unit at his hip and slid it over his hair.

Dillon lifted an injection gun. "Ready for serum?"

Nervousness had prevented Nick protesting the absence of his corpsman. It was happening too fast, too soon. But he nodded, felt a prick in his arm, and yielded to the billowing warmth. He meditated, slowed his breathing, and centered his thoughts on Terry.

Exhilaration and fear heightened his sensitivities. He found strange comfort in his vampire-like colleague's omen that he'd feel superbly alive when connected to the deadly cat.

Feline and man as one. Connected. Heartbeat rising–fast–faster than human. Imperceptible odors becoming real–pungent–fierce. The forest alive in his snout. Consciousness alive–feline in body–human in awareness–hybrid in instinct.

Nick's sky became moonlit brilliance through the feline's vision. Scents of small animals caressed a sensitive snout. Through Terry's ears, he heard the breathing of each marine. He was no longer an intruder but sensed himself welcomed in his natural habitat.

Strong hands grabbed his snout and released his collar.

Dillon's face materialized before him and nodded. He tensed strong neck and shoulder muscles to scan her surroundings, but the marine's hand held her head straight. "Go."

Feeling the power in Terry's hindquarters, Nick leaped into thick foliage to search for American prisoners.

Within Terry's body, he stalked through the woodlands. The terrain was rocky with sharp elevation changes, but he steered her with the speed and ease of an instinctive hunter. His heart beating after covering a kilometer, he reached the fenced perimeter to the enemy communications compound where the pilots were last seen.

Through her sensitive eyes, he spied two armed patrolmen, and he crouched as they passed. Resuming his hunt, he trotted through dense underbrush to a dirt path heading from the compound. He stopped and sniffed, and the scent of jet fuel caught his attention. Again, he sniffed, discerning the stale canvass parachute stench. His targets, a downed reconnaissance aircrew, were close.

After following the scent to a fork where footprints broke in multiple directions, he lowered Terry's snout and discerned the scent of leather from the rightmost path. He trotted her to the right as drizzling rain beat cool dirt into mud.

Slime spat from under his paw pads. The scents grew stronger, and he could smell American sweat–beef from the aviators' preflight meals. He ordered Terry's body to leave the footpath, hide, and await his return.

Groggy with serum, he reentered his body, and Dillon's hawkish face appeared above him.

"What've you got, Doctor Slate?"

"I smell the pilots. Here." Nick tapped a laminated map.

"How many enemy soldiers?"

Nick inhaled, stimulating his memory of Terry's snout. "It's hard to tell. They're all on the same grass-fed chicken diet. By the smell and footprints, at least three. Maybe four like our last satellite view said."

Dillon turned the map to his troops. "The Doc may have found the path to Omega. There's high ground where we can set an ambush. Keep your optics trained on the scene so I can see what's going on. Move out!"

Five marines raced away.

"Look, Doc. My marines and American pilots could die if we ambush a full platoon. You can't be wrong. Get me an exact number of hostiles."

Nick rolled his eyes shut, and his awareness rode a radio wave into the leopard's mind. Entering Terry, he found her resting in the moist grass with raindrops tickling her coat. He felt guilty interrupting her repose as he pressed her onward.

Stalking within her, he reached a fork where another path fed into his. Boot prints riddled the intersection, and the scent of many men lingered, but he discerned the distinct American odors. He sent Terry back into the woods and brought himself before Dillon. "Lieutenant, I think a second group joined the hostile escort team. I don't know how many, but there's a lot. Maybe four or six more."

Dillon nodded and pulled a microphone to his mouth. "We got extra players, people. Change of plans. Shift to ambush plan Bravo."

"What's plan Bravo?"

"Your cat takes out the guy in the rear. With extra patrolmen, we'll need the distraction."

Nick panicked. "She was only supposed to find them."

"You trained her to kill."

"Not yet, I haven't!"

"But you can do it."

"Theoretically, sure."

"You're on a Marine Corps mission. Adapt or go home."

Nick wasn't sure he could force a kill, but he accepted he had no choice. "I'll adapt." He sent his awareness into the leopard and spurred her into a gallop. His lungs heaved, and he raised his snout. The scent of men grew stronger and then he saw two men in khaki camouflage.

He bounded into the underbrush and maneuvered her up to a high ledge. Below, he spied four armed men marching in front of two hooded prisoners. Four additional soldiers trailed the American pilots.

Nick returned to himself. "Lieutenant. There's eight hostiles. Four original escorts, then the pilots, then four more escorts."

Dillon lifted the map. "Where is she?"

Nick had studied the satellite photos of the terrain and knew his leopard's location. He recognized the ridge and pointed.

Dillon returned the gesture. "The ambush team is here, ninety meters ahead in an elevated position. You attack the trailing man and escape into the woods. The ambush begins on your attack."

Nick hesitated.

"What's wrong?"

Nick stared at the stars.

"What's wrong?"

"Nothing!"

"Bullshit. What's wrong?"

"I'm scared."

"It's not your ass on the line."

"It's emotional feedback. She recognizes my anticipation. She senses danger. I can't hide that from her. She knows this is real."

"Can you get it done or not?"

"Yeah. Yeah, I think so."

"Do it!"

Nick invaded Terry's mind. He jumped from the ledge and silently trailed the prisoner's party toward the hidden marines.

He broke into a sprint. Forepaws tugged at mud. Hind legs sprang horizontally. Graceful balance complemented violent acceleration. A deep sawing roar echoed as he leaped.

A forepaw to the jaw knocked a soldier to the ground. Claws ripped through neck veins. Nick rolled through the leap and finished his victim with fangs through the windpipe. Scrambling to his paws, he darted into the woods.

Gunshots rang as she pranced through the underbrush. Stinging pain erupting from his leg distracted him from the sickening taste of human blood. He tumbled and heard her howling in pain.

Nick returned to his human body. His hands clasped his thigh and his throat hurt from screaming.

Dillon slammed a palm over Nick's lips. "Quiet!"

"She's been shot! Why am I in my body?"

"I shook you out of it. I aborted the mission when my team had visual. The pilots are rigged with pulse collars."

"What?"

"Pulse collars. They sense the heartbeat of the hostile escorts. If we'd ambushed, the collars would've lost the heartbeat signals and blown our guys' heads off."

"How do we get her back?"

"I've called my team back."

"I asked you, how do we get her back?"

The marine sounded remorseful. "We don't."

Although unlinked, Nick felt Terry's pain echoing in his nerve endings. He sensed her fear. "We sent her in! We owe her a chance!"

"The Osprey will be here in five minutes. My team will be here in seven. If you want her back, you've got seven minutes to make sure she's not followed."

Nick linked in and rejoined Terry. The leopard's body galloped on three legs, the bleeding back right leg dangling. He calmed her and slowed to listen, look, and sniff. Each sense indicated she was alone, her pursuers evaded. He headed toward the clearing where the Osprey would await.

His pace waned as adrenaline yielded to agony. Haze clouded his mind, and he couldn't keep the leopard's body from collapsing.

Grimacing and panting, Nick returned before Dillon. "I think the bullet nicked an artery. She's collapsed. Nobody's following her. We can still get her!"

"I'm not risking the pilots. We can get out of here undetected and let them blame the kill on a wild animal." Dillon ripped the antenna from the earth, severing the link between Nick and Terry.

Nick voiced a groggy protest. "No."

The marine stood and pulled Nick to his feet. "You've got to board the Osprey." Dillon tugged him toward the aircraft.

Nick staggered and felt himself being hurled up the ramp.

Dillon's voice overpowered the rainfall's metallic resonance against the fuselage. "You sit tight, Doc. I'm securing the area while I figure this out."

Nick fell back against a foldout seat but felt an urge to help his cat. Her emotions jabbed him, and he yielded his mind to irrationality. He stood and fumbled through the munitions locker.

He crept down the aircraft's ramp into the moonlit darkness. Rain sprinkled his hair. As his boot squished damp ground, a rifle barrel materialized inches from his nose.

Dillon hissed. "Don't sneak up on me! Get back in the Osprey!"

His thumb depressing the firing pin, Nick extended a hand grenade.

Dillon's gaze remained steel as he lowered his rifle. "Don't flinch or you'll kill us."

"I won't flinch if you bring her back."

Moonlit shadows cut across Dillon's face. "You've lost your mind."

"No. It's still mine–and hers. I had no idea how powerful an intelligent animal's emotions were until I drove one to its death. I can't let her die. Bring her back."

Keeping an eye on the outstretched grenade, the marine exposed a map. After the doctor pointed to Terry's position, Dillon gave an illogical order. "Continue to the extraction point."

Nick thought he misunderstood. "What did you say?"

"I ordered my team back here."

"Without her?"

"Without her."

"You don't believe me?" Nick raised the grenade.

"I believe you. Give me that grenade, and I'll get her myself."

"Why should I believe you?"

"Because you just reminded me that she's part of our team."

Nick handed him the weapon.

A minute later, the fifth marine lowered his rifle as he boarded the Osprey.

Nick looked up from his seat. "Any word?"

The marine shook his head.

Nick looked to the figures seated in the cabin's red lighting for solace but found scowls. He couldn't tell if the marines were angry at him for threatening their leader, concerned about Dillon's safety, or both. A minute passed in lethargic agony when Nick heard enthusiasm in a marine's voice. "He's got her."

Another minute later, two marines flanked the open door as Dillon materialized from the darkness atop the ramp. He flipped Terry's body from his shoulders into the arms of his waiting comrades. A marine tended to her bleeding while Dillon approached Nick. "We made it back without being seen. We'll get her to the carrier for treatment and–"

Nick had something different in mind. "No."

"What?"

The door clicked shut and Nick reached for an overhead handgrip as the aircraft ascended. "Heal her."

"The medical support on the carrier–"

"No! Suture her wound. Then touch down on the beach and let her go."

"You have no idea what you're doing."

Surprising himself, Nick trembled. "Yes I do."

"I'll tell you this once, and you'd better listen. I have the authority to neutralize you or the cat by any means necessary, if I determine that you're operating outside of my control. Got it?"

"I know what I'm doing. I'm ruining my life's work."

"That's good that you recognize it, but I question your motivation. Who's in control now?"

Nick felt a tear roll down his cheek. "I don't know."

"Sit down."

Nick obeyed, and Dillon crouched beside him with a softened face. For the first time since meeting the marine, Nick knew he was talking to a human being.

"How bad do you want this?"

"I need this. I can't explain it. I know it doesn't make sense, but I just need this."

"Okay. Hold on." Dillon huddled with his marines and spoke with soft intensity. Heads nodded with intermittent glances toward Nick. The huddle disbanded with two marines tending to the cat.

"Marines never lie except to protect each other, and this is one of those times. Since she took a bullet for us, she's one of us. We're going to tell one story at the mission debrief, and then I'll tell Colonel Meyer the truth and let him decide what to do about it."

"So what do we say?"

"You agree that you didn't give me back that grenade until we touched down on the beach."

Nick nodded and lowered his gaze, accepting that he'd plead guilty to a felony.

The Osprey landed on the beach. Her wound closed, the leopard hobbled off the craft without a parting glance. As the Osprey flew over the South China Sea, Nick extended an empty hand toward Dillon. "Here's your imaginary grenade back."

Marines drew his arms behind him and bound his hands. "Doctor Nicholas Slate, you are under military arrest for mutiny."

As the emotion drained from him, Nick staggered.

Dillon reached for him. "Help him to his seat."

Nick succumbed to exhaustion.

He awoke in a hospital bed inside the carrier. An orderly entered the room, checked his vital signs, and made a polite departure.

Dillon entered.

Nick grunted. "I suppose you're pissed."

"You weren't entirely responsible for your behavior. It looks like mind control works both ways."

"What happened to the pilots?"

"Pulse collars are banned by international treaties. We sent photographs to the right politicians on both sides of the ocean, and they agreed to release them."

"Then the mission succeeded?"

"Yeah, it did."

"What about my punishment?"

"Not happening. Your cat found the path to Omega camp, and we're getting our pilots back."

"I don't believe it."

"Believe it. Colonel Meyer isn't exactly thrilled about how you did it, but he covered your ass." Dillon extended his hand. "You and your cats are welcome on my team any time."

Three nights later in his stateroom, Nick reflected upon Terry. Remembering how she'd learned to trust him and how that trust had added bitterness to her pain, he doubted he could risk betraying another animal.

He fell asleep and dreamed in vivid lucidity.

Grass cooled soft fur. Blood flushed extremities as his paws stretched outward with the laziness inspired by a belly full of a goat meat. Stiffness in a hind leg signaled healing.

Nick was again a beast at home in the wild, and the creature once called Terry was free.

CHAPTER 22

Endless impulses tormented Joe Slate. He likened himself to an antenna tuned to the frequencies of humanity.

Since childhood, he suspected his hypersensitivity, and he'd hoped to outgrow it. But as he matured into adulthood, he became more aware of the emotional noise around him.

Whether he sensed someone's joy or happiness, it hit him like the pounding surf–until he became close enough to a person for the sensations to strengthen into burning spikes of agony. Keeping distant from meaningful relationships staved off much of the suffering, and alcohol and marijuana numbed the residual gnawing.

His unofficial employment since leaving prison fed his ingestion addictions, providing him cash and access to drugs. He followed instructions and delivered product to the gang's dealers, earning steady pay and protection.

The cops even left him alone after the police officer who attempted to squeeze him into catching ranking gang members had suffered a near-fatal stomach virus.

After Joe had strung together a few months of savings, he was able to buy his own trailer and approach a life of comfortable solitude.

Despite the fear of hypersensitivity, he endured a connection with his brothers, and his resentment towards them was more than paranormal. It was also practical, stemming from their successes at his expense. As the youngest in the troubled home, he believed he'd needed the most attention and received the least.

After years trying to ignore distant signals from his siblings, his receipt of Jake's pain during the hydraulic accident on the submarine had clung to him, and he could find relief only by talking about it with Nick. His firstborn brother's voice had soothed him until the husky brother's episode had passed, but Joe sensed Jake's continued anger and fear.

After smoking a joint, he grabbed a beer from his refrigerator and sat in the trailer's living room to watch television.

Without warning, he felt a rush of fear from his husky middle brother. It stung, and after an hour of accelerated drinking, it receded to a dull throb. Unsure if he could credit the alcohol for the lessening of the intensity, he called Nick.

The call went to voice mail.

Joe drank himself to sleep and felt freer of his brother's fear when he awoke. Unsure if being hung over helped his desensitization, he called Nick for his assessment.

Again, immediate voice mail.

Over the next week, Joe sensed Jake's fear slipping into anxiety. Then, in a cathartic moment, euphoria, followed by nothing.

He wondered if that was what death felt like.

When his emotions stabilized, Joe sensed peace. Where he would have expected a void caused by absence, he was aware of his brother. Still alive.

Jake had survived his danger.

A third call to Nick proved fruitless, and Joe returned to his life of minimizing human contact.

*

Father Lewis sat behind his office desk and studied his latest exorcism candidate. Like most cases, he expected the outcome of prayers, blessings, and sacramentals to help the candidate, a frail girl in junior high school, resuscitate her faith and dedication to God. Though commonplace and mundane, such outcomes merited his time as a servant of the Lord.

A glance at a clock showed the girl had held disguised holy water in her stomach for eight minutes. Seeing no signs of possession, Lewis prepared to conclude his investigation and move towards the explanation phase. Her parents, hunched beside her, deserved an accounting of how they'd mistaken her behavior as possession.

Then the girl vomited.

She looked to him with dark eyes and spoke in a deep, two-tone sinister voice–in Latin. "I hate holy water."

Lewis stood. "In the name of Jesus Christ, tell me your name."

"One more powerful than me sends you a message."

Caught off guard and outside the bounds of his training, Lewis continued his ad-libbed counterstrike. "In the name of Jesus Christ, tell me your name."

"You want a name? I have one for you." The demon uttered the appellation Lewis feared–his nemesis, the demon of the archangel's visitation. "Stunned into silence, priest? With your mouth shut, perhaps you'll listen. You seek him. We hear your conversations. If you find him, he will defeat you. He is waiting."

"In the name of Jesus Christ, tell me the sign of your departure, so I'll know when you have left God's servant."

Silence.

The girl writhed in reptilian rhythm, and the priest regained his composure. He looked to his psychologist. "The Rite of Exorcism. Doctor Morris, help me prepare."

The demon growled in English. "Don't bother. I've made my point. I leave of my own free will."

The girl fell into her father's arms.

As the sun set, the terror of the demon's warning stayed within Lewis' flesh. His back pain became unbearable, and he thought about drinking. But he'd avoided alcohol for more than a year, and he instead doubled the dose of his prescription narcotic.

Afraid of the demonic nemesis, he recalled that he'd let a year pass without approaching the youngest Slate brother, his last clue to hunting his unnatural enemy. "I'm guilty of sloth. I'm guilty of doubt. Why did I doubt the visions? I'm a faithless coward."

"I think you're being a bit harsh on yourself."

Surprised, Lewis turned to see the imposing figure of his pastor at the bottom of the basement stairs.

"I appreciate the support, Father Mark, but you're being too kind."

Mark Brown's tone was compassionate. "Remember the forefathers. Many were troubled and flawed. Paul's possible speech impediment, and maybe Moses, too. Peter's denial three times in one night. Matthew, a tax collector assumed to be skimming money prior to meeting Jesus. Thomas' doubt until he touched for himself."

"That may be true, but I can't keep failing my Lord."

"If you keep your focus on God and make a prayerful effort, you'll see his will through."

"You make it sound easy."

"Do you mind telling me what's wrong?"

"I need to face a demon, and I don't mean a proverbial one."

"Exorcists deal with that all the time."

"But there's one demon in particular I must face. I've seen it in my visions. I was embarrassed to mention it earlier because I thought I was suffering delusions, but it's true."

"How do you know?"

Lewis closed the paperback he was reading and shoved it aside. An idea promised to both liberate and confuse him. "Now that you mention it, I don't. A demon confirmed it today, but as I reflect upon it, he may have been lying."

"They'll do that as often as they tell the truth, won't they?"

"His only evidence was overhearing my conversations about it. There's no way he can know my dreams or visitations, whether they were visitations or not."

"Then you're not sure if you need to face this demon?"

"You're right, Father Mark. I'm not sure. I'm not sure of anything at the moment."

As Lewis lay in bed reading a book, his vibrating phone invoked a name he hadn't seen in months. He lifted the receiver to talk to the pastor of an Ann Arbor parish. "Father David. To what do I owe the pleasure?"

"Father Lewis. After what I tell you, you may not call it a pleasure. You remember asking me to inform you if I heard anything from the authorities about Joseph Slate?"

Lewis recalled having done so long ago. "Of course."

"The Red Cross just contacted the police in my parish. His brother was killed in a naval accident. The police asked if I want to send someone who might know him or his family to accompany the notifier. I thought immediately of you."

The exorcist's heart pumped through his chest. "Isn't the older brother the next of kin? Does he know?"

"Nobody can get a hold of him. He's a military contractor and may be out of the country. This will be a difficult first sharing of the news with the young man. I wish I had better circumstances to for you."

"No. It's fine. I'll handle it. I've been wanting to talk to him for years. Ugly as it is, this is my opportunity."

Gulping coffee to stay awake, Lewis drove to the Ann Arbor church. The local priest greeted him and introduced him to the Navy notifier, a plain-looking female lieutenant commander with a placating voice. "My driver will take us to Joseph Slate in the limo."

Lewis noticed a uniformed police officer standing behind the open door of his car. "Is he coming with us?"

"Where we're going, you'll be grateful for the escort. I have a corpsman and a military police marine in the limo to help with Mister Slate if needed, but you'll want someone with jurisdiction over the neighborhood."

The driver parked the limousine outside Joe's trailer. Lewis accompanied the officer to the structure, and she knocked on the door.

A man in a jeans and T-shirt answered. He was handsome, and

through the doorway, Lewis noticed a tidiness that surprised him for a young, troubled parolee. He also smelled cannabis and saw artifacts of the occult.

"A naval officer and a priest. This can't be good."

"Mister Joseph Slate?" the officer asked.

"That's me."

"I regret to inform you–"

Joe interrupted. "I'm not much for visitors. Given the hour, I assume you're here to tell me that Jake's dead and that you can't find Nick to tell him about it."

The officer held her composure. "That's unfortunately what I'm here to tell you."

Joe nodded. "Don't worry. I never liked Jake much anyway. Sorry you had to come out all this way for nothing."

"It's no trouble. We're here for our service personnel and their families. Can we at least give you the contact information you need to handle the aftermath of this tragedy?"

"Sure."

She extended a packet.

He accepted it, turned, and flung it onto a couch.

"Can we offer you any counseling for your grief? This is a difficult time for you. Whether you were close to your brother or not, it is a loss."

"Not so much. I don't mean to sound harsh, but he never gave a damn, and I didn't really want him in my life. I'm more concerned about how Nick's going to take this."

"We think he's out of the country. There's a notification team trying to contact him, but it's possible that he may contact you before he knows."

"I'll be gentle if that happens."

Lewis reckoned that the smug look on Joe's face said otherwise, and the young man's tone bothered him. He needed to speak. "I've been friends with Nick for years."

"Friends? You and Nick? He doesn't have many friends, and I sure as hell doubt it would be a priest."

"I may have overstated our relationship, but we've been acquaintances for a long time. He let me interview him about his research."

The young man's eyes narrowed. "You're the exorcist."

"Yes. Lewis Bannen."

"No shit. This is how we finally meet."

"I suppose it is."

"See, the problem is, Nick may not like priests, but I have a real problem with them. You could say I need your kind to stay away from me."

"I assumed that. That's why I haven't bothered you, though I've wanted to talk to you for some time."

"Well, shit. As long as you came out here, five minutes. Alone."

During a silent prayer, the exorcist followed the occult worshiper into his trailer and sat on a cloth couch. He noticed a lack of chairs, confirming Joe's disdain for company. "You think that pretty much anything good that's happened in Nick's life or mine is the result of some demonic possession, don't you?"

The bluntness was a challenge. "I can't know unless I examine you."

"Examine me. Now. Give me some holy water to drink or stick a cross up my ass, whatever it takes."

"That's not how it works. It takes time. It's subtle, usually. Some demons can be obvious, but the strong ones can endure holy pains for short durations."

"You know I don't believe any of this shit. I follow the powers of the universe, and they're taking pretty good care of me."

"I know we believe in different things. I do, in fact, attribute those powers of the universe you experience to demons."

"At least you're consistent with your crap. I'll give you that." The young man's tone softened, and he eased into the couch. "Do you know why I'm not concerned about Jake?"

"I believe you when you say you don't care about him. I think it'll hit you later, but I believe you now."

"It's more than that. I don't think he's dead. I still feel him, and he's fine. Does that make sense to you?"

Lewis questioned the presence of great evil. "It makes perfect sense to me, because it aligns with Church teachings. If you have this paranormal ability, it's either a charism of the Holy Spirit, or it's deception by a devil."

"Do you know how crazy that sounds? Step out of your shell, and maybe you'll see why I live my life my way instead of your way. Don't I seem a lot more at peace than you?"

Recognizing an impasse in the debate, Lewis rubbed his forehead. "You have a point. My only counterpoint would be a long-winded sermon, and I doubt you want to hear one."

Joe smiled as he stood.

The exorcist took the hint and moved towards the door. He probed his mind for a last-ditch effort to maintain contact with the young man who offered his last clue to find his nemesis demon, but he found nothing.

"That's the smartest thing I ever heard a priest say."

"I'm afraid that's all the wisdom I have for one night, slim as it is."

Joe opened the door to let the priest exit, and his face darkened. "One question before you go."

"Of course."

"Just for the sake of argument, if I had demon problems, what would they look like?"

Biting his lip to avoid cracking his face with a hopeful smile, Lewis grabbed a notepad and pen from the naval officer who'd remained outside the trailer. He wrote down the major symptoms that Joe or his colleagues might see, and he left his email address and phone number.

Silently thanking God for the toehold on the young man's life, he escorted the officer to the limousine and resigned himself to a late night of grateful prayer.

CHAPTER 23

Joe believed in Jake's safety despite the official story. The Navy had announced that his brother and three other crewmen had volunteered to scuttle their submarine off the Atlantic coast to avoid a meltdown as its reactor had failed.

Joe considered the incident a distant curiosity except for its effect on his older brother. Per his paranormal sensitivities, the supposed loss of Jake coincided with Nick's transformation into an emotional zombie.

Never before had Joe experienced numb nothingness from Nick, and the strange desensitization allowed for their proximity. Joe could tolerate his brother's presence in his catatonic state, and he reckoned he owed the firstborn sibling a small debt of hospitality.

When Nick had asked if he could stay in his trailer while he analyzed his life, Joe had agreed.

After finishing a delivery run to his dealers, he returned to his trailer to find Nick sitting on the couch. His once ambitious sibling had brought his life to a halt in front of a television.

Unsure if his gesture arose from pity, malice, or curiosity, he offered to get his brother high. "You want to smoke some weed?"

The firstborn sibling showed himself to be human after all. "Sure. I got nothing better to do."

*

An hour into smoking, Nick felt the soothing calmness of cannabis. "I can see why people smoke this stuff."

"You've been missing out, bro."

"I see that. I was always scared of the long-term health effects, but I don't need my brain anymore."

"Time to live it up."

"I guess so. It's not like I have to worry about working. I don't have any money problems with what I've saved up and now with Jake's life insurance." He recalled a conversation in which Colonel Meyer had expressed an understanding of his departure from the program he'd saved. Shocks like the one he'd felt with the leopard had accounted for the attrition of the prior participants, and the marine was more appreciative of Nick's successful missions and earning of continued funding than disappointed in his departure.

Before he could decide about crawling back to the CIA for a paycheck, the Navy had informed him of Jake's death. Compounded by his quandary with Deborah, he'd retreated within himself, and nobody was better suited to exemplify that lifestyle his baby brother.

"I was surprised I got half of Jake's shit. I thought for sure he'd write me out of his will."

"He didn't have a will. I would've shared with you anyway."

"I don't need anyone's pity money."

"I forgot. You're making a living as a dealer for a gang."

"I'm not a dealer, and I'm not in a gang. I distribute product to the dealers for a gang. There's a difference."

"In my world, we'd call that being a contractor."

"Whatever."

"At the end of the day, it's not a guarantee of your safety."

Joe inhaled from his joint, held his breath, and then blew smoke. "I'm not dumb enough to think I'm free of the gang. I've had to make a few deals and sign up to deliver   a few favors. I didn't like it at first, but I got used to it. I know how to keep the leaders happy and keep the cops away, and that's all that matters."

"I'd feel better if you got a real job to keep you from burning through all your insurance money."

"I'll take your advice under consideration."

"Don't be sarcastic. You should be grateful you've got the

money from his insurance."

"How am I getting half, if he had no will?"

"You have a letter explaining it."

"Does it look like I read it?"

"We're getting the even split by law as his survivors."

"He probably thought he was immortal and didn't need a will."

Nick wondered if the marijuana played with his feelings, but he couldn't recall any sixth sense about Jake dying. "I know you don't think he's dead, and I'm starting to see it your way. It's just hard when all the evidence says he's gone."

"I know he's alive."

"How can you be so sure?"

"I've never been wrong."

Nick glanced at Joe to see the face of arrogance. He considered it the most disgusting human trait, and he expected it to make his handsome brother appear ugly. But he jumped when Joe's face contorted into a distorted raven-like image.

Joe's nose elongated into a sharpened beak, and then it returned to its human form. "What?"

With alcohol and cannabis clouding his mind, Nick doubted the validity of his hallucination. "Nothing. Sorry."

"Don't freak me out like that. You made me think I was bleeding from my eyes."

"I must be seeing things."

"If you are, it's in your own screwed up mind. This shit we're smoking is pure. I've been smoking it for days."

As a movie ended an hour later, Joe grabbed his car keys. "We're running low on munchies. Let's go."

Nick sat in the passenger seat of his brother's beat up pickup truck. Fearing the police would catch them for impaired driving, he remembered Joe's claim that the cops gave him leeway.

As they passed a convenience store, he protested. "Why aren't you stopping?"

"I'm going to the grocery store. Better selection and prices."

Nick pulled his phone from his pocket and noted the hour. With the drugs in his system, he'd lost his perception of time. "I thought it was much later."

"Lucky you. When we get back, you'll have more time to chill. We'll fire up a new joint."

In the trailer, Nick ripped open a frozen pizza box and tossed the pie into the oven. He then joined his brother on the couch.

Joe was selecting a movie while chewing corn chips. "So what's up with you and that chick you were dating?"

"Which... chick?"

"The one after the CIA chick. I figured you banged her enough times that you were done with that CIA chick. Or vice versa, from the way you described her. She sounded hot and scary."

The misogynistic words abraded Nick's mind. "That was... wow. Do you always talk like that?"

"Like what?"

"Never mind." Nick reconsidered his brother's word choice. "I think calling Andrea 'hot and scary' is accurate. She was hot, and I'd be scared to piss her off. And stop calling her 'CIA chick', or she'll send a SEAL team for you. She's probably listening. But the last young lady I was dating was real cool. I've known her since school, but we didn't date until after Andrea."

"Sounds like a disease. You can't get rid of her."

"Love's a disease." Nick sank into the couch.

Joe shot him a sideways glance. "Love? Like you're thinking about marriage?"

"Remember I'm a few years older than you. I need to think about settling down."

"I hope I never have to, but if getting married's what you want, go for it."

"I wish it was that easy."

"What's wrong?"

"She's still hiding. Her ex-husband is arrogant and has a vicious temper. He's threatening people, including her family, to not get involved in the annulment."

Joe lifted a joint to his lips and lit it. "What's he hoping to achieve? He can't force her to love him."

"It's not about love. It's about control, dominance, and ownership. Arrogance has turned him into a monster."

"This isn't a cultural thing, is it?"

"No. Her parents are still in denial, but her friends and siblings would help if not for the intimidation. This is all about an asshole being an asshole regardless of race, creed, or religion."

"And she won't remarry until she has the annulment?"

"She might, but it would be only for legal rights. She won't consider herself married for real until it's with the Catholic Church."

Joe extended the joint. "I suppose she needs help for that to happen, and that's what her asshole ex is blocking?"

"Exactly. She needs witnesses to the lack of virtuous marriage intention of both parties at the time of their vows."

"It sounds hopeless without witnesses."

"She was smart, though. She did a stunt before her marriage and pretended she was possessed."

"Seriously?"

"That's how I met Father Lewis. Now he can use his records to show her state of mind before the marriage, and he even has in his notes that she said she was marrying against her will. He'll share them, since he's not the type of guy to back down if her ex challenges him. Looking back, she was brilliant to think of it and pull it off. She was saving her life."

"So the annulment is possible?"

Nick dragged from the joint. "Yeah. She thinks it'll happen. It's still going to take at least another year because of the delays, but with Father Lewis helping, it went from hopeless to probable. She tried giving her friends and family a chance to do it the right way, but I understand why they're scared. Now the priest is her best shot."

"That's good, but if you marry her without the annulment, that would mean no sex, right?"

"That's true."

"What's the point of being married if you're not really married?"

"I don't know. I'm getting ahead of myself anyway." Wrestling with sadness, Nick opened a beer and tipped it back.

"How so?"

"There's the problem where she may not want to marry me at all since I'm not Catholic. That's a huge issue for her."

"Why are you wasting your time? You've got the whole world of ladies to choose from."

"I don't know. I guess you're right."

"Pull your head out of your ass."

"I'm not sure it's that easy."

"Let me cast a spell for you to help you find a good woman."

"Does that really work?"

Joe's glance was harsh. "How do you think I've survived?"

"Can you do it now?"

"Not while I'm stoned. I take this shit seriously. You need to take it seriously, too."

"Maybe I will. Maybe I've turned a blind eye to the forces of the universe even while I've been using them."

"No shit, dude. It's about time you realized it."

"Okay, I'm realizing it."

"If you'll make the effort to get proficient in the right arts, you'll get the girl and have success in anything you want. Do you still do Reiki?"

Nick had stalled his healing energy efforts when the CIA had recruited him, but he retained his desire to help people and wanted to return to it. "It's been a while, but I want to get back into it."

"Study spells with me, and it'll help with that. Also, do you remember when you used to grab people's hands and tell their future?"

"I haven't done that since high school, and it wasn't telling the future. It was just crude premonitions."

"Well, do that with your Reiki, pick up skills in a few fortune-telling spells, and you could open up a wellness studio."

"I don't see why not. I was looking for something to do now that I had to quit my job."

Joe lowered his beer to the coffee table. "You never told me why you quit."

"I can't. Not completely. It's classified."

"Even between brothers?"

"Yes."

"What can you tell me?"

"You know that I was experimenting with seeing through the eyes of animals, right?"

"Yeah."

"I found some flaws in that line of work. I need to take some time off."

"How long?"

"Maybe forever. You've got me interested in the art of witchcraft now, anyway. That sounds better than what I was doing."

Joe twisted over the corner of the couch, rummaged through stacked books, and then lifted three to his lap. "Now that you're serious, it's time to become a student. If you read these books and practice a few spells with my help, I may introduce you to the experts who've been teaching me."

"You'd do that for me?"

"Sure." Joe tossed the books on the table, and a folded paper glided to the floor.

Reaching for it, Nick thought it was notes from one of his brother's witchcraft gurus.

"Give me that."

Nick grabbed it and treated it like a runes of mystical power as he handed it to his brother.

"Don't be afraid of it like it's a secret spell. It just doesn't belong here."

"What is it?"

"It's the list Father Lewis left with the symptoms of demonic activity. I guess you can have it if you want it."

"What the heck?"

Nick glanced at the list and considered it oversimplified.

"Sounds like there's wiggle room here for subjective interpret-ation."

"Sure. You want to keep it? I don't need it."

"No. Father Lewis had his chance to prove whatever he was trying to prove. I say we stay away from him from now on."

CHAPTER 24

A year later, Nick worked his hands over a client's chest, channeling his healing energy into the removal of a tumor.

Reality had kept his success rates below sensational, but his yield in giving people results had earned him a growing Reiki practice.

He finished, and his client looked to him with hopeful eyes. "I feel better. I think it helped."

Nick had seen few cases where his work saved lives, and he considered the successes to be more than coincidence. "We can never be sure. But I think we've turned the corner. A few more sessions, and we may be able to get that tumor to shrink."

"I want to avoid chemo if I can."

Nick escorted the client to the front of the small rented space and accepted payment. With hours separating him from his next scheduled guest, he turned his thoughts towards reading another book about his arts.

But a silver-haired man wearing leather boots, jeans, and a flannel Abercrombie and Fitch shirt walked in the door. The surprise visitor seemed desirous of blending in with Ann Arbor natives, but his dress appeared too impeccable and his demeanor too precise.

"May I help you?"

"On the contrary, I am here to help you." The French accent confirmed the entrant's foreignness.

But Nick kept his guard against a pesky sales call. "I'm not buying anything."

"I am here to give you something. I would call it a gift were it not already rightfully yours. I am merely the messenger."

"Okay."

"May we speak in the privacy of a treatment room?"

Nick escorted the man to the recently vacated room. The small space lacked windows, aligning with his expectation of the stranger's intent.

"Jake is alive."

An emotional whirlwind brewed inside Nick. "Who are you? How do you know?"

"The less you know, the better. He wishes to protect you with ignorance."

"What happened to him?"

"I cannot tell you the full story."

"What can you tell me? Right now you sound like a liar."

"When you were in junior high school, he sought your advice before asking Karen Miller to a dance. You refused to meddle, but when he grabbed you, you had your vision, and you warned him of the rejection. Despite this, he ignored you and suffered the embarrassment."

Comparing the description to his memory, Nick agreed it was accurate–but insufficient to prove authenticity. "Joe knows that story, and there's no telling who he told."

"But Joe doesn't know that Jake pushed you backwards onto your bed when you told him he would be rejected. You banged your head on the wall and cried."

"Jake promised he'd never tell that to anyone. He always protected me, and it was embarrassing for both of us."

"I trust you can forgive him for sharing that now, given the circumstances."

"What circumstances? All you've done is given me evidence that he's still alive."

The man withdrew a tissue from his trousers and used it to pluck a folded note from his shirt pocket. "This is the number for your Credit Suisse bank account. In it, you will find two million Euro. Jake trusts you to distribute as much to your younger brother as you see fit."

Nick grabbed the paper and opened it. He was eager to test his guest's claim against the account number. "That's a lot of money."

"He wanted you to have it. He expects you to study the rules governing withdrawals to avoid drawing attention to yourself. If you fail in this, you will jeopardize his safety and yours. He expects you to show restraint."

"I can do that."

"He's not sure if an agent like me will contact you again on his behalf, but you cannot seek him. And, of course, you can tell no one of this conversation or of Jake's survival–not even Joe." The stranger walked out of the treatment area and headed for the establishment's door.

Nick followed. "Is that it?"

"No. Your brother wanted me to tell you that he's sorry for what he did."

"Which was?"

"He conspired with my organization to steal his submarine."

The news shocked Nick. "He would never do that."

"He was a victim. There was an accident on his submarine that nearly cost him his life. During the blood transfusion, his commanding officer donated blood but also placed his cut finger into your brother's blood as a ruse."

"A ruse for what?"

"HIV transfer. Your brother's commanding officer was homosexual but used the accident to make your brother appear to be. In his warranted anger, Jake threatened retaliation, which garnered the attention of my organization."

"What organization?"

"We are arms brokers. We wanted the nuclear weapons from his ship, and we recruited him."

"Are you saying my brother sent Trident missile warheads into the black market?"

A shadow cut across the man's face. "No. In fact, he failed. He came very close, but it's true that his ship was lost at sea. The rest is a cover story, but the only subterfuge about which you should concern yourself is that your brother survived."

"Where is he?"

"In hiding, of course. And he's wealthy. We paid him well for his effort."

"This still doesn't sound like Jake."

"He told me you'd say that. He also told me to tell you it didn't feel like he was doing it. He said it felt like he was an observer outside himself while he was possessed by an evil force he didn't understand."

"Wait. What?"

"He begs your forgiveness and hopes you'll understand that he wasn't himself."

"Why does he beg my forgiveness?"

"He said you raised him better than this."

"How can I forgive him when I don't know the details?"

"You know enough."

Nick searched his heart. "Well, yeah. He's my brother. No matter how bad his actions are, I forgive him."

"He'll be relieved to hear it."

"I want to talk to him."

"I'm sorry, Mister Slate. You can't, and I have said all I could say. I have already stayed too long."

The messenger departed.

Alone, Nick verified his account and his new wealth. He memorized the number and then photographed and burned the paper.

He pondered the money's significance. Even while sipping from it, the amounts he could withdraw would be assurance against unpaid bills while protecting his remaining insurance money. As his thoughts expanded, he realized he could use the sum to change his life.

His Reiki business became secondary as he rekindled hopes of his first love–animals.

He fantasized about buying a home and building his own lab to use falcons as search and rescue tools. But he realized the rarity of needing to find lost people, and he transferred the lessons he'd learned to a civilian environment.

Law enforcement.

Secretive law enforcement, since public knowledge of his ability to control animals would attract unwanted attention.

His mind worked over defining the riddle of his life's purpose as it crunched through possible solutions.

The vision took form, and he called his old adviser.

Ross sounded happy to hear from Nick. "How are you, my old friend?"

"Good. How are you doing?" After muddling through some pleasantries, Nick asked the pertinent question. "Do you think you can help me set up a private lab using the university's services?"

"I'm sure that's possible, if you have the funding."

"I do. I've got that covered."

"I would caution you on spending your own money. I would hate to see you driven into bankruptcy for the love of research."

Nick lied. "I have backing from investors for a private project. Unfortunately, I can't tell you the details, but I want to use an eagle."

A pause suggested Ross' reflection upon Nick's intent. "I wish you could tell me what you're doing because this sounds fascinating."

"I wish I could, too. I'll need some help getting hold of an eagle, a female preferably, and getting the surgery done."

"I still have the contacts for that. I assume you'll want my help getting the electronic equipment and setting up space in the aviary with a trainer?"

"Yes, but I want to move the bird from an aviary to a wildness over time."

"Now you're really piquing my interest."

Nick reminded himself that everything he was doing, including using Jake's money, could attract people who killed for information. He needed to avoid an international money transfer. "I have one last request. My investors want to pay in Euro, and they're only comfortable moving the funds within Europe. Do you know of a way to make that happen?"

"Oh boy. You just asked the hard question. Engineering and science I can handle. Accounting is a different story, but I know a couple people I can talk to. Let me see what I can do."

With his life changing by the minute, Nick needed a friend–his only friend. He called Deborah and was relieved when she answered.

Her voice was silk to his ear. "Hi, Nick. How are you?"

"Fine. You?"

"Fine. How long's it been?"

"At least six months, I guess."

"More like nine. What's on your mind?"

"I was thinking through some life changes and wanted to talk to you."

"That sounds deep. Are you thinking about converting to Catholicism?"

He realized he'd drifted farther from her belief during their time apart. "No. Sorry."

"Don't be sorry. You believe what you believe."

"But you believe I'm wrong."

"Misinformed."

"Call it what you want, but I didn't call to argue about it."

"You're right. I'm sorry. But you know how important it is to me if we're together."

"I know."

"So what do you want to talk about?"

Nick wasn't sure what he wanted to discuss. The person he needed most in his life was giving him a chance to regain her, and he adapted. "I guess we're on the right subject now. I think we were too emotional the last time we talked about it, but I would like to talk about it now if it's okay with you."

"Sure."

"It's about our future together. Is that even a possibility?"

"We've got a lot of issues to work through. I do have some good news, though. My annulment finally came through."

"That's great. I wish you could've told me about it, but I see how that would've been awkward."

"Yeah."

He blamed himself for her hesitance to tell him about her complete freedom. It would've felt like an invitation, putting her in a weak position. He appreciated that she was too strong for that. "If I was Catholic, how easy would this be?"

"Real easy."

"I don't know if that makes me happy or sad. A little of both I guess. So where does this leave us?"

"We're talking marriage now?"

"Yes. I don't want to waste your time talking about anything less."

"By Church law, I either marry a Catholic or marry someone who's willing to make his personal beliefs secondary to my faith and let me practice it, including raising any children as Catholics."

"Sounds oppressive."

"If you blend the belief systems of a husband and wife, you create a new belief system that violates both originals. If you want to turn right, but I want to turn left, a compromise sends you straight over the cliff. Compromises can break things."

"I guess that makes sense. I don't really have any strong opinions one way or the other about any beliefs, though. I just go with what works."

She sounded upbeat. "That's reasonable. It's open-minded and flexible."

"That's part of the problem, though. I was raised Catholic, and I know what it's about. It's not open-minded and flexible."

"How about we study philosophy together and see where it goes?"

"I admit I haven't studied philosophy much, but I'd be shocked if it led me to Catholicism. I mean, I already know I don't like it."

"That's okay as long as you remain flexible. I need permission from the Church to get married, and you'd have to go through some detailed interviews on your perspective of marriage."

"Not to be rude, but that process failed you the first time."

"But I wasn't doing it with you last time."

Having labored through a philosophical subject, he wanted to cover something concrete. "What's the possibility of us getting together soon?"

"Whenever. I can come by your place."

"I have a house in Ann Arbor. Will you feel safe so close to your ex-husband?"

"He must have conceded defeat, now that the annulment is complete. I can't live my entire life running from him."

Nick respected her courage and looked forward to exploring a life with her.

Six months later, Nick examined his basement laboratory. Knowing he would work alone, he considered automation a necessity. He had replicated the CIA's reclining bed as best he could, and he had microphones placed throughout the room to accept his voice commands for the entire system.

His old adviser had come through with the equipment, funneling the funds into the university through a European bank, and he had brokered the surgically-altered eagle. A falconer had trained it to nest in a local park.

Anxious, Nick reclined in the chair and slid the soft helmet over his head. "Energize system."

A computerized female voice answered him. "The system is energized."

"Energize the transceiver relay."

"The transceiver relay is energized."

"Steer the antenna towards Nancy. Maximum power."

He had named the bird after his favorite president's wife. "The antenna is aimed. Relay is ready."

"Inject me with ten milligrams of serum."

"Injecting."

The prick startled him, but the warmth consumed him. His consciousness floated in the nothingness on the fringe of reality, and he sought awareness in the female eagle.

Having seen the world through her eyes at the trainer's aviary, he made his first attempt at control.

But he hesitated.

A receded dark memory burst into his awareness. The physical and emotional torment of a black leopard became acute. Fearing a repeat of the feline's backlash, he comforted himself with the safety of the bird's unsophisticated mind.

He nudged her from a branch and ordered a simple circle over the park. The manipulation was easy, and he released Nancy to her own will.

That night, he took Deborah to dinner.

Her dark eyes were captivating. "How's your new research going?"

Unable to hide the equipment in his basement from her, Nick had to venture onto the slippery slope of half-truths. "So far it's okay. I'm just setting up my basement to match what I had before. I'm just about there."

"Are eagles harder than falcons?"

"A little. Their brains are little bigger, but bird brains are bird brains. I'm more interested in how you're doing."

"I found out there's an opening in the Arts and Entertainment department for the Chaldean News. I should be able to pick up a job there easily."

"I hope that pays better than waiting tables."

"Not by much."

Nick was willing to risk his pride and her physical proximity to his secrets. "You should move in with me."

She smiled and agreed.

CHAPTER 25

As he scanned the police channels, Nick had heard his first opportunity for assisting with law enforcement.

An armed burglar had outrun the responding cops and was escaping through a suburban neighborhood. The police helicopter had just taken off, but the officers faced long odds in finding and catching the assailant.

Nick entered Nancy's mind and flew towards the crime scene. After minutes of flight, his raptor eyes saw moonlit movement below. The fugitive was running between yards and over fences.

It was too easy.

Unwilling to administer a punishment outweighing the crime, Nick rejected the quickest resolution of crashing the eagle's talons into the runner's head. The impact could prove fatal to the human, and he refused to risk damaging his bird.

Knowing he would surprise his target, he chanced a more elaborate maneuver. He dived, redistributed the stoop's speed into a low-altitude level flight, and then aimed for the human's buttocks. He extended her talons and reached for upper hamstring muscles.

Furiously flapping to stabilize her flight after impact, he looked back and saw the man on the ground. With his hands clasped around his leg and writhing in pain, his escape had ended.

Nick sent Nancy home and awoke in his basement.

His next opportunity to play hero felt epic.

Upon learning of the situation, he'd entered Nancy with hopes of making his biggest impact outside a military environment.

Observing the chaos from above the Chase bank, he flapped her powerful wings and drove the eagle into combat. Keeping one fovea, a center of visual focus, on one gunman and the other fovea sideways to assess his descent, he angled the bird's body downward.

Body armor absorbed police bullets as the gunmen's rifles chased the officers behind cruisers. A policeman reached for an injured colleague, and an assault weapon's fury dropped him to the pavement.

Wings retracted, Nick plummeted at two-hundred miles-per-hour and scanned the parking lot with raptor-clear vision to verify that the known third assailant remained indoors.

He identified the head armor that could neutralize a concussion attack and aimed his talons at the chattering weapon. He spread his wings and leveled his dive.

Talons strong enough to crush bone extended, opened, and slowed the descent as Nick passed over the robber's shoulder at highway speed and crashed into the barrel. With precision beyond his human abilities, he hammered talons into the weapon and then pulled them away to avoid burns.

As the rifle hit the concrete, the bird lurched, extended her wings, and flapped them.

Nick raced over a sedan, dove behind it, and opened distance before climbing again. At the tree line, he pumped for altitude and arced over the bank. Above the building, he began his stoop for another sideswipe attack, but as he saw his rearmed victim scanning the sky with a shotgun, twin black circles sited him.

He extended his wings, leveled, and defied the man to shoot. He judged his elevated distance beyond a kill shot, but the muzzles blasted, and Nick tucked his wings to minimize his cross section. Seconds later, he recovered from his free fall and darted behind the bank.

He circled high, flapped downward, and turned the plummeting raptor into an aerodynamic teardrop. Blind to his target, he spread his wings and angled over the building, absorbing violent accelerations with an avian hunter's grace.

Noticing extra police vehicles and renewed energy in the proper side of the standoff, he sensed hope for the law enforcement team. Officers lowered masks over their faces and pumped teargas canisters.

Nick slid the eagle's translucent film over its eyes and cut between gas plumes. An armored head appeared, and he rammed it. Talons braced the shock, but the eagle rolled. He sought level flight but slammed into a squad car.

He awoke in his basement and noticed his chest heaving as he reclined in the meditation chair.

To help him focus, he had kept the room's speakers silent, but he needed to listen to a report. "Energize the speakers."

From a broadcast of the police channel, Nick was relieved to hear his eagle had survived the impact and had flown away. But he also learned that one of the assailants was escaping.

He adjusted the soft helmet that sensed and magnified his brainwaves. "Give me five more milligrams."

A jet injector gun hissed and pricked his arm. He winced and then relaxed with the serum's warmth. He meditated, slowed his breathing, and centered his thoughts on Nancy.

Like dancing on the edge of consciousness, Nick drifted to pseudo-sleep, awoke miles away gliding at five thousand feet, and turned the eagle around.

The light bones and thick plumage felt healthy during the turn. Nick judged that the talons and beak had protected the bird's body as it had hit the police cruiser.

Accelerating with gravity and pumping wings, he drove toward a lone gunman who sent suppression fire at the posse crouching behind a cruiser.

Avian creature and man as one. Connected. Heartbeat rising—faster than human. Imperceptible perception becoming real, clear, and fierce. Wind over feathers. Wings pumping for speed. Heat from a deadly barrel rising as a mirage. Consciousness alive–bird in body–human in awareness.

Nick rammed the eagle's talons into the assault rifle's barrel, knocked the weapon to the pavement, and cut back with the intent to kill the gunman with a beak through his armor's eye hole.

But a policeman's shotgun erupted, and the robber fell back. Rolling to his knees, the assailant reached over his back to rearm, but another round sent him to the ground.

Nick veered the eagle away as uniforms swarmed the gunman, and he vectored Nancy towards her home.

He awoke in his basement and ripped the electro-magnetic interface helmet from his head. "Oh my God, did I really just do that?"

His shaking hands provided the answer.

He waited several weeks for his adrenaline to subside and for the story of the heroic raptor to drift from the headlines. While cooking a surprise steak, potato, and broccoli dinner for Deborah's return from her job with the newspaper, he considered scanning the airwaves again.

He had the itch to play superhero with his bird.

But a dark feeling overcame him, compelling him to turn off the grill and lay down. He fell asleep waiting for his girlfriend.

The phone rousted Nick from his slumber. He lifted his head from the couch and felt a sinking feeling when he noticed the time.

The voice on the phone sounded tentative, but it started spitting out a litany of injuries and prognoses. As he hung up, he digested that Deborah was recovering from a beating in a hospital bed.

In a trance, he drove to the emergency room, and the sterile austerity of the hospital hallways numbed him. He stopped feeling as an orderly escorted him to the bandaged, swollen face, and he became a zombie hovering over his closest friend.

He slid into a chair as a nurse emerged from a curtain and uttered a dirge about Deborah's pain medications holding her unconscious. Falling in and out of sleep by her bedside, he rolled to his feet when a uniformed police officer appeared.

The cop explained that she'd been attacked and robbed behind the newspaper's building. He promised that the department would follow every clue to identify the perpetrator, but Nick kept his expectations low as he dismantled the message—there were no leads and no reasons to expect any.

He fell asleep in the chair until a doctor woke him and convinced him to go home.

At home, adrenaline kept Nick alert as he reclined in the meditation chair. "Energize system."

The computerized female voice answered. "The system is energized."

"Energize the transceiver relay."

"The transceiver relay is energized."

"Steer the antenna towards coordinates that I've entered into the system. Maximum power." The coordinates were his best calculation of the bedroom of his girlfriend's ex-husband.

"The antenna is aimed. Relay is ready."

"Inject me with ten milligrams of serum."

"Injecting."

The prick startled him, and he sought awareness in the vision of his first human victim.

Speculation had allowed him to conceive of the idea. Expecting nothing but the unexpected, he rode his anger towards the lawyer's sleeping mind.

The self-issued warning he heeded was brevity. If he had the tiniest shred of success in invading a human mind, he would get in, and he would get out. Fast.

The power of a human mind revealed itself with the strength of its signal and the ease of locking on it.

He landed in the lawyer's subconscious mind.

"Who are you?"

Having no visual information but experiencing the clarity of shared audible thoughts, Nick lied. "A friend."

"You don't feel like a friend."

He concealed his anger and guilt as he continued his charade.

"It's okay. I'm just here to listen."

"Listen to what?"

"Whatever you want to say. I know there's something buried inside you. You hurt. You want to tell someone."

Deborah's ex-husband gave his first admission. "Angry."

Nick baited him. "I understand. You have a right to be angry, after all she's done to you."

"She's a stupid bitch. Leaving me for some scrawny faggot who doesn't make in a year what I make in month."

"I agree. She's a whore."

"Thinking she can divorce me."

"A real man wouldn't let her get away with it."

"Hell, yeah. I paid some punks to rough her up behind her office. Punks owed me a favor after I got them off a rape charge. All the bitches want it and cry rape after they get it."

Nick awoke in his brother's basement, made a fateful decision, and promised himself to try to reverse that decision before it manifested into action.

After tossing in bed during a sleepless night, Nick showered.

He tried to calm himself, but his anger churned. He had learned to swallow his own past victimhood, but with someone he loved being victimized, he locked onto revenge. "There's got to be a legal way. A peaceful way. A just way."

His solitude reminded him that Deborah lay unconscious in a hospital bed. He continued his monologue while studying a map to his future victim's house. "No. This guy's a lawyer. He knows the prosecutors. He already screwed her in the divorce. He's insulated from repercussions. There's only vigilante justice."

He toweled off, dressed into jeans and a hemp shirt, and then marched down stairs to the basement. He rolled onto the recliner and slid the helmet over his head. "Energize system."

The computer responded and followed his subsequent orders to point the antenna at his eagle.

"Inject me with ten milligrams of serum." He slipped into mediation and awoke in flight.

The joyous feel of flying fell flat against Nick's anger. He grew impatient and flapped his wings hard. Reaching the lawyer's home, he circled above it, watching the driveway with raptor-like clarity. Minutes passed, and he heard the front door slam.

He banked and angled down. Three rapid flaps, and the hunter's silent speed drove him toward the man's head. He extended a talon.

The back toe pierced the victim's skin, and three forward toes wrenched clawed at his throat. They glanced off the windpipe but seized the jugular vein. As the bird's wings extended for stabilization after impact, talons ripped flesh.

Flapping to maintain flight over the lawyer's SUV, Nick crossed the driveway and whipped the eagle above the street and back toward the house.

The man clutched his throat and fell forward into a pool of crimson.

Nick landed and walked the bird into the blood. He savored the horror in the man's dying eyes and watched until he lay lifeless.

He launched the eagle to the sky, vectored her towards her nest, and withdrew.

Awaking in his basement, Nick felt sick. After yanking the helmet from his body, he rolled to the carpet. The stench of his armpits was vulgar, and moisture covered his chest. He shut down the system and headed upstairs to shower again before heading back to the hospital to comfort his girlfriend.

He wanted to brag to anyone who would understand that he'd crossed the human-to-human connectivity barrier with an unsuspecting participant. He wanted to brag that he'd gotten away with murder. But he needed to guard his secrets.

His more immediate need was how to deal with his newfound indulgence for violence.

As hot water poured off his back, he reflected upon his first taste of bloodlust revenge.

To his disgust and satisfaction, it felt good.

CHAPTER 26

Nick stopped at the doorway to Debra's hospital room. A small crowd had gathered around her bed, and two young adults passed by him as they exited. An older couple lingered, and he approached his girlfriend.

Awake, she turned and grinned as she recognized him. The gesture made her grimace while agitating the bruise on her cheek. "Nick! You're here!"

"I was here until late last night."

"That's what the nurse said. Oh, these are my parents."

The elder couple smiled, and Nick walked around the bed to shake their hands. "I wish we could've met under better circumstances."

The mother grabbed his hands. "Thank you. God bless you."

Her father spoke in a foreign language while Nick returned to his girlfriend's other side.

Deborah translated her father's greeting. "His English isn't good. He thank you and blessed you."

"That's nice of him. How are you feeling?"

"Like shit. In case you forgot, two guys mugged me yesterday. I don't really want to talk about it."

"You don't have to. At least your sense of humor's intact."

The father spoke again, and the ladies chuckled.

Deborah howled. "My ribs. Laughing hurts."

"What did he say?"

"I need to catch you up on current events. My ex-husband was found dead in his driveway this morning."

Nick feigned surprise. "What? Are you serious?"

"Yeah, but as you can tell, nobody's taking it too hard in this room. It's shocking, but I'm pretty much numb to the world's drama right now."

"This must be hard for you."

"Hard on me, maybe. But my dad just said he deserved it so much that even his own family's glad it happened."

Nick received the joke as a relief. "Wow."

"The two people who left when you got here were his brother and sister. They came to tell me about it and to pay their respects to me."

"That was nice of them. They didn't seem sad, though."

"They just admitted that he was terrible all his life. He used to beat his sister and mother, and they knew he was mistreating me. They were afraid to speak out. They're sad, but it's as much because he was a horrible brother as much him being gone."

Any guilt Nick had retained for his bird-enabled murder slipped away. "Do they know how he died?"

"His throat was ripped open. They're not sure if it was an animal, or a weapon, or they're not telling anyone if they do know."

"That's terrible, even for him."

"Yeah. I actually felt some pity for him."

"Really? What if I told you he was responsible for you being in this damned hospital bed?"

As her parents excused themselves and moved to the exit, Nick realized he had raised his voice. "I didn't mean to be so loud."

The mother pursed her lips and waved. "It's okay. We need to go."

After they left, Nick looked to Deborah. "I didn't mean to drive them away."

"They were looking for an excuse to get to their package store. They usually spend all day there since my dad doesn't like leaving my brother in charge."

"Sounds like a tough family business."

"Tough but profitable. Anyway, what's this about my ex being responsible for this?"

"Nothing. I was just speculating."

"Why would you even bring it up?"

Nick probed the sheets for her hand and held it. "I have something to tell you."

"What?"

"I accomplished something recently that's all me, and just me. Nobody else helped, I did it on my own, and I can tell anyone I want. I believe I am learning how to read human minds."

She raised her chin. "Oh? So you're a psychic now?"

"I mean it."

"After what you accomplished with your birds, it's hard to doubt anything you claim."

"So you believe me?"

"I believe that you believe it."

"Fine. You can ask Joe, but nobody else."

"Ask him what?"

"About the sixth sense we shared with each other and Jake when we were growing up. This is just an extension of that sense."

She reached towards a desk for her phone. "Should I call him right now?"

"No, silly. It can wait until you're better. It's best done in person anyway."

"Okay. So you can read minds. How did you come up with your theory that my ex did this?"

"I read his mind. My equipment helped me lock onto his thoughts from far away."

"You know how far-fetched that sounds?"

"Just trust that I'm sane."

"You're dating me. So that's already one strike against you. Why would you hang out with such a mess like me?"

He reached into his pocket and fiddled with the ring he'd purchased a week earlier. His intent had been a proposal over a romantic dinner, until the mugging derailed his plans. "If I asked you to marry you now, would that be strike two?"

"No, you idiot. That would be strike three. Your mind-reading story was strike two. Propose to me when I get out of here."

"You don't sound surprised that I was going to ask you."

"I knew you were getting ready. It didn't take a genius. Just wait until I'm better."

"Okay."

He released the ring case. "Of course, I'll marry you, you romantic fool. Now give me a kiss and give me my ring!"

*

A week later, Joe heard a knock on his trailer's door. He lowered his beer and answered it. Wearing sunglasses to hide bruises, his brother's fiancée stood on his porch.

"Deborah?"

"May I come in?"

"Yeah, I guess. Where's Nick?"

"He's with a patient. I mean a client. The one with the cancerous tumor he's trying to help."

"Oh yeah. He asked me to cast a spell for that one. I hope it works out. What brings you here?"

"Nick told me to ask you something in person. So I'm acting on his request."

Joe stepped to the couch and sat. The room spun as he regained his equilibrium despite the chemicals in his bloodstream. "Okay. Sit down."

"Thanks."

"What can I do for you?"

"He said he can read minds and that you could do it, too."

"Oh, hell. Is that what he told you? I believe that the power of the universe lets anyone read minds, as long as you can tune into the right powers."

"So it's true, as far as you're concerned?"

"Mind reading? That may be an exaggeration. We could communicate between ourselves telepathically, but it was only feelings and minimal data. But to be honest, Nick wasn't ever as good as me. So I'm surprised he's bragging." In his inebriation, Joe wondered if he overstepped his bounds by sharing a family secret, but he convinced himself she was joining the family.

"Well, I appreciate your honesty. Do you mind if I ask a personal question?"

"The worst I can do is refuse to answer. Shoot."

"Nick said that Jake once had to rescue you from a priest when you were going through altar boy training. I don't mean to pry if you were a victim of physical abuse."

"Nothing like that happened, at least not that I can remember. But I don't know how long I was out."

"So can you tell me what happened?"

Joe reached for his beer. "I don't suppose you want one?"

"No, thanks. I have to drive."

"Right. Where were we?"

"Altar boy training."

"Yeah. Mom was late to pick me up. So the priest took me into his office to look after me until she showed up. I got bored and started checking out shit in his office. You know, books, rosaries, pen sets... anything that wasn't nailed down, I needed to grab."

"Makes sense for a child."

"No shit, right? But then I knocked his globe off his desk, and he got really mad. Said the Slate boys have the Devil in them. I got pissed off, and that's the last thing I remember until I saw Jake."

"The Devil in you?"

"I didn't think anything of it, especially since me and Jake were notoriously badly behaved in church. Always getting in trouble."

Her eyes narrowed. "You and Jake. But not Nick."

"No. And I didn't figure it out until years later. That priest wasn't complaining about our behavior. I think he knew about our special gifts and was jealous. I mean, he was living a life of stupid rules and leading a bunch of sheep to a fake god. And he sees us Slate boys with a power he wished he had. We didn't know how to use it yet, but we had it, and he knew it."

"Amazing. Thanks for sharing. I didn't mean to barge in unannounced, but I wanted to catch you while Nick was busy."

"No problem. Any time."

*

Lewis let Deborah into his office and moved behind his desk. "Congratulations on your engagement."

"Thank you, Father. This isn't going to be easy, is it?" Her call the prior day had explained her desire to make her marriage a small and private affair, and she requested that he preside over it.

"It never is when we involve non-Christians. I'll need to acquire a Dispensation from Disparity of Cult from the bishop. It's possible, but it's laborious."

"He's not in a cult. His brother may be, sort of. I'm not entirely sure what to call his brother's witchcraft."

"I met Joe. Witchcraft is a fine term for it. But the dispensation is for anyone who isn't baptized in Christ. It doesn't matter if Nick is in a cult or not."

"He's not." She appeared to be holding back a matter of interest, and he let her reflect until she broke the silence. "But I need your opinion on something."

"I am your servant."

"Since I've known him, he's done things that add up to one big scary mess. I love him, and I know the Church can handle anything evil that's bothering him, but I'm scared."

"His visions through birds' eyes?"

"Yes, but that's the least of it. That at least has a scientific explanation. It's the other things. He said he can read minds. He said he read the mind of my ex-husband before he died and that my ex admitted to having me mugged. That's disturbing."

Lewis' mental alarm sounded. "Disturbing, indeed. The Church's position on psychic abilities is that they're caused by either a charism of the Holy Spirt or by demonic intervention. In Nick's case, the odds are demonic. Demonic interventions span the Bible from its oldest book to the New Testament."

"It gets worse. I didn't tell Nick, but my ex-husband's family told me the wound to his neck was caused by talons or claws, possibly from a large bird-of-prey."

"But Nick deals with small falcons, doesn't he?"

"He picked up an eagle for his private research."

The priest's chest tightened. "Did you confront him about it?"

"I didn't want to accuse him."

Lewis tried to avoid jumping to the obvious conclusion. "It's not necessarily Nick's eagle who was involved."

"You would call it a coincidence?"

"I'm afraid to call it anything. But the evidence is building for Nick's involvement."

He admired her resolve as she sat straight and continued. "It gets even more worse. His younger brother admitted that he once blacked out in the private office of their childhood priest and that their other brother had to break down the door to get him out."

"Oh dear. Not molestation, I pray?"

"He doesn't know because he blacked out, but the priest used to say that the Slate boys had the Devil in them. I was going to write that off as colorful wording, but then I researched their childhood parish. Their priest became their bishop and then died of a brain aneurysm a few years later when he was confirming Joe. Joe didn't get confirmed, but he had a feinting spell as the bishop was dying."

Lewis concluded that the coincidences stopped being coincidences. "Oppression, infestation, and possible possession. And it's been practically all their lives."

"You don't think Nick's possessed, do you?"

"I doubt it, but this demon is sly."

"Wait. You know the demon?"

He considered sharing his visions with her but decided she'd ingested enough paranormal data for one conversation, if not for one lifetime. "There's usually a lead demon that controls the rest. It's rare that just one demon attacks. I know many of them from experience, and it wouldn't surprise me if this one is familiar to me."

"Okay. But if Nick isn't possessed, that leaves Joe."

"We can't rule out the third brother, though he's deceased. It's also possible that the demon shifts between the brothers."

"I've never seen Nick do anything suspicious, and you know I know the symptoms."

"Yes, I remember. You faked it well enough many years ago. Demons can hide, but I agree that Nick's an unlikely victim."

"Does any of this give you an idea of what to do?"

"Take heart, sister. This can be solved by bringing Nick and Joe into the Church. Sacraments, sacramentals, faith, hope, and prayer are the cure. If need be, I can perform the Rite of Exorcism, as well. The tools are at our disposal."

She frowned. "The chance of getting both of them into a church is about zero."

"Don't give up so easily. Remember, we have a wedding coming up, and I believe we're discussing the fates of the groom and the best man, if I'm not mistaken."

"If you can get permission from the bishop."

"I think I hold enough sway with him. Why don't we pencil in your wedding now so that we have something to look forward to? I think you'll make a lovely June bride."

CHAPTER 27

Standing at the altar, Lewis examined the wedding party.

At Deborah's request, he'd limited the number of attendees, but he kept several volunteers, strong men who'd assisted with exorcisms, moving about the church in preparation for the up-coming vigil Mass.

Keeping the affair subdued, the bride wore a sun dress while Nick wore khakis and a blazer. Deborah's sister stood beside her as the maid of honor, and her brothers and parents sat in the first pew.

The groom's side of the aisle was empty, Joe Slate being his solitary supporter as his best man. Lewis noticed the groom's brother fidgeting and wondered if a starched collar or some-thing nefarious caused the discomfort.

After the betrothed received their rings, Lewis exchanged a knowing look with Deborah before deviating from the standard routine. "Before the couple exchanges their vows, they wanted candles held by their sides." He turned, and with Father Brown keeping stride, he walked to the altar.

Each priest lifted a small sacramental candle and tipped its wick into the unity candle. While Brown delivered his tray to Deborah's sister, Lewis brought his to Joe.

Keeping the waxen image of the Virgin Mary facing away from the best man, he extended the pewter platter with its dancing flame. A dangling crucifix hung from the tray. "Please hold this, Joe."

Nick's brother held the candle near his chest.

Lewis climbed the steps. "Now, for the vows." He coached Nick and Deborah through the standard oaths as they ex-changed rings. After blessing the congregation, he glanced beside him for his pastor's opinion of Joe's possible possession, but a slow head shake confirmed Brown's agreement with the lack of signs.

Nick was flushed. "Can I kiss her now?"

"Hold on. Let me get the holy water for the final consecration." Lewis moved to the altar and then returned with an aspersorium filled with the liquid. Grabbing the aspergillum, he raised it high and shook holy water over the party, making sure that droplets hit the best man's face. "You may kiss the bride now."

The couple leaned towards each other, and thunder clapped as they kissed.

Clouds blocked the summer sun's rays from the sky lights, and the stained glass windows blackened. The dark room became ominous and silent, and Lewis drew courage from the Eucharist behind him. "I hope that's just testimony to the power of your love."

The small crowd laughed nervously, except for Joe, who appeared calm.

Lewis smelled burnt sulfur and heard rain pelting the roof along with wind howling over the building. A set of double-doors opened, and rushing air whistled into the space. As he held out hope that the phenomenon would subside, he noticed movement on the windows.

Dark fluid poured from the eyes of stain-glassed saints as blood, but upon a double-take second glance, the fluid disappeared.

Lewis glared at Joe, and dilated pupils stared back. The sacramental candle with its crucifix lay toppled on the floor, and Lewis made his determination. Having staged his book of the Rite of Exorcism on the altar, he darted for it.

But then the rain subsided, the wind died, and sunlight bathed the carpet. The scent of an extinguished candle's smoke filled his nostrils.

Joe stooped, balanced the candle onto the tray, and placed the sacramental on the top stair. "Sorry about the mess, Father.

That thunder startled me. I'll leave it here so I don't get clumsy again." The man's pupils appeared smaller in the sun's illumination.

Lewis retraced his steps to the couple. "That's fine, Joe." He surveyed the party, and each person appeared recovered from the scare. "Ladies and gentlemen. Mister and Misses Slate."

*

Nick aimed the car towards the highway, pondering nature's noisy announcement during his nuptials. "I think the universe was applauding our union."

"Doesn't it bother you how loud and sudden that was?"

"If it was before we were married, I might've taken it as a warning. But what force of nature could possibly warn me away from you? No, that was wild, but it was harmless."

"You don't think it's strange that within two minutes of Joe taking a blessed candle into his hands that all that happened."

"Strange? Maybe. But what if it's the universe telling the Catholic Church to back off from him, and from me for that matter? Let us live our lives in peace, and keep religion out of the way."

She folded her arms.

He collected his thoughts as he entered the ramp to the interstate. "Come on, honey. We're on our honeymoon. Let's start it right."

"That freaked me out."

"I understand. I was surprised, too. It's not like I have some magical answer to this. I was as surprised as you were."

"Maybe my expectations are unrealistic. You can see through the eyes of birds and read minds. You can't blame me if I don't know what you're capable of."

"I'm not entirely sure I know what I'm capable of."

"Have you thought about what to do with your life? We should talk about this. I don't know if I want to write for a niche newspaper the rest of my life, and how long can you go on spying on people through birds' eyes?"

"You have a point. I'm giving up birds for a while. I may go back to just Reiki so I can help people. That's what it's all about. It's about the contributions we make." He accelerated into traffic.

"That's a great attitude. That's my noble husband."

"I like when you call me 'husband'."

"It sounds good, doesn't it?"

"Yes, it does, my wife."

"Maybe we should chill out and be thinking about our honeymoon."

"Excellent point. We are celebrating our love, and that's what we need to focus on. I believe love is the strongest power in the universe, and we need to honor ours."

*

The next day within his trailer, Joe stood in his circle of protection with his arms above his head. "I ask that the God and Goddess bless this circle so that I may be free and protected within this space. So mote it be."

Before he could begin his casting, he sensed his guiding spirit communicating with him.

The familiar spirit was subtle, but its meaning was clear–as always. He quieted his mind and breathing to focus on the message.

To Joe's surprise, the spirit recreated a repressed memory of childhood when a priest had sequestered him into a private office. The priest had done terrible things to him.

The clergyman had said prayers and had invoked the name of that terrible Jesus Christ in ordering the spirit to leave Joe. He had rubbed holy water on Joe's forehead and had traced the shape of a crucifix across his chest. He had lain his hands on his shoulders and had called upon the assistance of Michael the arrogant archangel and of that wretched virgin whose name made demons vomit.

The spirit expressed gratitude that Jake had interrupted the dangerous childhood episode that would have expelled him from Joe.

It then revealed its reason for allowing Joe this memory.

It was to remind him to avoid priests and to make sure to stay far away from Father Lewis.

*

Three days later, Lewis awoke to a feeling of horror. Fitful sleep had invoked the chronic back pain, and he reached for a bottle of narcotic medication.

Reconsidering the drugs, he grabbed the crucifix from his nightstand and rattled off a prayer to Michael the archangel.

A successful session the prior day had rid an energumen of an unwanted demon, and the exorcist had expected a restful night. But God worked in mysterious ways, rousting him with insight.

He thought about waking Father Brown to talk about his new idea, but he decided to reflect upon it and pray until he fell back asleep.

In the morning, he found his pastor preparing pancakes and pulled him into a conversation. "Can we talk about Slate wedding?"

Brown's voice was deep "Of course."

"When you helped me talk through it afterwards, I was afraid to draw any definitive conclusions."

"The family history is dangerous, and the ceremony was bizarre, but neither of us saw irrefutable evidence. I know enough about the signs of possession to know that we can't check any of the boxes. Joe showed no unnatural abilities, no unnatural linguistic skills, and no unnatural knowledge."

Lewis swallowed. "I saw a sign, but I didn't tell you about it."

"Why not?"

"I couldn't be sure."

Another priest walked into the kitchen and asked if the conversation required privacy.

Brown answered. "Can you give us ten minutes?"

The young priest nodded and departed.

"Couldn't be sure of what?"

Lewis mustered the strength to share his doubts. "I saw the saints crying blood on the stained glass windows. It was just for a second, but I saw it. You didn't happen see it too, did you?"

"No. I'm sorry."

"But you believe me, don't you?"

"Of course. That's the preternatural evidence you need to determine a possession."

"I know. The other signs were questionable. The weather was abnormal but not supernatural. His dropping of the sacramentals could be just clumsiness. Compelling, but circumstantial. But the tears of blood from the saints was preternatural."

Brown furrowed his brow. "Then why didn't you exorcise him right then and there? You had everything staged, and you could've done it after the bride and groom left the church."

"It didn't hit me until now."

"What didn't hit you?"

"The signs of a possession were around Joe Slate the whole time, but Joe Slate himself has shown no signs of being possessed."

"That's true, now that you mention it. That's odd."

"It's inescapably odd. He shows no signs of suffering the unwanted company of a beast."

"What's that mean?"

Lewis felt his breathing accelerate. "I feel foolish for taking so long to figure it out, but I understand now. It's not a possession like we're used to fighting. It's something much more rare and dangerous."

"What?"

"It's an integration. Joe wants the demon within him."

Brown gasped. "God help us. I remember hearing of such a thing. It's a wretched event."

"An integration explains everything from his childhood and that of his brothers to the wedding day."

"This poses a threat to his community. Maybe beyond."

"Beyond, indeed. A demon could spend all of Joe's lifetime building his trust and training him to use his paranormal powers for attacks against humanity beyond our reckoning."

"Is there a chance you're wrong about this?"

Lewis surprised himself with his answer. "No. I'm right."

"How can you be so sure?"

The exorcist recalled the images of the night's slumber, and he accepted that he'd received a brief but powerful third visitation from Gabriel. The archangel's wordless message had been clear.

Lewis took the leap of faith and trusted his perspective and his God-given abilities. "I had another visitation last night."

"Gabriel?"

"Yes."

"Did he tell you about Joe's integration?"

"No. He didn't have to, and I believe that would be cheating. God needs me to embrace my role as his servant in exorcising filth from his children, and that includes confidence in my ability of discernment."

"Well, how do you feel about it?"

Lewis tried to generate courage. "Terrified. I've never dealt with an integration, but I know I must face the demon within Joe Slate. I believe I know the demon's name, and I should expect victory based upon that alone."

"But?"

"But this demon knows me and has sent a messenger to taunt me. I fear I'm walking into a trap."

"What will you do?"

"God has chosen me to protect people from all demons and has equipped me to do so. Against Joe's will or not, I know my purpose. I will send that demon away."

*

Sitting at a dinner table overlooking Lake Michigan, Nick let the setting sun's reflection hypnotize him. Beside him, he heard Deborah's phone ring.

After a quiet conversation, he grew curious and turned his head towards her. "Who is it?"

Deborah lowered her phone. "Father Lewis."

Her concerned expression told Nick that the priest had called for reasons other than checking on their happiness. "Does he want to talk to me?"

"Yeah."

Nick took the phone. "This is Nick."

"Hello, Nick. It's Father Lewis. I trust you're well."

"I am. I hope you are, too."

"I am, thank you."

"What's wrong? Is everything okay?"

"I don't know a delicate way to say it, but I need your help. I think Joe is possessed by a demon and has willingly accepted that demon as part of him. It's called an integration, and it's a most dangerous scenario. I need your support to give me the best chance to save him."

Nick absorbed the words as an accusation and an attack. "You're telling me this now, on my honeymoon?"

"I'm sorry. I just realized it."

"You realized it only because I've shared my life events with you. You'd have no basis for this accusation if not for my candor."

"It's not just your sharing. I've seen other signs."

"Like what?" The hesitation after his simple question convinced Nick he'd hear a dubious story.

The priest obliged. "Angelic visitations and demonic visions."

"I'm open minded, but that sounds like a load of crap. I appreciate what you've done for my wife, but you used up the last of my patience for your demon hunting experiments."

"Please believe me. The signs are clear. You don't know it because demons are cunning and patient, but you and your brother are in grave danger. You have been your entire lives. Your powers are part of the demon's ploy to manipulate you."

"Manipulate me into what?"

"I have no way of knowing, but surely you can see this is wrong. This is dangerous."

Nick's heart pounded. "What is? My life's work?"

"No, not all of it. You made true scientific strides with your falcon visual recognition, but controlling birds is demonic. You crossed a line, and you're a victim of oppression by the same demon that's integrated into your brother."

Nick refused to believe his gifts were evil when he could fathom using them only for justice. "I think it's time that you left me and my family alone."

"You're in danger, Nick. So are Deborah and Joe. God only knows who else. God only knows the limits of the demon's power through Joe and through you. God only knows how much leeway you have with Joe to hurt people."

Anger clenched Nick's throat. "Stay away from Joe."

"I can't promise you that."

"Good bye, Father Lewis." Nick hung up and handed the phone to his wife.

"What's going on? Father Lewis' accusation is a big deal."

"But you got it right when you called it an accusation. And that's all it is. Do you even believe in demonic possession?"

"I'm not sure. I studied it only enough to get my parents to take me to Father Lewis before my first marriage. It's really nothing I've ever considered as real."

Nick reflected upon the threat the exorcist posed. If the Catholic Church wanted to challenge him, he'd excuse the beliefs of his wife and others who sought spiritual refuge within its structures. But its clergymen who would use its powers against him, to strip him of his abilities, were his enemy.

His powers were his birthright, and he'd be damned if he'd give them up.

Then he sensed it. The danger. "We need to get back and protect Joe."

"From what?"

"From Father Lewis."

CHAPTER 28

Lewis looked to the speakerphone as the priest from Ann Arbor squawked back at him.

"The same boy you informed about his brother's death? You can't be serious?"

"I am gravely serious. I need to force myself into his trailer for an emergency exorcism. The man distributes marijuana. Surely you have a relationship with local law enforcement to allow me entry."

"This is highly unusual."

"I know. I have Father Brown here to confirm my story." He looked to his pastor.

"The evidence as Father Lewis explains it justifies an exorcism against Joe Slate's will. I've seen a good deal of the evidence myself."

"A good deal, you say."

"Enough. I'll accompany Father Lewis, if you'll help us."

"Pardon my doubt, but why rush? This has been happening for years, and now you want to catch him in his trailer tonight."

Lewis regained control of the conversation. "His brother may also be a vessel for a demon. I'm not sure if his brother is possessed or is just oppressed, but I'm sure the evil presence is stronger when the brothers are together."

"And the brother is elsewhere tonight?"

"Yes. Up north on his honeymoon. This is the time to act."

The Ann Arbor priest hesitated but acquiesced. "Our bishops will have to agree while we put this in motion."

Brown jumped on the comment. "I'll call ours, and he'll take care of it with yours before we begin the rite."

"Very well. Prepare your team, and I'll talk to the police sergeant. God help us if you're wrong."

*

A flash of awareness hit Nick, and he released the car door handle.

From the passenger side, his wife looked up. "What's wrong?"

"We're not going to make it in time. Joe's in trouble now."

"How do you know?"

"You've known me for years, and you still have to ask?"

"Are you sure you need to head to Joe's trailer, anyway? I mean, how dangerous can Father Lewis be? He's a good man. Think of what he's done for me, and he just married us. Is it really worth ruining our honeymoon?"

The voice inside Nick told him to take swift action, but the long drive between to Joe prevented his direct intervention. Then he remembered his ready-made backup plan. "I've got an idea. I'll connect with Nancy from our hotel room and fly her to Joe's place."

"You can reach your eagle from here?"

"I setup my basement lab for remote control. It's sluggish with the latency over the Internet, through cell towers."

"You're calling your bird on a cell phone?"

"Yeah. It's nowhere near as good as using the higher frequencies, but it works."

Within minutes, Nick sat in the hotel bed and withdrew a soft helmet from his backpack.

"You seriously made your own travel helmet?"

"I paid some college kid to build it."

"Why?"

"You never know when crime happens."

"This isn't a crime."

"To me it is."

"What about your serum?"

"I've got an injector gun with one dose."

"Is that enough?"

He plugged his helmet into his laptop and then slipped it over his hair. His keyboard and mouse commands energized the system in his home's basement lab and the associated antenna on his roof. Then he pricked his skin with the gun. "Maybe. Lay next to me and hold my hand. Match my breathing rhythm and see if you can help me meditate."

"I don't think I can."

"Come on."

"Fine. I'll try."

Nick's fear of losing his supernatural power delayed his relaxation as he reclined and meditated by his wife, but it came.

He was flying.

As a test, he banked the eagle left and then right. Counting a delay of two seconds in his recognition of her movement, he divided by half to account for the round trip of the information he shared with her. It left him with a one-second delay in his commands before she would act—sluggish, but acceptable.

He sent Nancy towards his brother's trailer in Ann Arbor.

*

Lighting cracked, and Lewis looked out the sedan's passenger window. Appearing a sinister black, Joe Slate's trailer absorbed the receding shadows as the night's electricity waned. "I sense the demon."

The Ann Arbor priest grunted. "I only know when I feel the presence of evil. I'll leave the discernment of a demon to you."

The familiar voices of his exorcist team from the back seat comforted Lewis.

Fear of a rushed attack against an integrated demoniac seeped into Brown's voice. "He's usually good about such discernments. I suspect we'll be in a battle tonight."

The physician brought the evening's proper purpose into focus—freeing Joe Slate. "Keep in mind the young man's health. If he's a drinker and a drug user, and he's been under demonic influence for decades, his strength is questionable."

Lewis let the comment linger as the Ann Arbor priest stopped the vehicle behind the police car. The four men exited the sedan, and a car drifted to a stop behind them. Two strong men from Lewis' parish stepped out, and the six-man exorcism team approached two cops in front of the trailer.

In the moonlight, the exorcist recognized the sergeant from the Ann Arbor police department. Beside him, the other officer looked young and handsome with sharp features and swarthy skin.

The Ann Arbor priest addressed the sergeant. "You're sure you're okay with this?"

Scoffing, the sergeant shrugged. "No, but I'm willing to look the other way. I'm a believer. Though he's new to the department, Officer Malak assures me he is too."

The young rookie nodded.

The sergeant continued. "Stay out of sight of the door and give us a minute before entering."

Huddling with the exorcism team beside the trailer, Lewis watched the cops knock on the door. Seconds later, Joe opened it and acquiesced to the search warrant for illicit drugs.

A minute later, Lewis marched forward. "Follow me." He found the door unlocked and barged into the living room. The strong men from his parish brushed by him and rushed towards the startled Joe, who hovered outside the bedroom the cops occupied.

"What's going on? You can't do this."

Lewis barked the order. "Hold him down in the recliner!"

"Help! Police! Come on guys, I'm being assaulted."

The sergeant answered Joe in a sarcastic tone. "Sorry. I'm in the bedroom. I can't hear you. Did you say something?"

"This is bullshit!"

With the alleged energumen restrained in the chair, Lewis began the instructional phase of the Rite of Exorcism, leading with the Lord's Prayer, the Hail Mary, the Athanasian Creed. He then touched Joe's neck with the hem of his stole while pressing his palm on the boy's head.

He followed with a series of requests to saints for intercession to set the tone for the exorcism and then powered through the routine prayers with the zeal of a man who sensed his life's greatest challenge at hand.

Reaching the second phase, he began his first of three series of commands to the demon. "In the name of Jesus Christ, tell me your name."

"I'm Joe Slate, you dumbass."

"In the name of Jesus Christ, tell me your number."

"What the hell do you mean? Six-six-six. Or would you prefer something less dramatic? This is stupid."

"In the name of Jesus Christ, tell me why you entered God's servant."

"The only fools serving an invisible god are you three dunces in your priest clown costumes and these musclebound apes holding me down."

"In the name of Jesus Christ, tell me when you entered God's servant?"

"I'm getting tired answering your dumb questions."

"In the name of Jesus Christ, tell me how you gained access to God's servant."

"No, really. Seriously tired. I'm not even mad anymore. You're just making fools of yourselves. Let me go and we'll forget this ever happened."

The denials fueled Lewis' determination. He sprinkled holy water over Joe and issued his commands anew. "In the name of Jesus Christ, tell me your name."

The smugness drained from his subject's wincing face.

Lewis cast holy water downward again, and unnatural sounds gurgled from the Joe's throat. He gasped when Joe's face contorted into a distorted raven-like image.

His nose elongated into a sharpened beak, and then it returned to its human form.

Lewis pointed. "Did you see that?"

Brown's voice was hoarse. "Yes. His face changed shape. There's indeed a demonic presence."

Shocked expressions on the assistants confirmed that they'd

seen the preternatural restructuring of the bones.

The exorcist pressed onward. "In the name of Jesus Christ, tell me your name."

The voice was shrill and demonic. "Never." Joe's eyes rolled back in his head, revealing the full whiteness of a possessed demoniac. The veins in his face and neck bulged, and then his eyes rolled forward with dilated pupils.

"In the name of Jesus Christ, tell me if you are held in him by necromancy, by evil signs or amulets."

"He wants us. We are in him to stay."

Lighting cracked, and the trailer shook. The front door flew open, and a large bird raced into the room. A dark shadow streaked across the ceiling, stopped at the exorcist's nose, and dug claws into his eyes.

Lewis dropped his Rite of Exorcism, curled downward, and protected his face. A talon tore the flesh under an eyelid, and half his vision turned red.

From his undamaged eye, he saw the sergeant sprint into the room and yank the eagle to the ground. As he fell to his knees, he saw the cop pin the bird's stomach to the floor under his uniform. The attacking raptor flapped its helpless wings.

The physician lifted Lewis' hands from his bleeding eye. "Let me have a look."

"I can't see out of it."

"I can stop the bleeding, but you need to get to a hospital."

The Ann Arbor priest spread his legs and stepped on the bird's wings to quiet it while the sergeant remained atop the animal.

The sergeant called out. "Officer Malak, call for an ambulance. We have an eye wound."

Brown closed the trailer's door. "Father Lewis is injured. We need to take Joe to the police station and hold him there until we can find another exorcist."

Inspired, Lewis protested. "No. I will finish this. God has given me this task."

"But I examined your eye. You need treatment."

"I have until the ambulance arrives. Help me to my feet."

As the physician wrapped a bandage around his head to hold gauze to his useless eye, Lewis lifted his book and continued the rite. "In the name of Jesus Christ, tell me the sign of your departure, so I'll know when you have left God's servant."

"We're not leaving."

The injured exorcist continued with his commands and started over with the command for the beast's name. "In the name of Jesus Christ, tell me your name."

"Sergeant Masterson says he awaits you in Hell. You should be there now in his place, but you're a coward."

A sting erupted in the exorcist's back, and he shifted his weight. Relief escaped him until he remembered he'd forgiven himself for being unable to protect himself and his Army comrade. His focus burned on the energumen, and he forgot the pain.

Then, deviating from the rite, he repeated the command for the name of the nemesis within Joe. "In the name of Jesus Christ, tell me your name."

"Don't you need a drink? I keep bourbon in the pantry."

Lewis recalled that God's grace had allowed his sobriety. "In the name of Jesus Christ, tell me your name."

"Never."

God's power swelled within him, giving him courage. "Then I will speak your name, and I will drive you out. I know you."

He inhaled and then yelled the demon's name.

Joe's body writhed, straining the hold of the assistants.

Lewis yelled the demon's name twice again and sensed the beast's horror. Dropping to a knee, he felt himself passing out. Father Brown and the physician stabilized him, but his mind slipped away.

In a moment of transcendence, he sensed his savior, Jesus Christ, offering him loving support. He knew he would defeat the demon, and he accepted that his life meant serving his Lord.

Rising to his feet, he towered over his subject and placed his cross on Joe's forehead. "I know you, and I know your name." He repeated the demon's moniker again, and then he yelled his final order. "In the name of Jesus Christ, I command you to tell me your name."

Joe lurched and screamed the beast's name three times.

With the beast broken, Lewis prepared to expel it and the lesser monsters that accompanied it. "In the name of Jesus Christ, tell me your number."

"We are six!" The voices from Joe's throat shifted among horrific, screeching beasts as each fallen angel called out its position within the hierarchy behind the leader–Lewis' nemesis. "We are one.. two… three… four… five… six!"

"In the name of Jesus Christ, tell me the sign of your departure, so I'll know when you have left God's servant."

The lead demon, the nemesis, answered. "I will scream in terror, and lighting will strike thrice!"

Lewis issued the order. "I adjure you, ancient serpent, by the judge of the living and the dead, by your Creator, by the Creator of the whole universe, by Him who has the power to consign you to hell, to depart forthwith in fear, along with your savage minions…"

Joe convulsed.

The exorcist continued. "Depart, then, transgressor. Depart, seducer, full of lies and cunning, foe of virtue, persecutor of the innocent. Give place, abominable creature, give way, you monster, give way to Christ…" As Lewis continued his commands, the world around him seemed to stop, except for the suffering demon.

Finally, the energumen howled, and three bolts of lightning ripped the night. After falling limp and then recovering his posture, Joe seemed to have a new awareness.

Lewis sighed. "Release him."

Freed, Joe ran his palms across his chest, and his lungs heaved before he burst into tears. "You took them from me!"

"It's best this way."

Joe buried his face in his hands. "No! No! No!"

Lewis waved his hand toward the wall. "Open the door and let the bird go. It's no longer under his brother's control."

His colleagues obliged, and the bird escaped into the wild.

Emerging from the bedroom, officer Malak stared into Lewis' eyes with orbs of intensity. "More like him will come. You must be ready to give testimony by your service to the Lord." The cop turned and disappeared into the bedroom.

Curious about the rookie's comments, Lewis wanted to follow him, but he saw flashing red lights through the windows and felt the sergeant's hand on his back.

"Before we get you out of here, tell me what you want me to do with him."

As Lewis walked away, he gave Joe a parting glance. "Leave him here, sergeant. He's suffered enough already."

In the ambulance, a paramedic peeled away the bandage from Lewis' eye. "This can be treated. I've seen worse."

"That's good."

Seated beside the exorcist, Brown addressed one of the night's many mysteries. "Did that speech by officer Malak strike you as odd?"

"You heard it, too?"

"Of course."

"I was afraid I was hallucinating."

"No. I heard him. He made profound statements."

Lewis recalled the image of the officer's nametag. "The name 'Malak' is Arabic for 'Angel'. I'm pretty sure his nametag said 'G. Malak'?"

"'G. Angel?'"

A chill billowed throughout Lewis. "Gabriel."

"Incredible if true. Hold on. I've got an incoming call." Brown lifted his phone to his cheek. "No. Officer Malak isn't with us in the ambulance. You can't find him anywhere?"

Lewis understood. "And they won't. He was the angel."

"If this is true, there will be more like Joe, who willingly accept evil in exchange for power."

"Yes."

"These are dark times."

Lewis recalled his training. "Scripture has prepared us. The war has been tense throughout salvation history, and it will now only intensify."

"At least you won this battle. You faced your demon and emerged victorious."

Remembering his final one-eyed glance at the sobbing demoniac, Lewis thought he'd seen Joe wink at him, causing him to question the depth and duration of his exorcism's success.

Would Joe Slate invite the demon to enter him again? Had the demon faked its departure and that of its fallen group?

Lewis was unsure if he'd defeated his nemesis or if he'd face the demon again. But from God's mercy and justice, a newfound strength–an unshakeable courage–rooted itself in the exorcist's soul, and his confidence readied him for a lifetime of combat against evil, no matter how long his maker would require his service.

THE END

Epilogue

Months later, Nick awoke with a start. He glanced at a desk clock and noted the hour as three in the morning.

Beside him, his wife stirred. "What's wrong?"

"I'm not sure." He recognized his surroundings as he examined the bedroom of their suburban home near Ann Arbor, Michigan. "I think…"

Deborah interrupted. "Don't think. Just try to remember."

Following her advice, Nick recalled his sleeping vision, but it was distant, dark, and blurry. "I can't remember."

She sat upright in the bed. "Can you tell if it was a dream or something else?"

Nick sighed. "I don't know."

She rubbed her eyes and then held his hand. "It's okay if your powers never come back. We have a life together now."

Connections with animals, links to human intellects, and command over healing energies had drifted into Nick's past after the exorcist's attack on his brother. "Yeah. We do have a life. I'm married to Ann Arbor's hottest new columnist, and I'm a wealthy, stay-at-home husband. No complaints." He hugged her.

She squirmed away and reached to the nightstand for her phone. "Since you woke me up, I'm jotting down some ideas for my next column that came to me late last night."

Nick fell back onto his pillow and tried again to grasp his recent visions. The dream that had rousted him remained distant, until its memory hit him. He gasped.

"What's wrong?"

"It's coming back to me." The once forgotten black dream, void of visual stimulation, replayed as an audio hallucination. He shut his eyes and listened, repeated the soundtrack until he memorized it, and then he shared with his wife. "You won't believe it."

"Married to you, I'd believe anything."

"My dream wasn't a dream. It was Jake. He contacted me."

She ceased her texting. "Jake's really alive? And he's contacting you psychically?"

He was certain. "Yes."

Apparently uncertain how to process the invasion into her marriage, Deborah slumped her shoulders. "What's this mean for us?"

"Jake's alive and in hiding. He said we need to find Joe."

"That's not an answer!"

"Sorry. But this is... I thought we'd lost our powers, and now we're communicating. Jake's alive for sure, and he's reaching out."

"And? What's this mean for us?"

"Our powers may be coming back, if they were ever really gone. We've got work to do."

"What work? Joe's running around the world God-knows-where, and Jake's on the bottom of the ocean, unless I believe in your powers over official reports from the Navy."

Nick flipped back the covers and stepped to the carpet. "Governments lie."

"And psychics can be wrong. Even you."

He marched across the room to the laptop on his desk. "We have to find Jake."

"We?"

"Me and Joe."

"Like finding Joe's going to be easy?"

"Easier than finding Jake. He's hiding from the world. Joe's only hiding from himself. I'll find him."

She inhaled deeply, and then her sigh filled the room. "Why?"

He chose his words carefully for her to understand the gravity of his premonition. "Jake told me more than to find Joe. He gave me a warning."

"I don't like the sound of that."

"Neither do I, but it's true. I'm not entirely sure how to interpret it, which is why I need my brothers. He said that we've been seen. Our psychic energy has attracted the attention of dangerous people, and we need to prepare our defenses."

"What people? What defenses? You've never mentioned any-thing about this."

A pit formed in his stomach, but he braced himself and stood tall. "I don't know who they are or what they're after, but they're coming. And we'll be ready."

About the Author

After graduating from the Naval Academy in 1991, John R. Monteith served on a nuclear ballistic missile submarine and then as a top-rated instructor of combat tactics at the U.S. Naval Submarine School. He now works as an engineer in the Detroit area when he's not writing.

ROGUE SUBMARINE SERIES	ARCHANGELS' WRATH SERIES
ROGUE AVENGER (2005)	*WRATH OF THE ANGEL (2016)*
ROGUE BETRAYER (2007)	Coming Soon:
ROGUE CRUSADER (2010)	WRATH OF THE BEAST (2019)
ROGUE DEFENDER (2013)	WRATH OF THE CHRIST (2019)
ROGUE ENFORCER (2014)	
ROGUE FORTRESS (2015)	WRAITH HUNTER CHRON-
ROGUE GOLIATH (2015)	ICLES
ROGUE HUNTER (2016)	*PROPHECY OF ASHES (2018)*
ROGUE INVADER (2017)	*PROPHECY OF BLOOD (2018)*
ROGUE JUSTICE (2017)	*PROPHECY OF CHAOS (2018)*
ROGUE KINGDOM (2018)	*PROPHECY OF DUST (2018)*
ROGUE LIBERATOR (2018)	*PROPHECY OF EDEN (2019)*

If you enjoyed this novel, please join John's Mailing List for discounts, promotions, and insights.

John Monteith recommends his talented colleagues:

Graham Brown, author of The Gods of War.

Jeff Edwards, author of Sword of Shiva.

Thomas Mays, author of A Sword Into Darkness.

Kevin Miller, author of Raven One.

Ted Nulty, author of Gone Feral.

John R Monteith

Wrath of the Angel

Copyright © 2016 by John R. Monteith

STEALTH BOOKS

THE NEXT GENERATION IN PUBLISHING
COMING IN BELOW THE RADAR...

www.stealthbooks.com

ISBN-13: 978-1-939398-66-6

Printed in the United States of America